The Passage East 1934

From colonial India
to wartime London

The Passage East 1934, published by The Blue Horizon Publishing, 2026

Print ISBN 978-1-9194383-0–6

Epub ISBN 978-1-9194383-1–3

Typesetting and cover design: Charlotte Mouncey, www.bookstyle.co.uk

Also by the author:

The Pickpocket's Letter

A Cobra's Bite Doesn't Hurt

The Bengal Tiger's Silent Roar

The Passage East 1934

From colonial India
to wartime London

Anil Nijhawan

My inspiration, my sons, Kavin and Rohit

PART ONE

Chapter 1

London 1927

What Damon was seeing from the steps of the watchmaker's shop was a boy in a shocking red jumper sitting in the middle of the lane with his legs folded beneath him, and his face buried in his knees. Standing over him was a woman in a white coat, begging him to come away from the road.

Damon came down the steps to see what was going on.

'Your friend, is he?' the coal merchant shouted at Damon from his dray and snapped the rein, 'Git him outta here.'

Damon shook his head. 'Not my friend,' he said and went closer still, walking around an omnibus that had halted just a few feet short, its engine growling in anger, and the passengers gawking out the window.

The woman saw Damon looking and asked for his help. 'He won't come home. Can you talk to him?'

'Hey, what's up?' Damon said to the boy and extended his hand.

The boy pushed his head back down between his legs.

The woman threw her hands up. 'All right, you win,' she said, exasperated, 'I'll speak to your father. Now come home, p-l-e-a-s-e.'

The boy looked up askance, as if to see if she meant it.

'Yes. I will.'

The boy got up onto his feet, grudgingly.

She prodded him on the back. 'Now get out of the way of the bus,' she said, and turned to Damon. 'Thank you so, so much.'

Damon shrugged, said it was nothing, and started walking away.

'Where do you live?' the woman asked.

'Just up the road,' he replied.

'Come over for a cup of tea.'

Damon didn't see the point of going, and he hadn't particularly liked the boy, who he thought was showing traits of a bully. 'Thank you, madam, but I must be getting home now,' he said.

'But I insist,' she said, 'come for a cup of tea and cake. Robert will like that too.'

So, his name is Robert. The other Robert, whom he knew in the class, was a drag. He was forever showing off his fancy collection of Beano and Dandy. No one liked him, yet he seemed unaware of it, which grated Damon even more.

The home was a short walk away. They guided him through the kitchen to a back room.

'What's your name?' she asked.

'Damon.'

'And what's your family name, Damon?'

'Finnegan.'

'Oh, the Finnegans,' she said aloud as if she wanted the neighbours to hear. 'Sit down while I make the tea. Robert, keep your friend company.'

Damon looked around him. Leaning against a bookcase was a full-sized cricket bat. Too large for Robert to handle, probably belongs to his father, he thought. On the floor lay a satchel with schoolbooks spilling out. He spotted a Beano and immediately wished he had declined the invitation to tea.

Robert picked up a rugby ball from the floor and held it up for Damon to see.

So, he's showing off his favourite toy, or is it the name scribbled on it he wants me to marvel at? It said: Robert Fletcher.

'I play rugby,' Robert said, 'do you?'

'No, but I like to watch. It's my absolute favourite sport.'

'I'm in the school team. I'll be the captain very soon.'

The stocky build and the excited tone of his voice convinced Damon he was telling the truth.

'Catch,' Robert said and threw the ball at Damon.

Damon put his hands out and fumbled cackhandedly. The ball fell on the floor. He giggled, making out he would have caught it if given enough notice.

Robert scooped the ball up. 'How old are you?' he asked.

'I'm thirteen. And you?'

Robert made a surprised face. 'I'm also thirteen.'

'Were you born in April too?' Damon said.

Robert's wide-open eyes stretched to the limit. 'Yes, April.'

The boys looked at each other's faces keenly, as if they were seeing mirror images of themselves, and it wasn't so bad.

'What were you doing sitting in the middle of the road?' Damon asked.

'They are forcing me to go to a boarding school,' Robert replied.

'You don't want to go?'

'No. I like it here,' Robert said, shaking his bulky shoulders. 'Do you want to go for a walk?'

'Yes, why not?'

They walked out through the front door without informing Robert's mother.

'Which school do you go to?' Robert asked.

'St Joseph.' Damon replied, making a face. 'It's a dump.'

'I'm at Islington Boys.'

They saw the Hare and Hounds pub and went inside on impulse.

'Out, out, out.' Miss Hardy yelled from behind the bar. 'You boys are too young to come in here.'

'She's a nympho,' Robert said on the way out.

Damon chuckled. 'It's hard to imagine her doing anything sexy with anyone.'

'Oh, yes, she is. I know.'

'How do you know?'

'My friend told me. He has seen her kissy-kissy David from the post office.'

Chapter 2

London 1934

'Christ, the room stinks,' Damon said, stepping over Robert's rugby kit, which was reeking of sweat and semen. He went to the window and threw it open. 'What are you doing during the holidays?'

'Playing rugby. We have inter-university tournaments coming up,' Robert replied.

'I am going to Calcutta. You want to come?'

Robert peeked from above the magazine he was reading in bed. 'India?'

'It'll be a damn good adventure. Uncle Fred has permitted me to stay in his house while he's here in London. He doesn't mind if I take friends along. We only need an airline ticket. Imperial Airways now has regular flights to India.'

'I've never flown in my life,' Robert said, then slumped back on the bed. 'Money is a problem. I don't have any.'

'You can ask your old man, can't you?'

'Ask my old man for money? Ha, ha, very funny.'

'Tell him how hard you are working at university. You deserve a break. Make him feel sorry for you.'

'Hold this.' Robert handed Damon the magazine. Walked to the wall and punched it hard. 'It will be easier to break through this wall than break into my old man's heart.'

'Then go back to the tried and tested method. Do a sit-down in the middle of the road.'

Robert laughed. 'That won't work now. What about you?

How did you manage to touch your father?'

'Na, I blackmailed my sister. I promised to keep her secret if she lent me the money.'

'Why didn't you ask your father?'

'We aren't on speaking terms. He's still angry with me because I refused to join the army after finishing school. Keeps on hammering about my grandfather, who was in the army.'

'My old man is the opposite. He doesn't care what I do so long as I don't ask for money,' Robert said, throwing his legs off the bed. 'Pass me the trousers.'

Damon picked up the grey trousers from the chair and threw them at Robert. 'Ever considered washing yourself?' he said, 'you stink of sweat.'

'It's the male odour. Didn't you know girls love it? It turns them on,' Robert said, pulling the trousers up his legs and buckling up. 'Let's go to the pub. I'll show you how to pick up girls.'

On the high street, noticing Damon's gaze fixed on a towering billboard advertising India Pale Ale, Bass & Co., Robert patted Damon on the shoulder. 'You don't have to go to India to drink India Pale ale, you fool. You can get it here in London in barrel loads.'

'It's not just about that. There's another reason I want to go to India.'

'What reason?'

'Because Dad doesn't want me to go.'

'Huh?'

'He doesn't get on with Uncle Fred. He is jealous because Uncle Fred is rich.'

'That's no reason for stopping you from going to India.'

'Uncle Fred is very fond of me. We are very close, I think it's because he doesn't have any children of his own. That's another thing which gets up Dad's nose.'

'Hah. It seems your old man is worse than mine,' Robert said.

Chapter 3

June 1934

Robert woke up to the chatter of fellow passengers, someone brushing their teeth, and others coughing and hawking. He sat up on the hardwood bunk platform, ran his hand across his face and felt the beads of sweat on his forehead. He yawned, feeling hot and disoriented. The sixteen-hour flight from London to Delhi with three stopovers in three different countries had kept him and Damon mostly awake. Now they were on the Delhi-to-Calcutta overnight express train. Dust and soot from the locomotive engine ahead were gusting in through the Pullman coachwork's open windows. He could see men working in the fields, guiding bullocks harnessed to ploughs. Women in saris were collecting water from a well a short distance away from a sun shelter made of bamboo and corrugated tin. He slapped Damon's knee. 'Have you ever tasted well water?'

Damon raised his head off the duffel bag he had been using as a pillow and glared at Robert. 'I have hardly slept all night,' he said, 'You were digging your ruddy knees into my back. My back's so stiff, I feel like an alligator with rigour mortis.'

'You will live, my boy,' Robert said and slapped Damon's knee again, 'Did you know alligators can live to a hundred years or more?'

'Never mind a hundred years, how much longer before we reach Calcutta?' Damon said, yawning.

'Four and a half hours by my calculation, if there are no obstacles on the tracks.'

A welcome odour of frying omelettes drifted into the coach.

'Breakfast,' Robert cried, craning his neck to see where the odour was coming from. 'You will definitely live once you have had some eggs and bacon down you,' he said. They monkeyed down quickly from the bunk bed and sat down on a bench to wait for the food to arrive. An Englishman sitting opposite clicked his fingers at the waiters in white tunics, who were emerging from the adjoining carriage carrying huge metal trays. 'Jaldi karo, quick, quick, this way.' His handlebar moustache stretching from one ear to the other reminded Damon of the lion tamer he had seen at the Ringley Brothers Circus, The Greatest Show on Earth.

Seeing the newcomers across from him, Handlebar greeted them with a flash of his eyebrows. 'Good morning,' he said.

'Good morning,' the boys replied in unison.

'No bacon with your breakfast,' he said and shook his head as if giving them bad news. 'They don't do bacon on trains because cooks are Mussalmans. They don't eat pork; it's against their religion, and Hindus don't touch beef for the same reason, against their religious belief.' He rolled his eyes. 'Damn inconvenient for us Christians.'

'So, what do we get?' Robert asked.

'Eggs, tomatoes and toast,' the man replied, 'no royalty fare here. This is the best you will get from a kitchen on wheels.'

After breakfast, stuffing tobacco into a pipe, his eyes dancing with amusement, Handlebar invited them to look out the window. 'This is how the coolie fellows live, take a dekho,' he said and bellowed with laughter. 'They are emptying their bowels. They call it tutti. He was pointing at a line of men on the raised embankment, squatting on their haunches, their pyjamas lowered to the ankles, performing the morning ritual while chatting with their neighbours.

A laughter further up the vestibule drew their attention. A group of four men were playing cards on an upturned suitcase in the middle of the aisle. Two men nearby had opened their chessboard and were staring intently at the arranged pieces.

Robert leaned back on the seat and shut his eyes to catch up on sleep.

Handlebar pulled out a book and began reading.

The train slowed as it passed a minor station. Damon pushed his head out the window. A family of six was waiting on the opposite platform. A boy waved at Damon before turning to follow a coolie abseiling slippery steps, balancing a stack of suitcases on his head.

'We're in Bengal,' Damon announced.

'See those trees with long trunks and fruits shaped like your rugby balls? They are coconut trees. Coconut is native to Bengal.'

Robert grumbled. 'Let me sleep.'

The commotion and increase in activity woke them from their sleep.

'We are in Calcutta,' Damon cried and put his head out the window. His breath caught in his chest, viewing a scene resembling a clip from a war movie: people rushing, crisscrossing each other's paths, lugging holdalls, dragging metal trunks, yelling at each other. A military band on the opposite platform, dressed in red coats with metallic ricracs around the sleeves and collars, was playing "Take Me Back to Dear Old Blighty". The locomotive coughed steam, screeched, shuddered, and finally stopped like a worn-out beast, ready to collapse.

They stepped onto the platform, hoisted their bags onto their shoulders, and followed the passengers streaming towards the exit.

Out in the open, the heat of the sun hit them like walking into a wall of flame. Blinded by the sun, Damon cupped his hand over his eyes. Panicking. When he opened his eyes, he found himself staring at the face of a cobra, its tongue flicking in and out furiously as if it were trying to reach Damon's nose.

'No bite, see,' the snake charmer said. He put the snake's head in his mouth and held it there for a few seconds. 'It no bite, *hanh*,' he said with a valiant smile and bowed to the applause from the audience. 'Touch, touch,' he said to Damon.

Damon quit breathing as he placed a finger on the snake's body.

'The country is teeming with cobras,' a familiar voice said.

Damon turned to look and found Handlebar with a pipe in his hand, grinning at him. 'You must watch your steps in case you step on one. They are devious animals.'

Damon nodded, trying hard not to stare at his moustache, at the pointed ends which appeared to come alive when he spoke, as if mimicking a cobra's flicking tongue.

'Where do you two young men wish to proceed?' Handlebar asked.

'A place called Alipore.' Damon took a business card out of his pocket and showed it to him.

Handlebar immediately pulled the pipe out of his mouth. 'Fredrick Finnegan?'

'He is my uncle. Do you know him?' Damon said.

'Who doesn't know him? Is he well?'

'He has had health issues. He's resting at this moment in London,' Damon replied, surprised at the coincidence of meeting Uncle Fred's friend on the train to Calcutta. Handlebar ran a hand over his moustache and regarded Damon up and down and then swept his arm around in an expansive gesture, taking in the entire Howrah station - the people, cars, horsedrawn carriages cramming the entrance, coachmen touting for fares, the banks of the Hooghly River a short distance away, dotted with bare-chested men bathing, buffaloes chewing curd half submerged in muddy water. 'What do you think of Calcutta?'

Damon hesitated. 'Sir, we have only just arrived. Isn't it too early to form an opinion?'

'Just arrived, quite so,' he said in agreement, 'I expect you are keen to get home after the long journey.' Without waiting for a response, he called a young Indian who was supervising the loading of suitcases into a car. 'Ganguli, did you bring two cars?'

'Yes, sir,' the young man replied smartly, 'just in case.'

'Do you think we can spare one to take our friends to Alipore?'

'Yes, sir. I will ask my men to load all your suitcases into one car,' Ganguli replied.

'So, there you are. My driver will take you home,' Handlebar said to Damon, and then he took his and Robert's hands in turn and squeezed as if cracking walnuts. 'Welcome to India.'

Ganguly loaded Damon and Robert's bulky bags into the boot of a white Morris Minor and held the rear door open.

'I don't think he was happy,' Damon said once the car took off and did a sharp U-turn.

'What makes you say that?'

'Did you see his face when I mentioned Uncle Fred was in London? He appeared flustered.'

'Naa, you are mistaken,' Robert said, 'why would he have offered us his car if he was unhappy?'

'Mark my word,' Damon said thoughtfully, 'there is more to it.'

The car stopped in front of a house in a leafy avenue of whitewashed mansions set in substantial plots of land.

'Wow,' Robert cried, 'this is your uncle's house?'

Damon said nothing, but he was equally amazed. He knew Uncle Fred was rich, but this was beyond what he had imagined.

At the metal gate, an old man stood with his feet firmly planted in the soil: dark, oily skin, grey hair, and a moustache.

Damon recognised him from the description Uncle Fred had given him. He looks older than he is, but he is sharp as a black crow and faithful, too.

Damon walked up to him. 'Are you Nath?' he asked.

The man released two streams of cigarette smoke from his nostrils and shook his head rhythmically.

'Are you Nath?' Damon repeated.

The man rocked his head again, with a little more energy.

'I think he means yes,' Robert whispered.

Damon unfolded a notepaper and held it to the man's face. 'From Fred Finnegan.'

The old man looked surprised at first and then began reading, mouthing the words silently. As if all was clear, he dropped the cigarette on the ground, scrunched it underfoot, and moved smartly to throw the gate open. 'Allow me the honour of carrying the suitcases. You must be tired after such a long journey,' he said, speaking fast, his Adam's apple bobbing, like a float on a fishing line.

He led them up a gravel path dividing the expansive green lawn. The crunch of shingles underfoot seemed to go on forever, culminating on a paved patio at the front entrance. Nath dropped the bags and fumbled for a key in his pocket.

A plaque on the wall read Burnham Cottage.

'Why has Uncle Fred named it Burnham Cottage?' Robert asked.

'He has named it after the village where he was born.'

A profound, warm, placid silence greeted them inside, like a long-held secret. The air smelled of dry leaves and distemper. As if this were his home, Damon started opening the windows, the drapes coming alive one by one.

Robert ran a finger on a hardwood cabinet with bulging fronts and curved legs. He lay down flat on a loveseat upholstered in jacquard fabric. He found himself staring at the head of a Barakhamba deer mounted on a wooden plaque, its majestic twelve-pronged antlers almost brushing the chandelier.

An oval table and eight chairs with buttoned-down fabric reminded Damon of the antique warehouse on Holloway Road, where he had visited with his father to repossess items for unpaid debts.

'How long will you be staying?' Nath asked.

'One month. Then we will fly back to London,' Damon replied.

'I'll send for the cook so you can tell her what you'd like to eat,' Nath said, stopping in front of a dark oil portrait of a country gent with a hunting rifle.

'A cook?' Damon whistled.

'She normally comes every day. However, since the sahib is away, she has returned home to the village. I'll send for her right now,' Nath said.

'But there's no need for a cook,' Damon said, 'we can manage, just show us the kitchen.'

Nath shuffled his feet as if he had been standing far too long in one position.

'Is there a problem?'

'But sahib, you'll have to go to the market for meat and vegetables and many other things.'

'That's not difficult. Is it? You tell us where the market is then.'

'No sahib, you'll not be able to do it. Things here are not like in your country, and Fred sahib will be angry with me if I let you go to the market. I also suggest that you avoid going out between noon and late afternoon. It gets hot here in Calcutta, dangerous for you.'

'Ah, he means mad dogs and Englishmen must not go out in the midday sun,' Damon said with a laugh. 'By Jove, he's right.'

Nath made a grave face as if to stress the danger. '*Ooph*, what heat in the afternoon in June and July. People die if they are careless, even my people who are born here.'

'That's balderdash,' Robert said with a wave of his hand, 'Look out the window. Do you see any dead bodies?'

'Come on, Robert, we should listen to this fellow. Uncle Fred has warned me too about the heat,' Damon said. He was about to ask Nath to send for the cook when he heard the clicks of a dog's paw nail on the marble floor. A spaniel appeared from the rear of the house.

'Oh, hello. Who have we here?' Robert exclaimed and bent down to pat the mane. The dog gave an ill-tempered growl.

'Easy, boy, easy now. What's his name?' Robert asked Nath.

'His name is Kutta. He's all right. Just misbehaving sometimes,' Nath replied.

'My friend Kutta and I will be going for long walks,' Robert said, 'we aren't afraid of midday sun, are we?'

Chapter 4

Robert, in pyjama bottoms, yawning and scratching his pale chest, came out on the balcony and stood basking in the soft rays of the early morning sun. A crow startled him, flying low over his head, its black wings flapping noisily.He followed the crow's flight and walked to the railing. Nath was watering the flower bed below with an old zinc-metal can.

'*Ahoy*, my good man,' he called Nath.

Nath stopped watering and looked up.

'Could you tell me where the action is in this town?' he said. 'We have been here three days and haven't seen any action. Do you know any place for a party?' He gestured, pouring bottled liquid down his throat, and did a jig of a Morris dancer. 'Action, beer, party.'

'Ah, you want to go to a party? Yes, yes, go to the Bengal Club. Fred *Sahib* goes there too. Shall I arrange a car for you?'

'Most definitely, my man. Go for it,' Robert said.

The car arrived after lunch, a black Austin with a dull lustre. The driver, an emaciated Bengali in an oversized white shirt, stepped out and stood to attention like a soldier on a military parade.

The boys slipped into the back seat as Nath gave the driver instructions for the Bengal Club. 'Now go,' he said, patting the car's roof, 'wait for them until they are ready to come back.'For half an hour, neither spoke as the car steered its way through

Alipore's crowded lanes heading for the maidan in the centre of the city.

'Do you know what kind of club it is?' Robert said.

'A good kind,' Damon quipped.

'Very witty. You ought to be a comedian, Finnegan.'

'Why ask when you know I have never been to this club?'

The driver revved the engine to overtake a slow-moving tram. As the car levelled with the tramcar, Damon had a clear view inside. He saw a woman at the window seat. She was in a red sari half-draped over her head, and a matching red dot on her forehead. Since arriving in India, he had seen women with this facial decoration. He was wondering about its significance when the woman looked out the window. Their eyes met. The woman blushed and looked away. Just then, Robert eased his buttocks and farted.

'Couldn't you have waited until we were out of the car?' Damon said and wound down the window furiously.

'It's that mutton stew I had for lunch yesterday. I can't stand foreign gribble,' Robert said, flapping his hand to agitate the air.

'Foreign? May I remind you that you are in India? This is their cuisine.'

'No, it's not. Indians don't eat stew and mash.'

'Then you should be thankful they are trying their best to accommodate you, a Johnny foreigner,' Damon said.

'They are not trying hard enough.'

'You know what your problem is. You're an ungrateful bastard.'

'I ungrateful?' Robert cried. He leaned forward over the driver's shoulder, shoving him aside, and pressed the heel of his hand on the horn. The horn erupted into a violent, drawn-out scream. A cyclist ahead wobbled and fell off the bike. Robert flopped back on the seat, guffawing with laughter.

Moments later, a familiar sound hit their ears. The clang and wail of an English fairground organ, the unmistakable mechanical tune of a Verbeeck. It's artificial cheerfulness, as out of place as the contraption itself, which would have been more at home in a park in Hackney.

Folks were pouring into a fenced arena. Brits, Anglo-Indians, Chinese, and Indians.

'Funfair,' Damon cried and ordered the driver to stop.

They dashed towards the fair, dust rising in miniature clouds around their feet. At the centre was a giant shamiana with haphazardly arranged stalls, raffling gifts and selling snacks and cakes. At the rear were the usual games of skill, coconut shy, and hook-a-duck. Robert stopped at the airgun shooting stall, paid an anna to have a go. He aimed and fired. Ping. The lead disappeared.

'The gun is rigged.' He heard someone say in a loud Irish accent.

Robert turned around to find two hefty Irishmen laughing at the way he was holding the airgun.

'We are from Fort William barracks, the Bengal headquarters of the Eastern Division,' explained the taller of the two. He was lean and blond, with a military moustache and the air of one born to intimidate. 'What brings you here?' he asked.

'We are on the way to the Bengal Club,' Damon replied.

The Irishmen exchanged glances and burst into laughter. 'You schoolboys want to go to Bengal Club, t-h-e Bengal Club?'

'We are not at school anymore; university.'

'University is it. I assume you ave black tie, tux, and de like in yer pocket, as you'll be needing them to gain entry. They are strict about the dress code. And will you be aware dat the club is a meeting place for judges, army officers, businessmen, and the like? Strictly whites only mind.'

'At least they meet one criterion,' the shorter one said, hollering with laughter. He was clean-shaven, steadied-eyed, and appeared older of the two.

Damon glanced down at his trousers, crumpled and adorned with dirt smears at the knees. Back at the university, it was a done thing to wear your clothes as ragged as possible in solidarity with people less well-off.

Robert asked if they knew of any pubs or taverns where they could have a glass of ale.

'Beer, you want. Ah, to be sure. Head to Bow Barracks, my friend. Full of very agreeable joints.' He winked. 'Anything you ask will materialise from the rear. You go easy. You don't want to end up rolling in the gutters.'

'*Ay,* don't listen to Paddy here. You go enjoy yourself. Matter of fact, we had in mind to go there ourselves.'

'Then you can come with us,' Robert suggested.

'Now that's a grand gesture, thank you,' Paddy said and immediately headed for the exit. He made his way out, shouldering people coming in.

'Where is your driver? I'll give him directions,' he said.

Damon pointed at the little fellow sitting on his haunches in the shade of a tree.

Paddy crooked his finger. 'Hey, you get up,' he barked, 'take us to Bow Barracks. You understand Bow Barracks, past the market.' He shook a fist at the driver's face. 'If you go near Chawringee Road, you'll get this in your gob.'

The driver produced a yellow-toothed grin. 'Yes, sir, Bow Barracks. No Chawringee.'

'The lazy bugger Gandhi-wallas have blocked Chawringee with their banners and megaphones.''Gandhi-wallas?'

'Haven't you come across them? You will, soon enough. They are everywhere, like cockroaches.'

Bow Barracks was not a barrack but a bustling street

lined with small cafes and eateries. At the rear was the Bow market, alive with early evening shoppers. Smoke billowed from coal-fired stoves on the pavements, roasting chicken, lamb and kebabs.

'Gangadeen, bring four Murree beers and make sure they are cold,' Paddy ordered and pulled the chairs out from under a table. 'Sit and enjoy.' The air was thick with laughter and loud-mouthed jabber; the language of Poles and Portuguese was clashing with Cockney English.

'Sailors from ships docked at the harbour. They are letting themselves go after months cooped up on decks.' He did a crude hand gesture. 'If you see my meaning.'

'Come on, Paddy, don't give the wee boys any ideas. The girls will suck them dry before they know what hit them,' Cleanshaven said.

Paddy bowled with laughter. 'You mean literally?'

'Enjoy, sahib,' the waiter said, setting down beers on the table.

'Yes, we will, Gangadeen. But do you know we'll be gone soon,' Paddy said.

'Going back home?' Robert asked.

'They are sending us to Malaya,' Paddy replied and looked at

Robert with smirking eyes, 'know where Malaya is? Did they teach you geography at school?'

'Of course, I know Malaya,' Robert replied, 'why are they sending you there?'

'Our government is worried about Japan. The country is getting too strong.'

'Why should we worry about that?' Damon said.

'If Japan succeeds in controlling the trade route to Manchuria, will it stop there? No. They are bound to want to come south to take over Malaya.'

Damon shut up to avoid betraying his ignorance of these geopolitical issues.

'You want to know why?' Paddy said. He pointed at a passing car, at the spinning tyres. 'Rubber. That stuff is more valuable than gold, and we control all the rubber plantations in Malaya and Burma too.'

So, it's all about rubber. Damon wondered if his uncle was into the rubber trade. Even so, why was rubber so valuable? He had heard Uncle Fred talk of timber, especially the hardy Burmese teak. 'My boy, it's a precious commodity. It can fetch the same price as gold in England,' he had said, slapping the dining table at which he was sitting. There was sparkle in his eyes as he said it. Damon, as a boy, had no doubt Uncle Fred was in the timber business.

A girl suddenly appeared beside their table. No more than nine or ten years of age, a pyjama-type tunic on her small form. She broke into a song and dance routine, her ponytail hopping at each step. Mature for a ten-year-old, she swayed her hips, pushing up non-existent breasts in a child's imitation of a temptress burlesque.

Two boys in tow began circling the tables, grubby hands outstretched, seeking donations for the song-and-dance show.

One of the boys eyed the bottle of beer on the table.

'Go away,' Paddy said.

'Go away,' parroted the boy.

'Shoo, go away.'

'Shoo, go away.' The boys were enjoying a game of turning mimicry into mockery. 'Hello, boss.' 'Come here.' 'Good.' 'Bad.' 'Fuck-fuck.' They happily flung every English word they had learned in their short lives.

'Bugger off, you two.'

'Bugger off, too, too.' The boys were now doubling over with laughter.

Paddy stood up and kicked one of the boys on the calf. 'I told you to clear off, you filthy urchins,' he bellowed aloud.

People at nearby tables turned to look.

A girl sitting at the next table half rose from her chair. 'Excuse me. There was no need to hit the boy. Was there?'

Paddy glowered at the girl. She appeared about seventeen years old, with slender limbs and long dark hair. Who is this slip of a girl daring to question me? 'I did ask them to go away, didn't I, miss?' he said in a slightly restrained tone.

'They would have moved on anyway if you had ignored them. There was no need to kick a defenceless child,' the girl replied.

'She is right.' A voice in the crowd.

Paddy sat up erect, his face fiery red as the flames in the pit. He looked around him to find the source of the jibe.

The crowd went silent. One could hear the hiss and splutter of grease dripping on the charcoal. A drunk Spaniard three tables away belched.

Damon pushed his chair back, slowly and gently. He looked at Robert to signal they should be ready to run if there was a fight.

Paddy turned his glare to the girl again.

The girl lifted the teacup from the saucer, slow and casual, and took a sip. The gesture reminded Damon of his sister. Like this girl, she expressed defiance by exaggerated body gestures, rather than words.

'Aargh,' Paddy gave a dismissive growl and waved the girl away with his mighty arm. 'I'm going inside,' he growled to his mate and rose clumsily from the chair. 'Gangadeen, bring the drinks over.'

The chatter in the crowd resumed as swiftly as it had stopped.

The girl called the boys over. Speaking to them in their native tongue, Bengali, guided them away with a gentle but firm push on the back. The boys ran away laughing as if nothing had happened.

She addressed Robert and Damon next. 'They won't bother you anymore.'

'It's all right, they were only kids,' Damon said. He struggled to tear his gaze away from her. She was reminding him of the girls on giant hoardings at street corners, advertising face creams, talcum powder and fragrant bathing soaps. Like in the advertisements, her complexion was fairer than most Indian girls, but her eyes and hair were dark.

'You speak Bengali very well,' Robert commented.

'Why wouldn't I speak Bengali?' she replied.

'I thought you were from back home, England.'

'Don't mind him,' Damon interjected, 'he's quick to jump to conclusions.'

She smiled but said nothing and settled back in her chair.

Butterflies flickered in his stomach. How to befriend her without appearing to do so. He remembered Uncle Fred's warning from a lengthy list of *do's and don'ts*: never try befriending a girl in public places unless you want a beating from her father, brother, or an uncle.

A beating? He had thought that was a bit excessive, but he still found himself scouring faces to see which might be a brother or an uncle.

Just then, the girl surprised him. She put the cup down and turned around, towards their table.

'Where are you boys off to?' she asked.

'We are going to Alipore after this,' Damon replied, struggling to keep his voice steady.

A fly hovered over her face. She batted it away with absentminded elegance. 'May I come with you?' she said casually as if addressing friends.

'Sure, you can,' Robert interjected. Assuming she wanted a ride home, he asked her where she lived.

She gestured vaguely toward a distant, dark building. 'It's an asylum for the unwanted.'

Back to the Victoria Memorial, the driver cut across the maidan, past the fun fair, which was now more or less deserted. The sun had already dipped across the city horizon, and soon it would be dark. This rapid transition from day to night, usually in less than an hour, disconcerted Damon. He had experienced nothing like it in England.

At Kidderpore Docks, ghostly hulks of barges and steamships came into view. Hurricane lamps swaying on masts. The headlights of a passing car illuminated a Union Jack pasted on the hulk of a barge.

'How do you cope with the Calcutta heat?' the girl asked. Cramped between the boys, she looked at Robert and then at Damon.

'Aw, it is hot, but I can cope,' Damon replied boldly.

'For me, it is a piece of cake. I am a rugby player,' Robert added.

'I know a place hotter even than Calcutta,' she said.

'Where's that?' Damon said quickly, eager to monopolise her attention.

'Rangoon,' she replied, 'there are only two weather types. It is hot from November to February, and extremely hot the rest of the year. The only way to survive is by sitting in a pool and smoking afeem.'

Robert erupted into a yowl. 'I'll give my arse to be able to dive into a pool,' he said, 'do you like swimming?'

'I don't know. I've never been in a pool,' she said.

'Love it. I go swimming every week,' Robert said, 'when I am not playing rugby.'

Lie, Damon wanted to shout, he has never been interested in swimming and refuses to go to the public swimming pool, only a mile from home. And then he spotted Robert's hand creeping over her shoulder. The rascal is trying to get into her knickers.

'What's afeem?' Damon said, trying to woo her away from Robert.

'Don't you know?' she said.

'Is it something you smoke, Indian charas is it?'

'No, you inhale or inject it in the arm. You boys are so naïve.'

'Not naïve, we're pure, virtuous,' Robert said and raised his hands like a priest blessing the congregation, 'untarnished descendants of Jesus Christ.'

'Yes, very true,' Damon added, 'we helped write the Ten Commandments.'

'Actually, there were eleven commandments, but one was omitted for the sake of brevity,' Robert said. 'Would you like to hear the missing commandment?'

'No, but I suspect you'll tell me anyway.' She regarded him with scorn, expecting to hear a smutty limerick.

'One can fornicate to one's heart's desire once a year on the twenty-third day of the Lord's month of June,' he said and cried with mock surprise, 'Oh, what a coincidence, it happens to be today, the twenty-third of June.'

The boys burst into laughter but stopped quickly when they saw she wasn't amused.

'I'd like you to know my father was a church minister,' she said.

'Oh boy,' Damon said, 'you're a preacher man's daughter?'

'Yes, no, he has resigned from the church,' she said, 'and don't call me oh boy. My name is Flora. What's yours?

'Damon.'

'Dum Dum. That's the name of Calcutta airport,' she said.

'I am Robert,' Robert said and raised a finger in the air as if a teacher had called his name in a classroom roll call. 'Not Rub Rub, if you please.'

'Rub Rub, I want you to know my father may have been Christian, but I am not. I've no religion.'

'Ye, me too. I don't care about religion. It stinks.'

Back at Burnham Cottage, Robert rattled the gate. 'Old boy, let us in.'

'Shhh, keep your voice down. Don't wake up the neighbours,' Damon cautioned.

Light came on in Nath's room. The door opened, and he came running to the gate in his nightclothes, a string vest, and a lungi. He saw the girl standing behind Robert and held the two halves of the gate firmly closed as though he intended to deny entry to the girl or all three.

Damon understood his reaction. Two bachelors escorting a lone girl home late at night. A scandalous act in Indian society. But there was nothing he could do to assuage Nath's disapproval.

They escorted Flora to the upper-floor balcony. 'It's cooler here,' Damon said and spread a sheet on the floor.

Flora sat down cross-legged.

Robert fetched a bottle of whiskey and glasses and dropped beside her. He poured a small measure into a glass and offered it to her.

'Oh no, I don't drink this,' she said, and just as Damon came out with a platter of sandwiches, 'I'll have that,' she said.

'Cheese, ham, and pickle. Very thoughtful of Nath,' Damon said and slid the platter in the centre.

Minutes passed. The only sound was Robert's ravenous munching, Crumbs dropping on his lap like confetti. Damon kept his eye on Flora as she ate her sandwich. She was biting into it from one side, working her way into the centre, keeping the outer edges intact. Once she had finished the central part, she started working on the rough edges.

Robert lit two cigarettes once they had finished eating and offered one to Flora.

Damon lit his own cigarette.

The time waltzed languidly as they smoked. Damon thought of Nath, that censorious look in his eyes. Does he think there's an orgy going on inside? He, too, would like a taste of it. Damon chuckled to himself, imagining Nath with a hand under the lungi, trying to subdue his throbbing penis.

Damon scrunched the cigarette butt in the ashtray and then lit another immediately. He wanted to charm Flora, make her look at him, and laugh at his jokes. But he didn't know how to do it.

He watched with dismay as Robert slid closer to the girl and stretched his legs.

'Do they play rugby in India?' Robert asked.

'No, I've never heard of rugby,' she replied.

'Have you heard of wrestling?'

'Yes, that I have.'

'Rugby isn't much different, only there's a ball involved. We fight to take possession of the ball. Like this.' He pulled an imaginary ball from the air, drew his legs in, and rolled over face down with the ball between his legs and stomach.

Flora smiled. 'That's not at all like wrestling.'

'Whoever has the ball runs to the touchline and drops it on the grass. Like this,' he said and placed a ball on her lap. 'And then we do a victory dance.'

He jumped to his feet and did a Morris dance jig.

She laughed. 'You're a fool, Rub Rub.'

Neither noticed as Damon crushed the cigarette in the ashtray and got up to leave.

Back upstairs, he kicked open his bedroom door. His other friend at school, Tim, wouldn't have been so selfish. I should have invited him instead of Robert. But Tim's family was not well-off enough to afford an airline ticket. His father was a habitual drunk. He remembered helping Tim carry home a fifty-year-old man from the pub, who kept protesting that he wasn't drunk.

Damon came down early the next morning. The smell of frying sausages, eggs, and bread toasting on an open fire had already drifted out of the kitchen into the dining area.

'Good morning, Damon,' Flora said, entering the room. Robert, in his pyjamas, followed.

'Good morning,' Damon replied without looking up at either of them, still sore from last night for failing to woo Flora to his bed and angry with Robert for not giving him a chance.

Robert sat down, screeching the chair forward, picked up a knife, and gave his boiled egg a sharp whack. The egg split into two.

'I don't like boiled eggs,' Damon announced.

'Why don't you like boiled eggs?' Flora asked.

'I have a phobia. Phobia of eggs once boiled.'

Flora laughed. 'I've never heard of egg phobia.'

'It's true,' Damon said, 'I don't know what they call it, but it started years ago when my cousin played a prank on me with a cockroach inserted in a boiled egg.'

Robert picked up his boiled egg and shoved it at Damon's face.

'Don't you dare,' Damon cried, threatening him with his fork.

'That's cruel Rub Rub,' Flora said.

Mrs P, the cook, came in with a plate of scrambled eggs. Her proper name was Priyamaya Dewi. The boys had tried and failed to pronounce the name. So, they had shortened it to Mrs P.

'Mrs P?' Priyamaya had given an amused smile and a head shake. 'Call me that if you like.' She, in turn, had found *Missus* difficult to pronounce.

'We are eating out today, proper Indian cuisine,' Damon announced. 'Will you come with us?' he asked Flora.

'I'll if you want me to. But there is a problem, I don't have any change of clothes,' she replied.

'Every problem has a solution,' Damon said, 'the wardrobe in the second bedroom is full of ladies' garments. Help yourself. I am sure you will find one that will suit you.'

Flora gasped. 'But I couldn't do that. Whose are they?'

'They belonged to my aunt. She is no more. I'm confident Uncle Fred wouldn't mind if you borrowed a dress. In any case, he would never know.'

'Alright,' she replied, 'but you will have to show me the bedroom.'

'But Indian food will kill us,' Robert cried and clutched his stomach.

'I know a place that doesn't kill,' Flora said.

'We're going,' Damon added firmly. He wasn't going to let Robert have his way this time.

Even from a distance, the restaurant stood out as a popular destination for foodies. A boldly painted sign above the entrance read "Khan's Authentic Mughal Dishes."

Stepping into a haze of cigarette smoke clotted with the smells of spicy cookery, Robert gasped and slapped the air with his hand.

'Die of suffocation or food poisoning,' he said theatrically, 'Take your pick, friends, Romans, and countrymen.'

'Stay with me, dear friend. You'll love it,' Flora said, going deeper into the bowels of the restaurant.

A party of Englishmen was sitting around a table laden with a mighty array of dishes. It was an amusing spectacle of red faces, pained expressions, and weeping eyes. Some of them were tapping their open mouths, as if that would blow away the heat.

'Look what love is doing to them,' Robert said.

'This place is renowned for authentic Mughal food,' Flora said.

'Renowned for death by chilli chapati? Where do they take the bodies?' Robert cried.

Flora placed a hand on Robert's wrist to quieten him and studied the menu on a blackboard fixed to the wall. 'What would you like?' she said.

'Roast beef and boiled potatoes,' Robert snapped.

She ignored Robert's whinging and ordered a few dishes from the waiter, speaking in Bengali.

'Have you got that?' she asked.

The waiter, a lad no more than sixteen in tight trousers and a trendy haircut, nodded yes while struggling to keep a straight face.

'Why was he so amused?' Damon asked after the waiter had left the table.

'He took me for an Englishwoman and was surprised to hear me speak Bengali. They find it amusing.'

At a neighbouring table, a middle-aged Bengali in a crisp white shirt and a robust moustache was stopping people passing by him. People were slapping his hand away, taking him for a drunken fool, until a young man paused. 'Dada, what can I do for you?' he asked respectfully.

The older gentleman took the boy's wrist and pulled him firmly down to his level. 'Sit down and listen to me,' he ordered, and then began a lengthy, grief-laden discourse with weeping sobs and long, cold breaths.

'What's bothering him?' Robert said.

'He has lost his son, gastroenteritis or something. Only ten years old,' Flora whispered, 'so sad. Don't you think?'

Robert thought for a moment and then shook his shoulder. 'These things happen. What can we do?'

'Robert,' she said a little sternly as if censuring him for lack of empathy.

'You expect me to get all weepy and melancholy. No thanks. I don't even know the man. He could be making up stories. Look at him, drunk as a skunk.'

'Now you know how we feel when you get drunk,' Damon said.

'Shut your mouth,' Robert said and clicked his fingers at the waiter. 'You, yes you. Do you keep beer in this hovel?'

'Oh no sahib, no beer,' the waiter replied.

'Why not?'

'We don't have a licence, try the banya shop over the road.'

The chair creaked as Robert stood up and made for the exit, elbowing people out of his way as if he had an exclusive right to the ground under his feet.

'Is he often like this?' Flora said.

A radio cackled and burst into a Hindustani song.

Damon raised his voice. 'He doesn't like people disagreeing with him.'

'How long have you been friends with Rub Rub?'

'We were about thirteen when we met. We live on the same street in London.'

'What's he really like?'

'What do you think?'

'What do I think? … Boy is cute but selfish.'

'In truth, he's extremely ambitious. Wants to become a banker like his father.'

'What about you?'

'I'm studying accountancy.'

'Is your father an accountant too?'

'No,' Damon said, 'that's why I've chosen accountancy.'

'Dum Dum, you're so strange. You chose accountancy because your father wasn't one?'

'We don't get on. I hate everything he stands for.'

'What work does he do?'

'He's a moneylender.'

Her eyes opened a little wider. 'Moneylender?'

'He lends money to people who can't afford to pay back, at an exorbitant interest rate,' Damon said, and looked out on the street. He spotted a shirtless little boy at the entrance, begging from people leaving the restaurant.

How could he tell her why he really hated his father? Hadn't told anyone about that afternoon. Ever. He was only ten. Father, an alcoholic, often came home drunk, breaking into laughter or howling, sometimes crying like a baby. His mother would then whisk him and his sister to the bedroom and lock the door. But they could still hear him downstairs singing and sobbing alternately until he would fall asleep where he sat. One evening, Damon came home from school, rain-soaked, with wet exercise books and soggy plimsolls. Mother and sister were out. He took off his shirt, hung it to dry on the clothesline, then went to the front room to stand by the fire. He had been there five minutes, taking in the soothing heat, when father appeared at the door. 'Dad, why are you home so early?' he had asked, surprised. Father did not reply. He stared at Damon for several seconds, as if Damon were not his son, but a stranger who had walked in from the street. 'I'd like to see you completely naked,' he said eventually, dropping his briefcase on the floor. At first, Damon thought it was another of his father's drunken jokes. But Father stood in the middle of the room, his smile melting away. To disobey him when he was drunk was dangerous. He could turn violent very quickly. 'Come on, do it.' Damon heard the cold threat and smelled the alcohol on his breath.

He should have protested, but that afternoon, for some reason, he didn't have the nerve. He closed his eyes and undressed. Father carried him to the bedroom. Relax, it won't hurt, he whispered with a heavy breath. A whisper that carried urgency and threat.

But it did hurt. He thought he had screamed. He wished Cissy, the family dog, would come to his rescue. The dog's barking used to madden Father. Once, in a drunken rage, he had attempted to stab her with a smashed whiskey glass.

Later, he heard sobs coming from his father's room, sobs of sorrow and pain. Father was crying. That terrified Damon even more. He sat slumped in the corner of his room for an hour, until he heard his mother's voice.

The following morning, at breakfast, he concealed himself behind a glass of milk while his parents ate in silence. He wanted to climb up the glass and dive down to its bottom, let the milk fill his body, and wash the stickiness and the blood away. You don't have to go to school today. You don't look well, Father had said. He was relieved, for he had not done the geography homework. Father lit a cigarette and then held him close. He could hear the breakfast in Father's stomach.

'Damon …'

'Yes.'

'I was asking about your mother. Do you hate her too?' Flora said.

It took him a few moments to control the screams and turmoil in his head. 'She's different. I love my mother.'

'She's ok with you becoming an accountant?'

'Oh yes, she always wanted me to go to university. Education was important to her. She used to walk me to school and talk to teachers to see how I was doing. During exams, she used to force-feed me walnuts. I hated them, but she believed they were good for the brain. Anyway, why am I telling you all this?'

'Because you like me. Don't you, Dum Dum?' She smiled, and little dimples appeared on her cheeks. When she breathed, her breasts breathed with her. He lowered his gaze quickly and scooped a piece of meat with a fork. As he chewed, savouring the strange taste, he pictured Flora naked beneath her knee-length dress, his hand creeping up her leg, to the smooth skin of the thigh, the fine curly hair, and the warm, moist flesh. He imagined the hair was black like her eyes. When he looked up, he saw she was staring at him and felt, with certainty, that she had read his mind.

'Tell me more about you,' she said.

'I've already told you. I'm studying accountancy and …'

'No, not your career. Your story. Interests, hobbies, fetishes.'

He struggled with how to pitch himself, which enthusiasm to embrace. It occurred to him that he had none. He saw himself as an introvert, afraid of taking risks and terrified of rejection. 'I am a pretty ordinary guy,' he said.

'I reject that out of hand, Dum Dum. Think of something you like. The first thing that comes to mind.'

'Reading?'

'What do you read?'

'Oh, everything – from action, adventure, mystery to classics. My favourite is Eliott.'

'Now tell me about your weird fetishes.'

'Fetishes? … I don't have any.'

'Oh, come on, everybody has them.'

He thought about it. It occurred to him that he did have a fetish, though he had never seen it that way. He loved bangles on girls' wrists. The tinkling of silver or glass had a strange effect on him. He had seen Indian girls with forearms covered. It turned him on. In bed at night, he would visualise a hand on him, the swift movements, the bangles jangling urgently.

Convinced that he was blushing, he tried to change the topic.

'I want to ask you something. Why were you sitting by yourself at the table on Bow Barracks the other day?'

'Why do you think?'

'I don't know. I am not a mind reader.'

'I am,' she said, 'I know what's on your mind.'

'What?'

'You are about to ask me where I would have gone afterwards if we had not met.'

He shut up. That's what he was about to do, though he hated asking questions like that. It made him like his parents, who always wanted to know where he had been, and when he would be back, and why he was so late.

They saw Robert coming in with a triumphant smile. A bottle of beer in his hand, held high like a trophy.

The restaurant owner came running with sheets of newspaper. 'Sahib, but you cannot drink it here,' he implored. 'You wrap the paper around the bottle. Don't let anyone see it.'

'Bugger off, I don't need this,' Robert said, slapping the paper away. 'I'm not drinking. See, I'm only holding it in my hand. I'll take it home.'

Damon was sure his friend would have swiftly downed a bottle or two standing in the shop.

'You will ruin me. Only last week, police raided the place. It cost me twenty rupees. The rascals are always watching and becoming rich.'

'Then don't pay,' Robert said, 'fight back. Like this.' He placed the bottle on the table, stepped back, and executed a rugby tackle, using the man as a prop.

The diners roared and clanked the crockery with metal spoons.

Amid this riotous scrimmage, Flora slipped a hand into the owner's back pocket, lifted the wallet, and slipped it into her cloth bag. She flinched for a split second, seeing the grieving man with the moustache looking her way.

Chapter 5

'Do you have any beer, my friend?' Robert asked Nath, who had come in to fumigate the rooms with DDT insect killer.

Nath scratched his neck, not offering a firm reply.

'Well, you have or not?' Robert said.

Nath lowered the spray gun and looked out the window at the peepul tree.

'Does the ruddy beer grow on trees?' Robert said.

'But I'm not allowed to tell you where Mr Fred keeps his whiskey,' Nath said a little apologetically.

'You don't worry, my man. I won't tell Mr Fred.' Robert said and slapped Nath on the back. 'This is just between you and me, eh?'

Nath still hesitated but guided Robert to the rear of the house into a dimly lit chamber, like an underground tavern. A long sideboard stood against the wall, canteens of silver cutlery, crystal glasses, and decanters, all meticulously arranged on top.

Robert dived to his knees and yanked the doors open, revealing more than a dozen bottles of alcohol, mostly whiskey but also rum and gin, stacked three deep. 'The rascal has imported them from Scotland.' He pulled out the bottle nearest to him. 'Authentic Highland – must cost a bob.'

Damon came dashing. 'What have you found?

'This.' Robert showed him the bottle, a golden hue reflecting against the light. 'Shall we? One or two shots. Uncle Fred won't mind, will he?' Robert said, his eyebrows skipping up and down.

'OK then, just a little,' Damon replied. He knew this room was forbidden to them, yet the guilt, coupled with their daring, made it an exciting venture. He took three glasses from the dresser and carried them to the balcony upstairs, to Flora. She was sitting on the floor with her back against the railing. Her flowing hair rested on her shoulders, and the sun behind her, like a halo, made her appear like an ancient beauty.

Damon's head went into a spin. He wanted to grab her, take her in his arms. Just then, Robert came dancing with the whiskey bottle and sat down beside her. 'Nath found us a brilliant twelve-year-old vintage. You'll love it.' He blew the dust off the label and held it up for inspection.

'You know I don't drink this stuff,' she said.

'I'll get you some tea.' He yelled for Nath, pulled the cork out, poured a measure into a glass, and then another for Damon.

'Salute, friends.' He sipped and smacked his lips. 'I could get used to this life.'

Damon opened his eyes. For a moment, he forgot where he was. He tried to move and found his head wedged in the curved wood armrest of the sofa. He freed himself, sat up and surveyed the room. Bottles, plates, glasses, and a water jug lay on the floor, among scattered breadcrumbs like confetti and remnants of pickled vegetables. He vaguely remembered Nath bringing in bread and strong cheese. Despite the foul taste, they had gobbled it all down.

He heard someone in another part of the house. In the confused state, he assumed it was Uncle Fred. He sprang to his feet and assessed the chaos again. How will I explain all this?

'Good morning sahib.' Nath's cheery voice hit his ears in a distorted note.

'Good God, man,' Damon cried, and sank back on the sofa, 'you gave me a fright.'

Nath smiled. 'You had a big party last night.'

'We did?'

'Yes. I could hear you even at the gate.'

'Where is Madam Flora?'

'She went to bed early,' he replied unconvincingly, for he could not have known if she did or not.

Robert came in with his hands pressed to his stomach. 'I have a runny stomach.'

'You're a disgusting man, Fletcher. Your problem is because of your excessive drinking.'

'Shut your mouth.'

'I will if you shut your backside.'

They sat quietly for several minutes, staring at the mess on the floor with droopy eyes.

'Where is Flora?' Damon asked.

'Still in bed.'

They heard footsteps on the shingles outside.

'Wow, you have a visitor,' Robert whistled.

An Englishman was making his way up the path, taking long, purposeful strides in baggy black trousers, a full-sleeve shirt, and a red-and-blue patterned cravat blooming from the top of a waistcoat.

Damon went to open the door. Perhaps a neighbour, he thought.

'Good morning,' the man said in a booming voice, as if he were speaking through a hailer. 'The name is Count Sinclair Blythe.'

A cockatoo with bright, colourful feathers was sitting on the frilly sleeve of the Englishman's right arm.

'Er, good morning,' Damon replied and blinked hard, wondering if the night's excessive drinking had impaired his vision, if the bird was a figment of his imagination.

'I know not if this moment is convenient for you to meet a stranger. Pray, forgive my audacity. I am eager to initiate an acquaintance at the earliest possible moment. As I mentioned, my name is Count Sinclair Blythe,' he said and paused.

Damon hesitated, wondering how to respond to the strange man with a bird on his arm.

'I can almost hear the thoughts unfurling in your heads. Is he really a Count? I must dispel any notion that I am a real Count. It's merely a name my parents gave me. Picture this: I am in my mother's womb, mere days from entering the world. My parents are in the company of a certain Count Sinclair of Dumbarton. Charmed they are by this gentleman. So, when I came along a week later, they didn't hesitate to name me after him. So, there I was, a babe of two days, unable to register my dissent. Still, I mustn't grumble, for it is fortunate that they hadn't met Count Dracula.' He hollered with laughter. The bird fluttered its wings as if in protest. 'May I be so bold as to enquire about you two?'

'My name is Damon, and this is my friend Robert,' Damon replied, still standing in the hall. He dared not invite him into the living room.

'A pleasure indeed.' He raised his arm higher. 'This dear birdy is Countess, on account of she's female. Say hello to our new friends, come, come, now, say hello.'

'Shut up … shut up … shut up.'

'Did the bird speak?' Robert's mouth opened wide.

'Behave, Countess,' Count said, scolding the bird, and to Robert, 'you must excuse her; she's an excellent mimic of words. My wife has corrupted her.' He spotted a framed photograph on the wall and stopped speaking. It was an old black-and-white photo of a young man in a bow tie and tails, posing in front of a marble balustrade with a jardinière sitting on top. He pointed a stubby finger at the photograph. 'You must forgive me, for I've been lax in giving you the real reason for my visit, which is to enquire about my friend Fredrick.'

'My uncle,' Damon said, 'is battling diabetes and soaring blood pressure. He wishes to stay in London until he's strong again.'

'Oh, that's distressing news. Still, he's in a good place for recuperation, unlike Calcutta. The heat here can lay low the strongest and heartiest of a man. How are you two faring in this weather?'

'We love it,' Robert said, 'May I offer you a drink of whiskey?'

'Oh no. I shouldn't,' Count said and thrust the heel of his left hand forward like a traffic policeman ordering a car to stop. 'You are young men, and you feel invincible. But heed my advice. Please don't overdo it, at least not for the next few days, until you're fully acclimatised. Don't go out in the midday sun. I've given the same advice to my niece, who is here searching for a husband.' He glanced fleetingly into Damon and Robert's eyes. 'I would invite you over to meet her, but truth be told, I can't because an unpleasant lady has taken refuge in my front porch. She killed her husband last week and ate him. I've been observing her for days now.'

'Shut up … shut up …'

'Shush.' He gave the bird a reproachful look and then continued. 'Before I alarm you out of your wits, let me clarify: the lady living on my front porch is a spider, a rare species not often seen in this part of the world. I'll, of course, catch her at some point and take her to Dr Brown at the zoo, who's an excellent entomologist.'

Silence.

'So, what's the news of London?' Count continued, 'I haven't been back in ten years.'

'Are you planning to go back?' Damon asked.

Count looked sideways out the window. 'I'll not be returning to Blighty.'

'Why not?' Robert said.

'I have my reasons. So now I must take your leave. Come on, Countess, we have work to do. Say ciao to your friends. Ciao, ciao.' He blocked the daylight at the door as he left. 'Do let Fredrick know I had called,' he said and was gone.

Damon and Robert looked at each other and broke into laughter.

'Strange man. He must be a circus clown.'

'Nah, he was too refined for that. He could be a real Count.'

'One thing is sure, he's looking for a match for his niece,' Robert said with a wink, 'here's your chance, mate. Get in there quick.'

'She must be desperate. I mean, who comes to India in search of a husband?'

Chapter 6

With Uncle Fred's dressing gown on his back, Damon descended the steps to the dining room. The sun's rays falling at an angle had divided the hall in half. And the clock on the wall said eight-thirty. 'I could do with a cup of tea, Mrs P.'

'Yes,' she said, wiping the table with a kitchen cloth as if dealing with years of accumulated grime, 'sit here all morning - waiting for you people to get up. Breakfast has gone cold. Sahib Freddy never does such a thing. He always let me leave on time to go to the temple for my morning prayer. Also, I want money for grocery shopping.'

'You're a good woman,' he said.

'Good. Yes. My husband also say that, but he no give me peace.' She returned to the kitchen, mumbling and began whisking something with a metal spoon, creating a racket like pellets fired from a shotgun.

Fifteen minutes later, Robert barged in, sniffed the sausages on the table, scrunched his nose, and yelled for Mrs P.

'Mrs P has gone. I've given her the afternoon off.'

'She serves us this cold breakfast, and you reward her by giving the afternoon off?'

'You should have risen on time if you wanted your breakfast hot,' Damon said, taking the last sip from the cup. 'She doesn't like to be late for the temple. Moreover, you need to start disposing of your whiskey bottles. Her faith prevents her from touching anything alcoholic.'

'Aha, she'll be rendered impure by a mere touch?' he cried, 'I expect you believe that crap.'

'That's not the point. We must respect their culture.'

'Respect culture? My fat arse.'

'At last, you're right about something,' Damon snapped.

'And what might that be?' Robert said. He knocked a boiled egg against the side of a bowl.

'About the size of your arse.'

Flora clinked her cutlery. 'Boys, please.'

After breakfast, they went to the balcony and settled down on the sheets under the canopy.

'What are you reading?' Flora said.

'Hemingway,' Damon replied, showing her the cover, 'Hemingway's debut novel about the adventures of a group of American expatriates in Paris drinking their way through life.'

'A bit like you then. Only you are English, not American,' she said with a smile and added, 'you are in Calcutta, not in Paris.'

'Ah, but I am not an expatriate. I am here for a mere four weeks.'

Robert, lying on his back with eyes closed, made a grunting sound indicating he disagreed with Damon.

Damon ignored him and turned to the back cover. 'Ernest Hemingway paints a picture of unrealised love, from the streets of Paris to the running of the bulls in Pamplona, Spain.'

'Drunk yanks looking for love?' Robert stated.

'Does this bit apply to you too?' Flora said to Damon.

Her sharp, piercing look pinned him to the wall. He struggled to respond.

A flock of blue-tailed bee-eaters descending from the sky.

They circled the peepul tree, turned, dived over the balcony, and flew away in formation.

'You, Finnegan. What's the collective word for a flock of starlings?' Robert said.

'These are not starlings,' Damon corrected, 'wrong colour.'

'I know that, but my question is about starlings.'

'I don't know and don't care.'

'Murmuration boy. A flock of starlings is a murmuration. Don't forget.'

'Yes, mister dickhead sir. Please, sir, may I be informed what a flock of dickheads be? Will it be mastuberation?' Damon said, snapped the hardback book shut and got up.

He went down, out through the kitchen to the pond in the garden, his trouser legs scraping the grass. Sun's rays reflecting on the still water hit his eyes. He caught a splash. A fish or a frog, he thought. The ripples dispersed slowly. The surface became still again, but for the dragonflies hovering a few inches above. He picked up a pebble and skimmed it across the water's surface. As he turned around, looking for another flat pebble, he saw Flora standing at the doorway, a hand cupped over her eyes.

For a small girl, she had such long legs and arms: an artist's impression of an ideal beauty, Madonna's dreamy eyes, and full lips.

'What are you doing?' she said.

'Nothing really, only skimming pebbles.'

'Can I have a go?' she said and came down barefoot, stepping gingerly over the grass. Her toenails, painted a light shade of rouge, matched the glass bangles on her right wrist.

'Be careful. The ground is rough here,' he said, handing her a small pebble. 'Throw it like this in underarm action.' He demonstrated how it's done.

She readied herself by pulling the arm back. The bangles jingled as she threw the pebble. 'I'm useless at this,' she said demurely with a disappointed smile and sat down cross-legged on the grass. Half her face was in the shadow; the other half glimmered in the sunlight. It revealed the dark tone of her skin, confirming that she wasn't entirely Caucasian.

She raised her hand and offered him her varnished rouge nails. 'Does this colour suit me?'

He was speechless for a few moments. 'Yes, it's a beautiful colour,' he said. He longed to touch her hand and the nails, a strange wanting, but his fingers wouldn't do it. Instead, he memorised the bluish veins on the back of her hand, which appeared to melt away into the wrist.

Neither spoke for a while.

'Damon, I want to ask you something,' she said, 'would it be all right if I stayed in the house for a few more days?'

He paused, contemplating. Why does she want to stay here, even though she has a home somewhere in the city? They had found her sitting alone the other day, surrounded by burly sailors. A thought crossed his mind and quickly swirled into a tempest. Is she one of them? No, it can't be. He dismissed the idea, cast it away with a firm throw of the pebble into the water.

'I suppose you can stay if Robert wants you to,' he said.

She appeared relieved, which pleased Damon.

'Thank you, Damon.' She puckered her lips and blew a kiss at him. 'I would like to pay my way. I've got money,' she said after a pause.

'Look, there's no need for you to contribute. You are here as our guest …' He shut up, seeing Robert at the kitchen door.

'There you are, I was wondering where you guys had disappeared,' Robert called.

'Thank you,' she mouthed quickly at Damon as Robert came bounding down.

Chapter 7

One night, a tropical downpour kept them awake. The staccato symphony of raindrops dancing upon the roof, the rat-tap-tap of liquid percussion, and water cascading down the gutters. It seemed to go on and on.

'That was a massive thunderstorm,' Damon said the next morning, 'I couldn't sleep a wink.'

Mrs P chuckled. 'That was nothing, sahib—just a rain. Look outside, nothing,' she said as she placed a teapot on the breakfast table.

Nath came in with a spray gun, bringing with him the odour of DDT.

'Nath,' Robert said, smothering his nose with a hand, 'this stuff is a killer.'

Nath smiled. 'You are right, sahib, it kills. But not big Englishmen like you. It kills little, little mosquitoes and insects.' He gestured with his thumb and forefinger. 'You may not know that after heavy rain, we get insects, big fat ones. We must kill them with this.' He pumped the gun with his right hand, releasing a fine spray of the chemical.

Outside the open window, a crow's full-throated cawing was competing with the cackle of the radio tuned to the morning news. The names Gandhi and the Congress party, the Swadeshi movement, were cropping up repeatedly and sensational reports of attacks on the English, Anglo-Indians, Christians, Chinese and anyone else suspected of being less than euphoric about the prospect of an independent India. Delhi was passing one law after another, hoping to kill the dissent. An official from Internal Security came on the air. The Imperial Police have the staff to protect everyone; no need to panic, he said, his mien as guileless as a fresher on an Oxbridge campus.

'I suppose you already know all that,' Robert said, addressing Flora.

She didn't respond but asked Mrs P for another cup of tea.

'Your friends? What do they make of it?'

'My friends are all Indian,' she replied and picked up a silver candlestick from the side table. 'They are naturally in support of the movement. In any case, you are hearing the sanitised version coming from the Viceroy's office. The reality is far more harrowing. I know, for I see it every day.'

'Have you been threatened?' Robert asked.

'No, that's because I know how to look after myself. I speak Bengali to let them know I am Indian. But you must understand that this hatred of the British didn't come from nothing. This anger and resentment cannot be divorced from the reality of your people's extravagant wealth. It matters when they see the English eating expensive meat joints in a country of dal and rice. It matters to Indians when they see you live in big mansions, sail to London and return with amazing goodies. People in the street feel humiliated and angry.'

An uneasy silence followed. The radio presenter continued reading the news, speaking perfect BBC English, but with an undertone of an accent: Prime Minister Baldwin is sending a commission to India, headed by Lord Simon, to decide India's political future. According to reports, the Congress Party and Gandhi intend to boycott the commission because there is no

Indian representation. Demonstrations are planned against Lord Simon when he arrives in …

Robert threw a hand up in the air. 'See, the Gandhi-wallas are at it again. You are on their side, aren't you?' he said, as if accusing her of betrayal.

'Wow, what a dumb question, Fletcher. Don't you see Flora *is* Indian?' Damon said.

'OK, tell me this. Do you want us to leave India?' Robert said, narrowing his eyes

'No, darling, Rub Rub. I don't want you to leave. You are welcome to stay as long as you wish. Only I want to see India governed by Indians and not by your countrymen sitting in London.'

'That's my girl,' Damon said, 'you give it to him like it is.' He reached for a leather-bound tome he had picked up earlier from Uncle Fred's library of books: Robert Clive, The History of the British East India Company.

'I was reading this last night,' he said, opening the book to an inner page and quoting a passage. 'Robert Clive's East India Company set up the foundation of the British rule of India. But Clive arrived in India impoverished by debt. In seventeen-fifty-one, they appointed him as Captain to lead a garrison. He scored an impressive victory at the Battle of Plassey in seventeen-fifty-seven and rapidly proved himself as a formidable leader. That was a turning point in his career. Later, he led a force of two hundred British soldiers and five hundred Indian sepoys on a sixty-five-mile march from Madras to the desert town of Arcot, then the capital of the Carnatic region. That enabled the East India Company to reach the Bay of Bengal, one of the country's wealthiest regions. Its abundant natural resources, gold and diamonds, as well as its textiles, astonished the British. Not long afterwards, the East India Company became the wealthiest capitalist organisation in the world.'

Robert interrupted Damon. 'So, it's clear that without Clive, there would not have been a British empire the size it is now. And we would not be sitting here enjoying comforts which we cannot even dream of in England,' he said.

'That is true, but it doesn't make it morally defensible. We manipulated them, waged wars, and plundered their wealth as if there wasn't a tomorrow. For what? So, a handful of people could become obscenely wealthy. That includes the Royal Family,' Damon said.

'So, what?' Robert retorted, 'he did what he had to do.'

Damon continued quoting from the book. 'William Pitt, the British Prime Minister, had described Clive as a heaven-born soldier in recognition of his military success at Plassey. Nor do historians dispute that Clive's victories against the Mughals marked the beginning of British rule in India.'

Robert yawned aloud.

Damon continued. 'By early seventeen-seventy-two, the public began to understand what lay behind the East India Company's vast profits. London's newspapers were reporting that Indians were dying in the streets and the fields. The published testimonies of Company's men who worked in India say Clive's governorship was the cause of near famine ...'

'All that is history, my boy,' Robert said, 'what matters is now, today, people are so comfortable, no more starvation.'

'Look around you, Robert. Most people in India are poor, only a step away from starvation. There is a vast disparity of wealth. You should ask Mrs P if her life is comfortable. The comfortable people, the rich, you're talking about are the English in India and their Indian hangers-on.'

'We call those Indians toadies,' Flora said, making a face.

'Ah, come on,' Robert said, getting agitated, 'there are people like that in every society. Don't we have them in England?'

Flora did not reply, while Damon turned the pages of the book.

Flora replaced the candlestick on the table. 'Would you like to see how the other half lives?' she said.

'You mean the native Indians,' Robert said, 'what is there to see?'

'I mean the English people Damon is talking about.'

'I would,' Damon said promptly.

Later that afternoon, Damon asked Nath to fetch a car from the private taxi company.

Flora gave the driver directions to the Great Eastern Hotel. 'But take the route through the old town.'

The old town didn't look that old; it was just heavily congested. Its unplanned narrow lanes wound haphazardly around houses and ancient trees. The driver began pumping the horn at every turn. Women were picking up their babies; men dismounted the bicycles to stand pasted to the walls. Two bare-chested coolies lugging a cart piled high with bales of merchandise pulled it into a ditch to let the car pass.

Heads were popping up at open windows. Children came out of the houses, half-naked and barefoot. They began running alongside the car, laughing and jeering, gawking at the occupants. Damon thought of his childhood. Mother would tell him repeatedly how privileged he was to have a good home, clean clothes, and schooling. But he would not be convinced. He felt deprived, seeing classmates with bigger toys and flashy clothes.

These children have nothing at all, yet they appear so happy. He wound down the window and waved. The children waved back, screaming with delight, as if he were a famous film star.

Suddenly, Robert made a fist and shook it threateningly out the window. The children slowed at once and stopped running, disappointed that the fun was over.

Damon saw the hurt in Flora's eyes as she glanced back at the dispersing children. It made him think. She has lived here all her life; why has she not become immune to scenes of deprivation? Who is she? Why does she say so little about herself and her family?

'Wait, I know a friend who lives around here. Would you like to meet her? See how they live?' Flora said.

'Yes, a good idea,' Damon said.

They got out of the car and entered a muddy back lane.

'Where does Laxmi live?' Flora asked a girl tending to a goat in front of a house. Her hair plaited into two tails and her pyjama-like tunic hitched above the ankles.

The girl stared, as if she had never seen Englishmen before.

'Do you know Laxmi?' Flora repeated.

'Through there,' the girl said, pointing.

They walked up the alley, sidestepping little puddles. At the end, facing a brick wall pasted with cakes of cow dung, Flora firm-stepped to a door. She was about to knock. The door flung open, revealing a fearsome-looking woman. Chapped pink lipstick and emerald eyeshadows, pronounced chin, she stood with her hands on her hips.

'What do you want?'

'I am looking for Laxmi. Does she live here?'

She eyed Flora scowling, chuckled. She looked at Damon and Robert, who were a few feet behind, and then back at Flora. 'Usually, men ask for her.'

'She is a friend. Is she in?' Flora said.

The woman shifted her weight onto the other foot and turned around heavily. 'She is in her room at the back. I think.'

'It's alright,' Flora whispered to Damon. 'This is a women-only house.'

'You mean one of those houses …?'

Flora nodded.

'Your friend is a prostitute?'

Flora did not respond.

'Interesting,' Robert said, suddenly keen to explore.

Her room was a shed behind the house. A marigold planted in a tin can was sitting near the steps beside a doormat, giving the impression of a houseproud owner.

Flora knocked. No response. She tried again. This time, they heard movement inside – a string bed groaned and then footsteps. The door opened a fraction at first and then swung open wide.

'Florence,' a girl screamed and threw herself at Flora, wrapping her arms around her neck.

'I'm so glad to have found you. It hasn't been the same since you left,' Flora said, smiling too.

'I couldn't go on living there forever, you know,' Laxmi said as if there was an age limit.' She saw Damon and Robert. The smile left her face.

'It's alright, Laxmi. They are my friends. We were passing

by and thought we'd stop by to say hello. I also wanted to see where you lived.'

The smile returned on Laxmi's face, an easy, little girl smile. Like Flora, she had an attractive figure, high cheekbones, and sharp, darting eyes. Unlike the woman at the gate, she didn't have any makeup on and looked better for it. Damon could see why she would be in demand by men.

'Come inside,' Laxmi said.

The room was small. Not quite enough height to stand without touching the ceiling, a string bed lay on one side with a rolled-up bedding at the top. The only other piece of furniture was an old chair and a table, which was pushed against the wall. On the floor were a few metal pots and pans.

'Shall I make some tea?' Laxmi asked.

Damon wondered how she cooked or went to the toilet. Perhaps the lipstick woman lets her use her house.

'No, tea. We are not stopping,' Flora said, 'I just wanted to see that you are well.'

'I'm alright,' Laxmi said, rocking her head, 'you know.'

'I'll come again,' Flora said.

The driver turned the car around and nearly ran over a dog, impatient to leave the old time behind. No one spoke for a long time. Feeling as if the silence had swelled into a fourth person, competing with Flora for attention. Damon kept his gaze out the window, seeing nothing.

The car entered a broad avenue with tram tracks, and suddenly everything appeared brighter. Gone was the spicy odour of steaming dal and fried fish, the raucous cry of street children and tinkling bicycle bells.

'Why did Laxmi panic when she saw us?' Damon finally broke the silence.

Flora thought for a moment. 'Englishmen only ever go there when they want to harass someone or have them arrested. Sometimes they do it to collect bribes.'

'Where did you meet Laxmi?' Damon asked earnestly as if he needed to know.

'In the home.'

'Home?' Damon said.

'It's a home for abandoned children. Nuns found Laxmi wandering the streets. She was only six at the time. She has no family,' Flora said.

Damon wondered why Flora was living in that home when she had already confirmed she had a family and that her father was a Jesuit priest. But he said nothing. It would be insensitive to ask, he thought.

The car turned into a broad tree-lined avenue, screaming affluence, with whitewashed villas protected by hedges, walls, and uniformed guards at the gates. 'This area is the preserve of first-rate men from second-rate towns like Croydon or Slough,' she said, 'they house administrators, military officers, and rich merchants. Endless rounds of golf, garden parties in gymkhanas, and gin on the veranda. Life is good here.'

'Wow,' Robert said, 'I wouldn't mind going to a gin party.'

'If you are willing to lead a pretentious lifestyle, show you have wealth and good connections, they will invite you every time. But if you slip once, they will dump you as if you were a station coolie.'

'I'd rather be a coolie,' Damon said.

'That should be easy,' Robert said, 'you already look like one.'

Damon ignored him.

'We are entering the financial district now. Ahead is Dalhousie Square. Government offices, banks, big merchant houses, the High Court, are all clustered around here.'

Finally, the hotel came into view. A sign in the fading light said: Great Eastern Hotel.

Cars were swinging over to the main entrance under the guidance of a uniformed constable in white gloves, a fresh-faced Englishman.

'A London bobby in Calcutta,' Damon cried.

'Damon, this is the Great Eastern, the finest hotel this side of Suez. This is where the cream of English society comes together to play. It would hardly be proper for them to receive caution from a native constable when they come out roaring drunk. Just think of the scandal.'

A doorman in uniform opened the doors for them and bowed. 'Welcome to Great Eastern,' he said as if he meant it.

'Thank you,' Damon replied.

Flora grabbed his arm and pulled him in. 'Observe the etiquette, Damon. One doesn't stop to thank minions,' she said, sarcasm evident in her voice.

The lobby was buzzing with small talk, shouted greetings, and laughter. Military officers in dress uniforms, businesspeople in buttoned-up tunics, and fashionable ladies in silk, satin, and decorated bonnets. Native staff, dressed in starched white, were flitting from guest to guest with trays of canapes. Feeling out of place in his everyday clothes, Damon hunched his shoulders as if it would make him obscure.

Flora led them to a side lobby with a dazzling display of mirrors and lights on one side, shops on the other.

Robert saw a camera shop and barged in.

'Can I have a look at that one?' he said.

'Kodak Junior, sir, an excellent choice,' said the Sikh shop assistant, dressed smartly in a navy turban and matching trousers. He handed the camera to Robert and moved on to deal with another customer.

Robert peered through the lens and flicked the shutters, making out he was a skilled cameraman, leaning sideways on bent knees to catch a good shot.

'May I have a look at that one?'

The Sikh brought down the Agfa Box 44.

'Not Agfa, the one beside it.'

This time, Sikh handed over a Kodak Brownie.

'Now this I like,' Robert said, turning the gadget over. 'Daddy has one too, and a Leica.'

'Let's go. We can't afford these things.' Damon tugged Robert's shirt.

'Wait.' He asked Flora to pose and clicked her from many angles.

'Enough,' Damon said and pulled him out of the shop.

Ahead was the Nightingale Bar. They decided to go in and explore. Here too, there was the buzz of small talk, laughter, tinkling glasses, and a fug of cigarette smoke. On a raised dais, an Indian dressed in a black tie was playing a grand piano. The entire wall behind the piano setting was covered with a mural of nightingales with spread wings above a Romanesque cathedral, giving the room an art gallery ambience.

'What grand place,' Robert said, 'let's have a beer.'

A waiter guided them to a table at the far end and pulled the chairs out for them to be seated.

A bunch of ladies was sitting at the table beside theirs, all in their finest evening wear. Their loud chatter carried to the tables around them.

'Have a drink, Mother,' the lady in pink said.

'I like to enjoy my drink slowly,' replied the older woman, her wavy hair straying from under the bonnet.

'How is one to see real India?' one said.

'Try seeing Indians,' replied the tall one in light green.

'As if one can avoid seeing them.'

The other three laughed.

A woman in grey swayed over to the table. 'Sorry, I am late.'

'I have avoided seeing them since landing,' the fourth lady said, 'except my servant, of course, who is a jolly nice young man.'

'Now be careful praising your servants. It goes to their head. Before you know it, they will start getting fresh with you.'

'Oh, how awful. Francis says one is better off employing women servants.'

'Oh, he would say so, wouldn't he?'

Robert chuckled, listening to their talk, as he drummed his fingers on the table.

'What I mean is I was a nurse before I married Richard. I used to come across them frequently in hospitals. A most unsuitable position for an Englishwoman. One's only hope was to hold sternly aloof.'

'Aloof from your patients?'

'Why, the kindest thing one can do to a native is to let him die.'

Flora put down her coffee cup and swung around sharply. 'Madam, didn't you know before you boarded the ship that Indians live in this country?'

'Oh, my.' The ladies shut up and huddled together as if they were on a crowded bus.

'Bitches,' Flora hissed, loud enough for them to hear.

Damon placed a hand on Flora's arm. 'Calm down. Look this way.'

She turned back slowly, her face flushed red and sweaty.

'Take a deep breath,' Damon said.

'Alright … I am alright … don't patronise me.' She calmed down slowly, looking straight ahead of her for several seconds. And then, as if she had seen something extremely disagreeable, she picked up her bag from the floor. The chair screeched as she stood up. 'Now that you have seen how the other half lives, let's go,' she said.

Back at Burnham Cottage, Robert went to the balcony and stood looking into the night sky. Fireworks were exploding nearby. Flashes of red, blue, and green, dressing the sky with floating glitter backed up by a lively beat of Hindi music. 'It's wedding season,' Nath had said the previous day, 'an auspicious time of the year for getting married.'

Robert struck a match, and as he brought the flame to the cigarette, he felt an arm around his neck. He turned around and found Flora standing with an expectant smile, arms behind her back.

'This is for you,' she said and whipped around a package from behind her.

'A camera?' he cried.

'Do you like it?'

'Yes,' he said, 'I have always wanted a Kodak Brownie.'

He opened the box, pulled out the camera and brought the

view screen to his eyes. 'Flora, this looks just like the one in the camera shop.'

'It's for you and Rub Rub. Take pictures of your holiday.'

'It's brand new,' he said, 'but I didn't see you buy it at the shop.'

She said nothing but continued to look at his face for signs of approval.

'Flora, tell me the truth. Where did you find it?

'I borrowed it,' she said, 'I'll pay them later.'

'Do they know?'

'No.'

'That's called stealing, Flora,' he said, incredulous, and then burst out laughing. 'I'll be damned. I didn't see you do it.'

'If you don't like it, I'll take it back,' she said.

He did not reply. Let her interpret his silence however she wished. He didn't care.

She waited for him to say more. Finally, she huffed her shoulders and went back in.

A mixed-up girl, he thought. A thief? Strange. She doesn't seem the type. What about the man in the bar? She was running away from him. If she's in trouble, I will not get involved. I can't afford to. But he needed to know more.

He went to look for her. She was in his bedroom, sitting at the marble-topped dressing table, combing her hair with Mrs Fred's silver-mounted hairbrush. Her dress hung loose over her shoulders.

He stopped at the door. She continued brushing as if unaware of his presence.

'Look at me. I've something to say,' he said.

'Go on, I am listening,' she replied without turning.

'Who was that man in the Nightingale bar?'

'Which man? As I remember, the place was full of them.'

'The man on the table behind us. You took off as soon as you saw him.'

'I don't know what you're talking about.'

'You panicked when you saw him. Damon saw it too.'

'He's wrong. I wanted to leave because of those awful women. You heard them yourself. Didn't you?'

'Yes, but …'

'Tomorrow I am going away. I must show my face, or they will think something has happened to me. But I'll be back in two days.'

'Show the pretty face to whom?'

'To the people at the home.'

'Is this something to do with that man?'

'No, nothing to do with him.'

'Who was he? I want to know.'

She stopped brushing. As if by accident, the dress slid further down her shoulders, exposing more of her breast.

'Come here,' she said.

He walked over to the dressing table.

She half rose from the stool and planted a kiss on his mouth.

Surprised, he looked down at her, at the exposed breast, pink, with veins just visible under the skin. He took her arm. 'Come here.'

'Wait,' she said and placed her hand on his chest, 'oh, you're so strong.'

'What's that supposed to mean?'

She stood up and kissed him again on the mouth, and then

pulled away, leaving him panting. She unclipped the dress at the neck, took it off and threw it on the back of the chair. She was braless. And then she lowered the slip to the floor, stepped out of it, sat down on the stool and began combing her hair.

He stood rooted to the spot, blushing and confused.

'Aren't you hot in those clothes?' she said, 'take them off.'

He fidgeted with the buttons at first, then took off his shirt and trousers. Down to his underpants and socks, he stood like a shy schoolboy.

'Take off the socks.'

He took off one, then the other.

'The underpants, too,' she said, 'want some help?'

He bristled. I don't need a girl showing me how to take off my pants. He pulled the pants down with a sharp tug and quickly placed his hands over the crotch.

'You shy?'

'What? Me?' As if it were a dare, he pulled his hands away.

'Kiss me,' she said.

He looked at her breasts.

'Not there, stupid, on the mouth.'

Chapter 8

The body was lying face up in an open sewer. Limbs at unnatural angles, chin on his chest, a thread of blood-stained spit dangling from the smashed jaw. The starched white dress shirt was ripped and bloodied, the black tie and tuxedo, once symbols of celebration, now shrouds of sorrow. And finally, there was the scrap of paper lying on the chest.

'If you're going to get yourself killed, you may as well look your best.' The voice was foreign to the rhythm of the street. Damon pivoted to find its source. There he stood, an outsider in every sense, taller than the rest, a thatch of dirty blond hair on his head, a week's bristle on his face. He was the only European amid a collection of gawkers, hawkers, and housewives, who were jostling for a glimpse of the corpse. 'I wouldn't hang around here too long. The stench will be unbearable soon. Strong enough even to turn the stomach of a Calcutta fishmonger.'

Damon realised the man was talking to him and Robert.

'Hello,' Damon replied. He didn't know what else to say. They had set out to explore Kalighat to see the temple, only to be caught up in the melee.

'A little peon discovered him while out on his rounds. Almost scared the life out of the poor bugger,' the blonde-haired stranger was saying.

Damon had never seen a dead body before. And now here he was with a dead Englishman in a Calcutta back street.

Klaxon call of danger was ringing in his ears. What if they got implicated in the murder?

'Word has spread. Murder is good entertainment the world over, and here in these back lanes, you can sell tickets to see a dead sahib,' the blonde said and then clapped with sudden excitement as if his theory had been validated. 'Look over there, look,' he said, pointing.

A street performer had hurriedly set up a stall. His trained monkey, dressed in a red waistcoat, was dancing on its hind legs, a dervish of desperation in its movements, while the monkey-master provided percussion backing on a damroo.

'Who is the man?' Robert asked, raising his voice over the din.

'A businessman. His name is Sinclair Blythe. He owns the biggest meat-processing factory in Calcutta.'

'Count Sinclair Blythe,' Damon cried and immediately swung around for another look at the corpse. But the dead man was already under the cover of a tarpaulin, and constables were setting up barricades.

'Ah, so you know him,' the blonde said, observing Damon with a keen eye.

'No, no, I don't think so,' Damon replied quickly and looked around him, as if checking for an escape route. He elbowed Robert in the ribs. The two turned around and began walking away.

'Did I say something to upset you?' the blonde yelled, 'Wait, where are you going?'

'Alipore,' Robert snapped over his shoulder.

'Do you know your way? Easy to lose oneself in these narrow lanes.'

They continued walking.

'I am telling you. You will lose your way,' the blonde said, catching up with them.

Robert slowed a little. 'Show us then, the quickest way out of here.'

'Sure, I will,' he said and overtook Robert and Damon to block their path. 'I'll get you out before the police catch up with you. But first, I want to know what you are doing here.'

'Police? What would they want from us? We had nothing to do with it,' Robert said.

'That could be so, but the point here is this. An Englishman is dead, and even before the spilt blood has cooled, two more Englishmen happen to be at the scene. Do you see, my friend, the reason the police will want to speak to you?'

Blood drained from Damon's face. 'But we were only just passing by.'

The blonde appeared to notice the fear in Damon's eyes. 'Don't worry. I will get you out of here,' he said and waved at them to follow him. 'Don't waste time.'

He set off at a fast pace, his baggy cotton trousers floundering as if tethered to his waist by the merest of threads.

'Did you see what was written on the note?' Robert asked.

'Oh yes. It said simply, Leave India or this fate awaits you all.'

'Work of fanatics, do you think?'

'It's possible but unlikely. Bengalis are hot-headed people. They take great pleasure in winning an argument. Like all armchair revolutionaries, they will shout abuse, even threaten to kill you. However, they are lazy when it comes to putting words into action … no, that note, it is … how you say … a red herring. This, I believe, is the result of a business deal gone wrong.'

'You do know we had nothing to do with it,' Robert said, with an emphasis on the word, nothing.

'What I know or not is irrelevant, my friend. What matters is what the police believe.'

'You were there before us,' Damon said as if implying he could be a suspect too.

'Yes. The truth is, police know me and know what I do,' he said.

'What do you do?'

'I am a journalist, a crime reporter.'

'Then let me get this straight. You knew a crime was about to be committed, so you got there in double quick time to catch it in action?'

Blonde threw his head back and laughed, attracting the attention of two men at the roadside barber's stall. 'It was pure coincidence, my friend. I had just left the Kali temple when I saw people running into the lane. I knew instantly something bad had happened. It's the instinct.' He tapped his head with the knuckles and made the face of an intrepid fortune teller. 'Sixth sense, you see. Do you believe in a sixth sense?'

'No,' Robert said, 'I believe only in what I see with my eyes.'

'You're not a sentimental fellow, like me. Sentimental and romantic.' He took out a tiny tin box from his pocket, twisted the lid off and held it to Robert's face. 'Do you know what this is?'

Robert peeked in and drew back sharply.

Blonde laughed. 'This is holy powder, not poison. Hindus smear it on their foreheads after the morning prayer. It symbolises that God has driven the evil away and blessed the wearer. I always carry it with me. I know it keeps me safe.'

'You have an accent,' Damon said, 'are you French?'

'Yes and no,' he replied, pedalling his hands alternately up and down. 'I was born in France, my father was from Denmark, but my mother's roots were deep in English soil. You see, I don't know who I am. But my name is Pierre. Of that I am certain.'

'Pleased to meet you, Pierre. My name is Damon, and my friend here is Robert.'

They walked in silence for a while. The blonde was guiding them through narrow passageways—women cooking in outdoor kitchens, impregnating the air with the odour of fried fish, dhal, and rice. Faces were turning toward the strangers.

'Bhalo achho,' Pierre shouted at a shirtless rickshaw puller seated on a stool and sipping tea out of a clay pot.

The man grinned and offered them a rickshaw ride.

'No, no.' Pierre jogged briskly in one spot. 'I must work my legs, or they will wither away.'

'We are nearly there,' he said to Damon and Robert, 'if you don't mind me asking, when I mentioned Sinclair Blythe, you appeared startled. May I know why?'

'The truth is,' Damon replied, 'we have met him. He came to my uncle's house the other day.'

'When exactly was that?'

'A week ago.'

'Merde, c'est mauvais, That's not good. And did he meet your uncle?'

'No. My uncle is in London,' Damon replied.

'I can tell you Sinclair Blythe has friends in the government, including LG.'

'LG?'

'Lieutenant Governor of Bengal, a figure second only to the Viceroy of India, a powerful man.'

'And we thought he was a circus clown.'

'Clown?' Pierre chuckled. 'He is eccentric, loves animals. He's a patron of Alipore Zoo. One thing is certain: his death will rattle people in high places. They will try to pin it on Indian nationalists, which I am almost certain isn't the case.'

'What makes you certain?' Damon said.

'Consider it this way. If they – how you say – want to put a lid on the truth, they will arrest a token few freedom fighters from the Indian National Congress and put them in jail for the murder.'

Damon remained silent, unsure of Pierre's credentials. How could he know so much?

'Here we are,' Pierre said, stopping outside a bicycle repair shop on a bustling main road, a tram track dissecting it in two halves. 'There is the bus stop,' he said, pointing.

He drew Robert and Damon close by placing a hand on each of their shoulders. 'See, I kept my promise. But, before you go, I would like to buy you a coffee. It's not often I meet people who hobnob with the upper class like Sinclair Blythe.'

Robert nodded. 'I could do with a coffee.'

The Bengal Coffee House wasn't a coffee house. Tea appeared as the beverage of choice. Smoke-filled and noisy, it was a debating chamber for the young. High not just on caffeine but on politics, too.

'Bengalis love their tea,' the Pierre explained, 'and they like even more to gather in groups to discuss how to solve the country's problems, how to rid India of the English.' He winked. 'No offence meant. But don't worry, these folks are harmless. If you meet them at a personal level, they will embrace you like a brother, invite you home to meet the family and insist you dine with them. And they will say, you're welcome to stay in India, but others must leave.'

'Do you have many Indian friends?' Damon asked.

'Oui, one or two. Only recently, one said, Pierre, you walk the streets like you were born here, don't you fear an attack by a swadeshi hothead? I replied, I don't, because I am not English.' He made an apologetic face. 'No offence meant, huh.'

'Who do you work for?'

'I used to work for the Daily Mail in London. After years of crime reporting, I wanted to move to politics. They said we can't have a Frenchman talking politics in England. Now, I am freelance. It suits me fine.'

Someone walloped a table at the other end of the hall, which was followed by shouts and screams.

'Relax, they are celebrating something. It's just a Bengali thing,' Pierre said, 'so, are you residing with your uncle?'

'Yes, while he's in London,' Damon replied.

Pierre contemplated for a moment. 'I am going to make an unusual request, which may strike as audacious. But I'll ask anyway. My landlady at the guest house has given me notice to vacate the room. She wants me gone as soon as possible. Could I stay with you until I've arranged alternative accommodation? This request comes from deep within my heart because I genuinely like you both. You are decent folks, unlike the hardboiled old hands who have made this country their home.'

'Why does she want you to leave?' Damon said.

'Let's say we have had political disagreements, not directly with her but with her husband. He's a rascal, a diehard colonial fart of the old school who believes slavery was an essential evil, and if legal today, he would practise it gladly. He says it is for the sake of the empire, which he believes is crumbling because of weak-kneed politicians and liberal fools.'

'He'll get on well with my father,' Damon said.

'He has been harassing his wife, poor Mrs Tebbit, insisting that she hand me an eviction notice.' He shook his head. The beams of his shoulder pressed against the flimsy shirt, which clearly had seen better days. His matted hair bore a fair amount of the city dust. Yet he appeared unfazed about his appearance. Behind those expressive eyes, the easy-going roll of the shoulder and the loud laughter, Damon could see he was a well-informed, intelligent man.

'If it doesn't suit you. It's all right, my friend. The old fart will have to put up with me a little longer.'

'What the heck,' Damon said, 'you can stay with us while you are looking for another accommodation. We have room to spare.'

The Frenchman appeared relieved. 'Merci beaucoup. I'll pay you back however I can.' He took Damon's hand and pumped it heartily. 'Can we do it today?'

'Why not,' Damon said, 'it makes no difference to me.'

Out on the street, Pierre hailed a phaeton and guided the driver to the guest house in Bhowanipore. 'It's a neighbourhood of English expatriates who have failed to make it big in the colonies,' he explained. The entrance was hidden behind upright palms and a coppice of bougainvillaea as if to shield it from the probing eyes of the natives. A board above read 'Marigold Tebbit Guesthouse'.

'You stupid ass, why did you invite him to stay with us?' Robert said as soon as Pierre went in to fetch his bags.

'I have my reasons.'

'What reasons?'

'He knows people. Can't you see how useful he could be if the police come to question us?'

'If police come, it will be to question you, not me.'

'And how's that?'

'That clown was a friend of your uncle, not mine.'

It was getting dark by the time they arrived back at Burnham Cottage. Birds coming to roost in trees had already set up their nightly racket. Pierre carried all his possessions in a small, battered suitcase, surprising Damon, for he had assumed journalists possessed a library of books and journals.

After dinner, they went to the balcony to sit in the cool breeze. There, they chatted into the late hour. Pierre, the raconteur, began weaving an elaborate portrait of himself.

'After my mother's death, I had the urge to travel beyond Europe. At the time, I was working for Agence Havas as their man in London.'

'Agence Havas? What's that?' Damon said.

'It's a news agency, like Reuters. One day, the foreign editor called me to his office. Do you know where Haiphong is? he said, I hear things are warming up there after the uprising by Vietnamese soldiers. There's so much merde reaching us. We need someone on the ground to tell us what's going on, and that someone is you, whether you like it or not.'

'I did like it, but I pretended I didn't. I made out I was doing him a favour by agreeing to go to the mosquito-infested hellhole. I planned to stay in Vietnam after my assignment was over and then move on to another country. In Haiphong I discovered very quickly that meeting people in government offices was a piece of cake. They were third-rate bureaucrats addicted to bribery and mahjong. A packet of Gauloise would set their tongues rolling like drunks in a downtown bar. Moreover, they wanted to feed me information which would show them in a good light back home.' He paused, lifted the teacup with his hands wrapped around it and took a sip. 'Nice tea. Do you know the origin of tea?'

'India?' Robert said without conviction.

'No, China. But we'll talk about that another time. First, let me tell you about my Vietnam adventure.' He paused again for another sip and then wiped his lips with the shirt sleeve. 'I had hardly settled down when I met a guy called Lai Lai. The fellow looked like a ghost with a bad gleam in the eye, but he was a good talker. I suspected he was a Surete secret service agent. He took me to a restaurant run by a French ex-convict. Over a bowl of noodle broth and frog legs, he asked me how much I earned as a journalist. I told him I wasn't complaining; there was enough to pay for the room and cigarettes, and the rice hooch, and, of course, the girls who were in the habit of doubling their rates whenever they saw a Frenchman. The man chuckled and said I was a fool. You could earn ten times that amount, or even twenty, by doing a little bit of work. I can still see his one beady eye, which he was in the habit of fixing on people without winking. The other eye he had lost in a drunken fight. He took a leather pouch out of his pocket and showed me its contents. You want to know what was in the bag? Yes, you've fucking guessed it. Opium.' Pierre paused for another sip of tea.

'Did you …' Robert said without completing the sentence.

'Well, I pretended to go along. I figured I could have some major scoops which I knew would be lapped up back home, and at the same time, embarrass the French pissheads in the colonies. Do you know what they did to the Vietnamese after the mutiny?'

Damon shook his head vaguely, and Robert looked away.

'Well, listen to this. They burned down sixty-nine homes, forced the villagers to pay extra taxes and levied corvée labour to rebuild French-owned properties in Lâm Thao. They prosecuted six hundred soldiers and civilians, handed down eighty death sentences, others were given hard labour for twenty years, yet more went to penal colonies of Poulo Condore and French Guiana.'

'Hold on,' Robert said, 'mutiny in the army ranks is extremely serious. You must know that. If not dealt with firmly, it can spread.'

'That's true, my friend, very true,' Pierre replied in a mocking tone, 'but remember the mutineers were Vietnamese wanting to liberate their country from the fucking foreign invaders, the French. Anyway …'

Robert got up, walked to the radio on the sideboard and began turning the dial.

'Am I boring you? I am sorry, my friend, I'll shut up,' Pierre said, 'I think I will retire for the night, if you could show me to the bedroom?'

The next day at the breakfast table Pierre started talking about opium. 'Did you know Indian opium is far superior to Vietnamese or Burmese?'

Robert shook his shoulder. 'So, damn what?'

'That's what I said to Lai Lai. But when he mentioned having contacts with Indians who supplied the merchandise, and that they were big players, I became even more curious. I wanted to find out who these people were. A scoop like that was bound to make a good story back home. How could I pass it by?'

'So, you had a scoop and got paid good money,' Robert said and left the room again.

'Don't mind him,' Damon said, 'I'd like to know what happened next.'

'Then I'll continue,' Pierre said. 'What else could I have done but get close to Lai Lai, make out I was his friend. One day, he took me to a fortune teller. You'll be rich, the fortune teller said in his Franco-Vietnamese dialect and ballooned his cheeks. In Vietnamese culture, fat people are envied; it is a sign that they are wealthy. You'll live an exceptionally long life, he said, and you'll meet a beautiful girl very soon and fall in love with her. He was so convincing. Only later did I find out it was a setup. Five days later, I met a girl in a bar, and we hit it off instantly; it was as if she had been waiting for me all my life. Her name was Huong. She liked to sit cross-legged on my bed beneath the bundled mosquito net and gaze at me as I worked on my typewriter. She even talked of marriage. One day, she asked me if I'd ever smoked opium. When you drink wine, and you feel like you're the king, opium is even better; it makes you feel like an emperor, she said.'

'You smoked opium?' Damon asked even though it was obvious to him that someone like Pierre would have seen it as an adventure.

Pierre nodded. 'I had to. How else could I've convinced them that I was one of them? She took me to a secret room above a café, all equipped with opium things. I didn't like it at first, but it started to blow my mind after the third. I was deep in it, and I didn't even know it. It was only after a chance discovery that Huong and Lai Lai were secretly working together to turn me into a junky that I pulled myself away. Next time, instead of inhaling it into my lungs, I held the smoke in my mouth and pretended I was gone. I did this for six weeks, listening and watching. What I learned was shocking. I discovered that the big players financing the operation were Englishmen, mostly based in Calcutta, respectable businessmen close to the government. Do you know who I am talking about here? Yes, you guessed it, people like Count Blythe.' He paused.

'No,' Damon cried in horror, 'you're saying that circus clown was an opium dealer?'

'No, no. I am not saying that. I am saying he could have been. I don't know. I am saying big businessmen like him were involved. They had an amazingly efficient supply chain setup all the way to China, Burma, Vietnam, and other countries.'

'That's frightening,' Damon said.

'Exactly. I realised I was playing a dangerous game. One slip and ...' He made a throat-slitting gesture. 'I decided to cut and run. I told Huong my head office wanted me back for an urgent meeting. The next day, her brother came and demanded that I marry his sister and take her to London. I had only two options. Marry the girl or die in a fight with her brother, who was a local gangster.'

'Since you're still alive, I take it, you married this girl,' Damon said.

Pierre unbuttoned his cotton shirt and pulled it apart, exposing an anaemic, skeletal chest with fine brown hair below the sternum as if it had been placed there as an afterthought. He turned around and showed Damon his back. 'They poured petrol over me and lit it. I am alive only because of my contacts within the ministry,' he said slowly and sat back, suddenly appearing subdued.

Damon marvelled at the Frenchman's ability to face dangers and surmount them. What an adventurous life he has led!

They were quiet for a while. Pierre sipped tea as if he had never had that beverage before.

'What I want to know is how you ended up in India?' Damon said.

'How did I come to India? It was a decision I made on a whim, just like that,' he said, clicking his fingers, 'I bought a ticket and sailed to Bombay on the Viceroy of India. From there, I went to Pondicherry.'

'Pondicherry?'

'Ah, you haven't heard of it,' he said and made a hand gesture to say it was understandable, 'not many people have. It's a piece of land on the southeast tip of India. For fifty years, it was a French dominion. And then the Dutch arrived in sixteen-ninety-three. They captured Pondicherry from the French and established a Dutch East India Company outpost. Six years later, the French launched a counterattack and regained control. They planned to move north to colonise the whole of India. But the French lacked the English's cunning. After the Battle of Plassey, Clive manoeuvred the French into a retreat south.' He paused and curled his lips into a scowl. 'Merde, if the French had pulled their fingers out of their backsides and fought properly, they could have defeated Clive. Do you know what would have happened? No? We would all be sitting here speaking French. Not English,' He smiled and then raised his hand. 'Sorry, no offence meant, eh. However, let me share another fact with you. Even the Austrians attempted to establish a base in India in the mid-seventeenth century. They sent a ship to the Nicobar Islands with six men and slaves with the intention of setting up a colony.'

'Six?'

'Yes, it is funny, eh? They had set out with grand intentions to send shiploads after shiploads of men, but lost interest along the way. And then came the Danish. They also sent a ship to the Nicobar Islands. Poor Danes, no dried fish, no snow, they also lost heart, perished of tropical diseases thousands of miles from home.'

Up at eight-thirty the next morning, Damon pulled the curtains apart, startling two pigeons on the window ledge. The birds eyed him nervously with their tiny buttons, ready to flee at the slightest hint of threat. He stood still and watched, fascinated by their twitchy head movements and how they dipped their necks when cooing. After a few minutes, he took slow backwards steps so as not to alarm the birds and left the room.

Pierre wasn't in the bedroom that they had allocated to him. He wasn't in the living room or the balcony.

Damon went down to the kitchen. Mrs P was grinding spices in a stone mortar. Her back against the window. In his blurry eyes, he had a vision of a sorceress of days gone by, concocting herbal potions.

‘Oh, sahib, you come for breakfast. I prepare something quick,’ she said.

‘It’s all right, no rush. Have you seen Pierre this morning?’ Damon said, ruffling his hair.

‘No sahib,’ she replied and reached for the pan of boiling water on the stove.

Damon wondered if Pierre had slipped out of the house during the night. So why did he move in here in the first place? He had talked of the opium dealers of Calcutta. Is he a dealer himself? Have I bought myself a bigger headache? For a moment, he stood still, feeling his armpits sweating up.

‘Tea, sahib,’ Mrs P said, bringing the cup to his line of vision.

He picked up the cup, left her standing with the saucer and went out through the kitchen door.

He took the path to Nath’s cottage. Seeing the door was open, he put his head in. Even though he had seen the room before, he was still astonished to see how Nath’s whole life was crammed into a tiny space—such frugal living. There was a bed in the centre of the room, the mosquito net still draped over it, like an elephantine ghost. Nath, bare-chested and wearing just a lungi, was sprinkling some form of liquid at the feet of his little idol of God Shiva.

Damon tapped the door for Nath’s attention.

‘Good morning, sahib,’ Nath said pleasantly.

‘Have you seen Pierre this morning?’

‘Yes, sir, only an hour ago. He went that way. For a morning walk, I am thinking.’

Damon went up to the gate, feeling the grit tickling his bare feet. He found the lanky Frenchman sauntering towards him, minus his black leather sandals.

'What a lovely morning,' Pierre called from a distance.

'You went for a walk at this unearthly hour?'

'Yes, my friend, the best way to tune your brain and recharge the batteries. The entire population takes to the street at six in the morning, and the only ones who don't are those interned in cemeteries or Hindus reduced to ashes.' He inhaled hard. 'I took the opportunity to check out Sinclair Blythe's house. It's only two streets away.'

Damon's fingers froze around the cup handle. 'Why did you do that? What if the police have followed you here?'

'There were no police at the house, nothing at all, hopelessly inefficient.'

'Why interfere with matters that don't concern you?'

'It's my job. I am a reporter, you see, my job is to interfere, find the truth and report it without fear.' He patted his chest solemnly with a closed fist. 'Everybody knows I am a journalist. They know I am a digger. My digging often reveals interesting facts. Consider this. Your uncle was a friend of Monsignor Blythe, a ruthless businessman who didn't believe in fair competition.'

'But my uncle is retired. He doesn't have business interests anymore.'

'Ahh, that's where you are wrong, my friend. Once a businessman, always a businessman.'

The words hit Damon with a force, and they constricted his chest, making him breathless. He now wished he hadn't gone to the Kali temple. He wouldn't have known Count Sinclair Blythe was dead, nor met this Frenchman. And yet, he would begrudgingly admit he was glad to have this man in the house. The man was resourceful, well-connected and lived by his wits.

Just what he needed in case the police came to question him.

'I am fully charged for the day. Let us go in,' Pierre said and again took in the morning air with a long, deep breath.

Nath was by his door with a beaker, sprinkling water on the steps of his cottage.

'What are you doing, my friend?' Pierre asked Nath.

Damon wondered why he called everyone his friend. Did he really see them as friends, or was it a figure of speech?

'I am sprinkling holy Ganga water here,' Nath replied.

'Why do you do that?'

'To cleanse my home and to stop bad spirits from entering.'

'I see. Nath, tell me this. Why do Hindus have so many Gods? Isn't one enough for them?'

Nath appeared surprised at first and then shook his head as if pitying Pierre for his ignorance. 'Sahib. There's only one God. We use Vishnu, Ganesh, Kali, Durga Mata, and others as physical manifestations of the supreme being up there, our God.' He pointed a finger at the sky. 'Even Mohamad and your Jesus Christ are emissaries of Him.'

'I believe you're wrong about Christ,' Damon said, 'Christ is God. He came down to earth to show us the path, bring salvation to us human beings.'

Nath shook his head in the usual noncommittal way, which meant he disagreed but wished not to offend his master by saying so. 'Have you read Bhagavad Gita and Mahabharat, Damon sahib?' he said.

'No, I can't say I have,' Damon replied, though he had seen a copy of a hardbound Bhagavad Gita in Uncle Fred's library.

'I have read the Bhagavad Gita,' Pierre said, 'it is a synthesis of strands of Indian religious thoughts, the Vedic concept of the bhakti and dharma. Dharma is the theory, and bhakti is the act of putting that theory into practice.'

Nath's eyes opened wide. 'You have?'

'Yes. We will talk about it sometime,' Pierre said, and then placed a hand on Damon's shoulder to lead him back in. 'Let's have some tea.'

Chapter 9

Damon accepted the deck – it was his turn to deal. The three were sitting around the table. Nath was standing, respectfully trying to keep in the spirit of the game. As a servant, it was customary not to sit with the masters at a table.

'Where did you learn to play cards?' Robert asked Nath.

'In the army only, when I was a young man,' Nath replied, 'young like you. There was nothing to do but play cards when we were not on duty.'

'You were in the British army?' Damon said, 'But you were born in Nepal.'

'Many Nepalis in the British army. Didn't you know? There is a Gurkha regiment too,' he said proudly.

Damon finished dealing and picked his cards. He was thinking of his father, who had harangued and cajoled, short of hitting him, to enrol in the army after school.

'Did your father force you to join the army?' he asked Nath.

'No sahib, I wanted to. My father was also in the army. They sent him to many countries – Africa, Aden, and that place Mesotama.'

'You mean Mesopotamia?' Pierre said.

'Yes, that one, sahib. He died fighting there. Gave his life for the country.'

Brave man, Damon thought. But there was a problem. He didn't sacrifice his life for his own country. He did it for a country he had probably never been to, a country he knew very little about. A country whose people would never accept him as their own. What a paradox. To hell with it. 'You know, if there is hell for people like us. It's not here, but back home, in England,' he said.

'Come on, my friend. Play,' Pierre said, 'this is meant to be a fun time.'

'I've been letting you all win so far,' Robert said, slamming his cards face down on the table, 'now I will show you who the master is.'

'Aha, no chance, my friend,' Pierre shouted, 'I have this.' He dropped an ace of spades and an ace of hearts on the table.

'Drat,' Robert cried, throwing his head back on the chair.

'Do you think they would have caught the killers by now?' Damon asked Pierre.

'Phooor.' Pierre made a face, throwing his arms out wide. 'They will never catch anybody. Do you know why? Because they know who did it.'

Damon shut up, realising he shouldn't have spoken about this in Nath's presence. Servants talk, and one never knows what rumours they would spread. He glanced at Nath and found him with an utterly blank expression as if he had not heard anything.

'I saw a car cruise past here the other day. The driver was watching the house,' Damon said.

'Just what are you talking about now?' Robert said.

'He also followed us to the Victoria Memorial. I'm sure he was spying on us.'

'Finnegan, you have been reading too many detective novels. Now play, it's your turn.'

'You remember Uncle Fred's friend on the train. He gave us

a lift home in his car. It was that car and the driver.'

'Makes no sense. You're being paranoid as usual.'

Chapter 10

'Why didn't you tell me before you wanted to drink wine?'

'I assumed wine wasn't available in India,' Robert replied.

'My friend, never assume anything until you have checked with Pierre. Come with me.'

They walked to the nearest rickshaw stand. Pierre inserted two fingers in his mouth and gave a piercing whistle. A cycle-rickshaw-wallah, waiting for a fare, jumped to his feet. 'Climb in, please.'

Fifteen minutes on the road. At the Ganesh temple beside the market, the rickshaw-wallah stopped pedalling. He dipped his head and said a silent prayer. The prayer finished, he pulled his head up and clanked the bell. The worshippers at the ochre-smeared entrance gave way, politely, seeing that the passengers were two Europeans. Past Maharani Vidyalaya School and the fruit market, through the air charged with children's laughter and the sweet odour of mangoes, guavas and temple incense, the rickshaw-wallah said, as if in reply to a question from Pierre. 'Business is bad. Nobody cares for us poor people.' With his thumb and forefinger, he tugged the sweat-soaked shirt clinging to his starved-mutt ribcage. 'This heat kills us. Sweat all day, just a few rupees, and still, bhanchod customers are haggling. They want free rides, as if I were their salaa uncle. And this thing needs maintenance all the time.' He patted the handlebars hard several times.

Pierre tapped his shoulder from behind. 'Have faith, things will surely get better.'

Rickshaw-wallah rocked his head, sun reflecting on his oily hair. 'If you say so, babu.'

'Simple folks,' Pierre said to Robert. 'Don't you think?'

Robert scrunched his shoulders, as if he didn't know or care.

The market lane led to an open space, like a village green. At the centre was a small church with lead glass windows, a cone-shaped roof with a pointed spiral. The front door was sealed with crossbars and a rusty padlock. Once whitewashed, the outer walls were now grey and mouldy, vegetation sprouting in cracks and crevices.

Jesus is coming, read a sign on an old billboard attached to the east wall.

To become a Hindu, someone had chalked underneath.

At the back was another four-walled structure, the presbytery, now a commercial warehouse.

'Wait here,' Pierre said to Robert, 'I'll go in and do the deal. How many bottles do you want?'

Robert raised his right hand, the fingers splayed wide. 'Five. I must replenish Uncle Fred's cupboard, or Damon will be damn furious with me.'

'I'll see what I can do,' Pierre said and went in.

Robert sat down on a flat rock, wondering who the priest was and why he had abandoned the church.

He went back to his childhood. The Monday morning assembly at the church, Father Gilbert reading from the school diary: God make me a channel of your peace, an instrument of your love.

A man came pedalling a creaky bicycle, braked, dismounted

and leaned his bike against the warehouse wall. That's when Robert spotted the slogans daubed on the wall. The message was clear: India sought independence from the British. And he had an uncanny feeling the slogans were for him personally, as if they had known he was coming. He looked around him. A line of crows was sitting on the power line, looking down, creating a racket. It seemed to him they, too, were cawing at him. *Get out of India!*

Two hundred yards ahead, near the west exit, he spotted a crowd of people gathered in a circle, facing inward. An ageing Bengali, a wizened birdman with spectacles, spotted Robert and beckoned him over. 'Please come, please come.'

Out of curiosity, and so as not to offend, Robert got up and walked over to the assembled crowd. The old man ordered a break in the circle so the Englishman could have a clear view. Robert smiled to hide his nervous tension. They took it as an endorsement of their activity. The break in the circle widened. 'Watch, watch,' the Bengali said, gesturing with his skeletal hand.

At the centre, a young Indian girl sat on a chair. She was dressed in a long frock and a blouse with laced sleeves. Her face was heavily powdered, and her hair curled and bobbed into a beehive. A crude caricature of English aristocracy. Directly behind and above her was a display of Christmas decorations - colourful tinsel, baubles, and ribbons. Sitting opposite her was a boy of similar age. He was attired in traditional Indian clothing, a simple shirt and a white cotton dhoti. The audience appeared relaxed and jovial.

'… why do you celebrate Christmas?' the boy was saying, pointing a finger, 'you are Hindu. You don't celebrate Guru

Nanak's birthday, Eid or other religious functions. So, why this love affair with Christmas?'

The girl replied, projecting her voice over the crowd, 'Because it's a tradition I've always upheld.'

'You are slavishly following the English, embarrassing yourself and all of us. It's because of people like you that we get a bad name.'

'No,' she screamed, springing from the chair, 'no, it's not true.'

'Then what's the truth?'

'If I want to celebrate Christmas, I will,' she said firmly, 'there's no harm in a bit of fun. Moreover, Christmas is a national holiday.'

'Who chose it as a holiday in a Hindu, Muslim majority country? … the British.' The boy turned to the audience again, urging them to speak up.

'British! British!' the audience responded.

To Robert, this simplistic street theatre had but one purpose: to whip up Indian nationalistic fervour. Yet a curious paradox – they were using the English tongue, the language of their oppressor, and as a legate of their enemy, they were not disrespecting him. He stood like a wooden dummy, unable to cheer or walk away, praying for Pierre to come out and rescue him.

'Don't you know these people you look to emulate don't want us? They address us by dirty names, like wogs and savages and coolies …. we will not put up with it anymore.'

The audience cheered.

'All you are doing is mimicking the British. Copycat, copycat.'

'Copycat, copycat, copycat,' the audience chorused.

He heard a lone voice. 'Damnation, copycat.'

Pierre was standing by his side, a hessian bag in his arms.

'Bravo. Bravo. Bravo.' Pierre made a show of clapping as the bottles rattled in the bag.

The actors bowed.

'Don't take it to heart. They are just kids having fun.'

'Fun? I thought they would lynch me.'

They climbed back on the waiting rickshaw. 'Chalo. Take us to where we came from,' he ordered.

The rickshaw-wallah dropped his bidi, straddled the bicycle, raised a closed fist in the air, yelled, '*Hindustan zindabad*,' at the crowd and began pedalling. For a small man with no flesh, he appeared to have a powerful voice.

'What did he say?' Robert asked.

'It means long live India.'

Chapter 11

The hessian sack in the left arm, Pierre opened the gate with the right.

They found Damon pacing the gravel path, kicking pebbles.

'What's the matter with you? You look like you have been jumped,' Robert said.

Damon turned around sharply. 'We have been burgled,' he said, gasping for air as if he had held his breath for the three hours that the other two were absent.

'What?'

'I said burgled. Are you deaf and dumb too?'

'All right, calm down. Have you called the police?'

'Call the police? How? I don't know where the station is. Nath isn't here.'

'Scoundrel. Disappears when he is needed,' Robert said.

'He has taken a day off. Something to do with meeting his son.'

Nath had left early that morning while the house was still asleep. An hour on the bus, followed by a mile-long walk to the village. The son and his wife were both out; one was working on the railway line, while the other was planting seedlings in paddy fields.

The neighbour was sitting on a cane chair at the front door, smoking a bidi.

'Nath bhai, kaise ho?' he said by way of a greeting.

'The same, nothing to complain, God willing,' Nath replied and waited for the inevitable questioning.

'Still working for the English family?' the neighbour said with a laugh and did a raking in gesture with his hands. 'Bringing in lakhs and lakhs of rupees, are you?'

Nath knew that beneath that haughtiness was jealousy. He, too, had tried to find employment with the English sahibs as a gardener or security guard.

Nath said nothing. If only this fool knew of the harsh reality.

Alone in his son's house, full of time and silence, dust motes spinning in the air, sunlight reflecting on a small mirror above a tiny wash basin, he sat down on a chair to reflect on what was going on back at Burnham Cottage. For twenty years, he had worked diligently and in good faith for the Finnegans. He had never faced a situation such as this. It was breaking his heart. They had threatened to kill him if he obstructed their entry to Burnham Cottage or even breathed a word to anyone. He believed them, absolutely, for he had seen with his own eyes poor Balraj Singh, stripped naked, beaten, and tied up. Later, they took Balraj to Howrah Bridge and asked him if he could swim. No. Too bad. Hee, ho, here you go. They had tipped him over the edge.

Better to live another day. He had considered going to the police. However, the men in uniform had no authority beyond catching petty criminals, managing road traffic, issuing fines and taking bribes. The people who wanted him out of the way were rich and powerful, all Englishmen. They had offered him money. He could still hear their derisive laughter when he had refused.

He had told Damon he would be back by nightfall. By then, whatever is to happen will have happened.

He went to the backyard. Worked the hand pump to fill a bucket of water. Stripped to the underpants and bathed.

Later, he brewed tea with milk. Poured it in a steel tumbler, sat down on the doorsteps and surveyed his son's vegetable patch. The brinjals were still green and small; the okras were ready to harvest; the papaya trees needed pruning. He spotted a line of ants marching from the rock to the papaya tree in a path cut in the dry soil. A stream of his bathwater was flowing towards the tree. Soon it would overrun the ants' marching route and set them off in a panic. He felt sorry for the little creatures. They will never know why their peaceful, structured routine was so cruelly disrupted. His face collapsed, and tears began rolling down his old, wrinkled cheeks. He sobbed freely and loudly. Wiped his nose with a gamcha. A goat wandered in. He clapped at it. 'O, God's child, go away. There's nothing here for you.'

Left alone, Damon had time to introspect. He had pulled fluff from his belly button, cleared wax from his ears with Uncle Fred's HB2 pencil, listened to Fred Elizalde's jazz on the radio while he lay on his back and did languorous bicycling exercises. He thought again of that place called Kanyakumari; Pierre had talked about it the other day. He said it was the southernmost tip of India. The place where land met ocean. It seemed incredible that there could be an end to India, one you could point to and identify on a map.

'What about the cleaner?' Robert asked.

'She was here earlier. I don't know where she is now. I was alone when they came.'

'Just what did happen? Go through it step-by-step.'

'I was sitting on the veranda reading a book when I heard a noise and saw this man dive into the hedge.' His lips quivered. 'I realised then they must have been inside the house.'

'What have they stolen?'

'They have ransacked Uncle Fred's bedroom.'

Robert and Pierre dashed upstairs.

'Careful. Don't touch anything until the police are here,' Pierre advised.

The epicentre of the disorder was at the far end of the room, where the wardrobe, the writing bureau and the filing cabinets were situated. Shirts, trousers, and jackets lay scattered on the floor. The drawers pulled out and tipped over. Uncle Fred's personal papers, bound documents, manila folders, some bound with ribbons and sealed with red wax, were lying in an unruly mess on the table.

'Have they taken anything from the rest of the house?' Pierre asked.

'I've checked. Nothing appears disturbed,' Damon mumbled, his gaze darting restlessly from the documents on the desk to the wardrobe and the windows.

'My advice is to lock the bedroom and call the police.'

'They have got what they came for. What can police do now,' Damon said.

'Damon is right,' Robert said, 'we don't want police snooping all over the place and alerting the neighbours. It's going to look bad.'

'Boys, boys, just grasp the gravity of the situation. These people are no ordinary thieves. They clearly knew which one was your uncle's bedroom. And they were looking for something specific. Any idea what that might be?'

Damon shook his head.

'Your uncle will have friends. It might be worth speaking to them.'

'I don't know any of his friends, except that circus clown fellow who …' He left the sentence hanging in the air.

Robert saw the antiquities in the wall cabinet and stopped to inspect them. There were Chinese and Burmese ceramics, prayer bells, and metal bowls studded with precious stones. He thought of his father's small collection of Delftware and Edwardian silver.

He found a cabinet under a desk with a solid wooden door. It opened easily. What he saw inside made his heart miss a beat. His first impulse was to leave quickly. Pretend he had seen nothing. But curiosity was the greater force. He crouched down low and picked up the shotgun. Sunlight reflected on the gun's metal and brass inlays as he held it up and felt the weight and substance. Real. Oh, yes. The name Webley & Scott was stencilled on the wooden butt. He was fourteen when his father had let him hold his gun for a minute, just once. After that, he had locked it away somewhere secret.

He aimed the gun out the window at the distant figure of a woman in a sari on the street. Blam. He saw her jerk and fall, kicking her feet. No, let her live. The gun was unloaded anyway.

In the moonless night, darkness had engulfed the house. Nath had just turned into the gate when Damon pounced on him. 'Someone entered the house uninvited and helped himself to your master's personal papers. What do you have to say about it?'

Nath held his head with both hands as if it were about to come loose.

'He is overreacting. Do you think this man is in on it?' Robert whispered in Pierre's ear.

'Can't say for sure. He's nervous because he knows in situations such as these, the suspects by default are the servants of the house.'

'Go and inform the police at once,' Damon ordered.

Nath nodded and hurried off.

'Where is Kutta?' Robert's alarmed cry made the air heavier with fear.

Each examined the other's face.

Damon spoke first. 'I haven't seen or heard him all afternoon, certainly not while the burglars were in the house.'

Silently, as if bound by an invisible pact, they went to the rear garden, which was Kutta's sanctuary. It was here Mrs P threw scraps of food at him, all the while complaining he ate too much. 'Even elephants eat less than him.'

Damon walked through the fruit trees, prodding the hedges, and stumbled on a discarded garden fork with a broken handle.

'Kutta, Kutta, here boy.' The call sliced through the still air.

'Kutta, Kutta, here boy.' A meek, fearful call.

They peered over the fence. The torchlight picked up rocks and ditches, a haven for frogs and crickets in the rainy season. A little further away was Nath's makeshift chicken enclosure, housing a dozen birds.

'There he is,' Robert cried.

Half-hidden among the rocks, Kutta lay on his side, legs pushed away from his body, a stance reminiscent of a dog stretching after a satiated sleep. But that deportment isn't permanent in live animals.

Nath came back an hour later. He saw Kutta lying on the patio floor, on a sheet of newspaper. 'Whoh,' he exploded and went down on his knees. He placed a hand on the dog's ribs, half to soothe the departed soul, half as if to check if he was alive. 'I'll kill them. I'll kill them.'

Robert immediately looked at Damon and Pierre and gestured: This guy knows something.

'Who will you kill?' Robert asked.

Nath did not reply. He continued shaking his head.

'Use your brain, Robert. He is just upset, that's all,' Damon said.

'I'm telling you he knows something,' Robert said.

Nath collected Kutta in his arms and left.

'You are a damn fool, Damon. Can't you see he is hiding something?' Robert said.

'Robert,' Damon screamed, 'Nath is a trusted servant. He has been with my uncle for many years.'

'Fine. You do as you damn well wish. It's you and your uncle. Not my business,' Robert said and turned to go back in. 'I've better things to do.' He slapped the wall searching for the light switch, forgetting it was on the other side of the wall.

'Boys, boys, calm down. You'll get nowhere by quarrelling,' Pierre said and helped Robert by switching on the light.

Four constables in uniform showed up in the morning, each holding an open umbrella. Three black umbrellas and one white traffic police parasol.

'Sorry, sir, we are a little late arriving on account that we had to walk from the station,' said the leader to Damon.

'Why didn't you use a vehicle?' Damon said.

'Inspector Jameson has requisitioned both the vehicles to ferry his friends to the Tollygunge Club on account of it being his birthday today. Still, we are here now. Not a particularly good day, but we promise to do our best. Please tell us what the problem may be.' He collapsed the umbrella and thrust it into Nath's hand. 'Give it a good shake, will you?'

Damon led the constables to the ransacked bedroom.

The constable surveyed the room. Walked around it. Visually inspected the files and folders on the table, garments lying bundled on the floor.

'Could you tell us exactly what's missing, item by item? My assistant here will take notes.' He clicked his fingers at the constable behind him. 'Notepad, pencil.'

'That IS the problem … er …'

'Senior Constable Banerjee, sir.'

'Yes, Constable Banerjee …'

'Senior Constable Banerjee, sir.'

'Yes, Senior Constable Banerjee, the problem is I don't know what's missing. The papers belonged to my uncle, who is in London. And I can't easily communicate with him.'

'Oh, I see, you can't easily communicate,' the constable echoed, 'but we will do our best to trace the missing items. Could you tell me who was the last person in the house before the thieves arrived, apart from you, of course?'

'That will be the cleaner. She was in this morning, but I don't know at what time she left the house.'

'Aha,' Banerjee said and clapped, 'you say this woman, the cleaner, was the last person to leave the house before the thieves arrived. Given there was no sign of forced entry, she must have deliberately left the doors unlocked. No, no, no, we have the accomplice for sure. If we can catch her, we have the culprits.' He clapped again as if he had solved the case. 'May I've her name and address, please?'

'You'd better speak to Nath about that,' Damon said, 'but I should point out the front door isn't kept locked when there are people in the house.'

'Oh, I see.' The constable's exuberance subsided. 'Still, I would like to bring her in for questioning, on account of one can't trust these types of people. They are often into all kinds of skulduggery.'

Nath burst into the room with Kutta in his arms, cradling it like a newborn. 'See, see, see,' he cried and thrust the lifeless form at the constable as if accusing him of complicity in its demise.

'Arre, arre, arre. What's the meaning of this?' Banerjee recoiled.

'What was his fault? He's only a dog. Kutta … Kuttu … Kutti,' Nath yodelled as if calling Kutta back to life and then lapsed into swearing in Nepali.

'What's this nonsense you're shouting?' Banerjee said, 'Close your mouth this instant.'

They trooped to the back garden. Damon and Banerjee ahead, followed by Robert, Pierre, and Nath. The constables followed at the rear, appearing as bored and tired as their uniforms.

'Found him there,' Damon said, pointing at a rocky growth.

'All right, stand back,' Banerjee said, bracing himself, and climbed over the fence. He walked around the rock, making a show of inspecting it from different angles, then bent down for a closer look. Just then, a green snake shot out of a crevice towards his feet. 'Orre, salaa,' Banerjee cried and jumped as if he were doing a high jump from a stationary position.

He climbed back over the fence hurriedly.

'Don't worry, sir, I'll solve this case very soon to your satisfaction,' he said, 'Is there anything you wish to say? No. We will be off then.'

He ordered his assistants to follow him. Marching in a single file. The shingles crunched underfoot. Umbrellas open, three black and a white traffic police parasol, even though the rain had stopped.

Pierre and Robert smiled and burst out laughing.

No one spoke for a while. Nath shifted his weight from one foot to the other. 'Sahib, I would like to say something,' he said gravely. His brown face had taken on a darker hue as he scratched his neck.

'Yes, Nath, say it. You're the keeper of this house in my uncle's absence,' Damon said.

'It's not my place to interfere,' Nath said, hesitating, 'but I suspect that Fred sahib's friend Blythe has something to do with this.'

'See, I told you. He knows,' Robert cried, pirouetting around to face him.

Damon studied Nath's face intently. 'How can that be. Don't you know Blythe is no more?'

'I know about that. But sahib, he has a partner who does all this kind of work. Bad people, gangster type.'

'Tell me more,' Damon said.

'This man is a junior partner, but he controls everything. If they want something, then they will get it.' He paused. 'I am telling you this because I want you to be careful.'

'This is getting interesting,' Robert said, 'are you saying we are in danger?'

Nath nodded slowly.

The pained expression and the upfront body language convinced Robert that he was telling the truth this time.

'Jesus Christ! How do you know all this?'

'I know the gatekeeper at the Blythe house. We are from the same village.' He lowered his voice to a whisper. 'The rumour is that Dr Aziz ordered his senior partner's …' Nath made a throat-slitting gesture with his thumb.

'Dr Aziz?'

'He is the junior partner.'

'If you know so much, why not tell the police?'

'No, never, sahib. Do you think the police can protect me from Aziz? Please don't tell anyone what I've told you.' He paused for a moment. 'Or you will find me floating in the Hooghly.'

'You don't have to worry, Banerjee has the case in hand,' Damon said.

Pierre interjected, 'My friend, this is Calcutta, not London. A constable from a local police station will not dare question anyone like Blythe or Aziz if he values his job. He may arrest a small-time crook. The fellow will feel safer going to jail than naming names. You'll have to use your own initiative if you want to help your uncle. Let me think how.' He picked up a cigarette packet from the table and tapped out a cigarette. 'Nath, my man, do you think you could organise some tea? I am famished. It's been a long day.'

'Yes, sahib.' Nath left the room.

Pierre lit the cigarette and inhaled. 'This is what I suggest you do. Go to Sinclair Blythe's house and talk to his widow. Say you have heard of her husband's death and have come to offer condolences. She, like her husband, is quite a character. This type of person is easy to draw out. There's a good chance you will pick up something.'

'I'll come with you,' Robert said instantly.

'I've never done this kind of thing. How, for Christ's sake, does one offer condolences to a woman you have never met?'

'Come, pull yourself together, man. I'll be with you,' Robert said and winked, 'I hope the niece is there.'

Nath gave them an update the following day. 'Madam Blythe has moved. She's living in a house in Chinatown. I have the address.'

Chapter 12

The sun was beating down hard by the time they arrived at Bow Bazar.

Pierre hailed a cycle rickshaw and gave the driver the address in Tangra, deep in Old Chinatown.

'Go and see Mrs Blythe and be back in two hours. I'll wait here,' he said. 'Good luck.'

The houses on the street were impressive, built by the Bengali aristocracy in the previous century. Now in disrepair, the Chinese community had moved in. They had set up shops selling handcrafted leather shoes.

The air smelled of raw leather as if they had entered a tannery. Robert wrinkled his nose. 'Oh, man, this is a dump of a street.'

Damon stared at a house with monsoon-softened edges and meandering old-age seams in white-washed walls. Surely, the Blythe can't be living here. Across the street at a Chinese café, patrons were sitting over bowls of steaming noodles. Others were smoking cigarettes. Matchsticks flaring as though pyromania, not nicotine, was the addiction there. In London, seeing a Chinese man was a novelty. Damon remembered, as a small boy, getting a smack on the head from his mother for staring at a Chinese couple.

'Go on. Knock.' Robert prodded Damon.

Damon stepped up to the green door and knocked three times. A bolt slid inside. Then another. The door creaked open slowly, revealing a shrivelled older man with Chinese features.

He stood stooped like a question mark. 'Yes?'

'Is Mrs Blythe at home?' Damon said.

'Wait, please,' the man said and slammed the door shut.

When the door next opened, a girl was behind it. Damon launched into an explanation, speaking rapidly. 'My name is Damon Finnegan. My uncle Fred Finnegan and Count Sinclair Blythe were friends. I heard the terrible news of Mr Blythe's ….'

'Err, I do believe you need to speak to Caroline. Come in, I'll see if she wants to take visitors.'

They stepped inside and waited. The street smell followed them in. The hallway was spacious and tastefully decorated, a sharp contrast to the building's shabby exterior.

Robert elbowed Damon. 'You fool, couldn't you see she was too young to be Blythe's widow?'

'Niece,' Damon blurted.

'By Jove, she's sexy.'

The girl came back and gestured at them to follow. Robert overtook Damon as if the girl had addressed him personally. She escorted them further down the hallway. The smell here was mellow, of affluence and cleanliness. She stopped at an inner door and pushed it open smartly. Cool air laden with moist hay burst in their faces.

The room was furnished with dark wood furniture, an Afghan rug at the centre of the floor, and heavy drapes blocking direct sunlight. A woman of about fifty was sitting on an easy chair, her hands resting on padded armrests. Wearing a wide, sloping hat, she epitomised the aristocratic Englishwoman Damon had seen in pictorial history books.

'My name is Damon Finnegan, and this is my friend Robert,' Damon began, keeping himself erect, arms by his side, as if in deference to royalty. 'We heard the sad news recently and have come to offer our condolences. It's what my uncle would have wanted.'

The woman regarded Damon from head to toe. 'Thank you for coming, Damon. Thoughtful of you. Tell me who your uncle is?' Her speech was bold and refined.

'Fredrick Finnegan, mam. I understand he and your husband were good friends.'

'Ah, Fredrick from Alipore. But I haven't seen you two boys before.'

'We arrived two weeks ago, a short visit,' Damon said.

'I thought so, you are recent arrivals,' the girl said from the back, 'I've been here three months.'

The girl was playing with a curl of hair on her forehead, twisting it around a finger.

Mrs Blythe said without looking at the girl. 'This is the problem with young people. They never know what they want. I've asked her to get married and settle down. But she's so restless.'

It took Damon by surprise. He couldn't see the relevance of that statement.

'Oh, Aunt Caroline, please.'

Mrs Blythe continued, half addressing Damon and Robert, 'the average Jones, Brown, Burton who comes to India with lofty ideas of doing good, quickly forgets their calling and loses themselves in the Club, playing bridge and gossiping, while the true India slides by unnoticed.'

'That's why I want to go back. I don't like playing bridge,' Pam said.

'Do you play bridge?' Mrs Blythe asked Damon.

'Aunt Caroline, please, you're being unkind to the guests.'

'Nonsense, my dear. I wasn't going to ask him to play bridge. Anyway, it's very sweet of you to think of an old widow like me. No young man that I know would take the trouble of offering such a gesture. It wouldn't enter their heads unless prompted.'

Damon nodded, feeling pleased with himself. It wasn't so hard after all.

'Since you have come all this way, how can I not offer you a drink. Do you like whiskey?' she said.

'I do, err, no. I am fine,' Damon said.

'What about your friend, Robert?'

'Er – maybe a little,' Robert said.

'Good. Could you call Chan, please,' she said to Pam, and then to Robert, 'Do you know how we make scotch and water in this house? We pour scotch in a glass and then call to mind thoughts of water, and then we mix the scotch with an abstracted idea of water.' She smiled and winked, which made her look younger.

'Aunt Caroline, should you be drinking?' Pam interrupted.

'Wee dram will not harm, my dear. Do ask Chan to fetch the bottle from the new batch. I hope they haven't pilfered that as well.' She turned to Robert. 'She thinks I've a drink problem.'

The word pilfer was the trigger. 'Is pilfering a major problem here?' Damon said, keeping a casual tone.

'Oh, yes, so it is. It's the servants. They take whatever they fancy, and when confronted, they swear by their God that they are innocent.'

'It must be distressing. We have had a burglary recently,' Damon said.

'Oh, for heaven's sake, you have had your whiskey stolen as well,' she said, 'it's an epidemic.'

'Not whiskey,' Damon said, 'someone broke into my uncle's chamber and stole his personal papers.'

'Oh, how awful. Personal papers. Now, why would anyone want those?'

'Unfortunately, uncle isn't here to vouch for what's missing,' Damon said, keeping a discreet eye on her.

'I expect the police were no help. No, they wouldn't.' She paused. 'When is Frederick coming back?'

'He's in ill health and wants to stay in London until fully recovered. As you may know, Aunt Frances passed away not so long ago. He's still in mourning.'

'Oh, I knew her all right,' she said, 'what God giveth with one hand, takes away with the other.'

'Yes, very true,' Damon said. He didn't know why he said it, for it had no meaning in the context. And then he caught her looking at him in a rather inquisitive way.

She was about to say something when the door burst open.

The old man they had seen earlier barged in. 'Madam, the police are outside. They want to come in right away. Five. There are five this time,' he said, speaking rapidly while his right hand was shaking as if he were whisking an egg.

A sudden silence descended in the room. Mrs Blythe straightened her back as if to get up. Her elbow caught the side table. An inkpot fell on the floor and smashed. The sound of breaking glass was slight, but within the confines of the room, it assumed the amplitude of an explosion.

'For heaven's sake,' she said, creases crowding her face like so many threadworms. She glanced over her shoulder as if looking for a way out. 'Don't let them in … no, wait … that will look bad.'

In the hallway, Pam's shrill voice rang out, 'I am telling you to wait. You can't barge in like this.'

'First, get these two gentlemen out of the way. Use the back exit. Hurry.'

'But madam, that …'

'Then use the warehouse exit, hurry up, will you?' She began rearranging her dress as if expecting an audience with essential guests.

Robert sprang to his feet and dashed for the door.

'No, no.' The old man grabbed Robert's arm. 'This way, please.' He hurried them into a long corridor towards the rear of the building. 'Go, stairs at the end. Up and down to the back exit.'

Suddenly, the world was upside down as they moved through semidarkness towards a distant azure glow. At the source, a small ceiling light was illuminating a cast-iron spiral staircase.

'Come on,' Robert said and took the stairs running. The stairwell reverberated with the smack of two pairs of shoes. The landing was a small antechamber with a battered door in the front. Robert charged at it. It flew open. They stumbled into a bigger room. The air was thick with the smell of pigeons nesting in the air vents. Old furniture lay scattered on one side. On the floor was an unmade bed. Hair oil stains on the pillow. Crushed cigarette butts nearby. Someone had been sleeping there. They were about to turn back when Damon spotted a door partly hidden by an upright string bed. It opened easily. They were now in another stairwell. The only way was down. They hurtled down, the sound of footsteps on metal-slotted rungs echoing like gunshots.

At the bottom of the stairwell were two more sets of double doors.

'For Christ's sake, which one is the exit?'

'Try this one.'

It opened, but with a protesting groan.

Chilled air blasted their faces, and then a stench clawed at their throats.

They found themselves in an enormous warehouse. Suspended from metal hooks on the ceiling was a sepulchral assemblage of skinned animals. No heads or limbs, just bare carcasses slit open in the middle. The obsidian floor beneath was littered with congealed blood. Against the wall was a row of worktops, the wood's grain serrated and stained with blood. Machetes, knives, and handsaws lay scattered on benches as if the workers had only just downed tools and fled.

'Hello, is anyone here?' Damon croaked.

No response. No sound other than Robert's urgent breathing.

'Is anyone here?' Robert raised his voice.

Silence, still.

Damon turned around to leave. The door would not open. It rattled but stayed obstinately shut.

'Pull,' Robert said and searched for a handle or a latch. He could find none. In desperation, he clawed at it, jammed his fingernails in the slits. It was hopeless, like trying to pick a lock with paper clips.

'Let me have a go,' Damon said and clawed hard at the narrow slit between two halves of the door. 'Open you damn pig.' He became aware of his own voice echoing in a hollow chamber. Sweat dripped from his face despite the chill. After repeated tries, he turned around and stared into dark corners, searching for signs of another entrance or exit, a window. But all he could see was the stony face of the upright walls.

'We are buggered,' he said, imagining freezing lifeless in this chamber of death. Like these animals, he too could become a vessel of emptiness, a corpse. He became aware of his heart pounding against his chest and sank to the floor, utterly stalled, as though he had run out of gas.

'Come on, stand up, we will find a way out,' Robert said, but there was no energy in his conviction.

It felt like hours before they heard distant footsteps.

'Shush,' Robert whispered and stood very still, listening.

A door opened and shut somewhere. The sound of footsteps again. Steadily getting louder. Heels tapping the concrete, as if the person were in a hurry. It stopped at their door. Someone was outside. They could sense it.

Robert took a pace back, staring at the door, ready to fight. Damon was beyond caring by then. He didn't even lift his head when the door opened with a groan and a gush of warm air.

'Ah, so you found a hiding place,' the Chinaman said, cackling. His jagged teeth stood out, as if designed to tear into raw meat.

Robert clenched his fists. Spittle flew from his mouth. 'No, you fat ass. You gave wrong directions and got us locked in here.'

'Locked? Ohhh, I see,' the Chinaman said. He looked surprised at first, and then his shoulders shook up and down. He was laughing silently as he shuffled sideways and pointed at a small circular bolt at the hinged edge of the door. 'See this. You pull. Door open.'

'You get us out of this damn smelly hole.'

Chapter 13

'I have explored every rat hole of the market six times over. Even the rats are beginning to take me as one of them,' Pierre fumed. 'Why are you so late?'

'Well, they are not entirely mistaken,' Robert said.

'Now you watch your salaa mouth. I am here only to help you. I didn't have to come. Maybe, I'll go home now.' He raised a hand to summon a rickshaw.

'I am sorry. We got trapped in a slaughterhouse,' Damon said.

'Slaughterhouse?' Pierre cried, 'stop fooling with me or I will slaughter you.'

'I'll explain later,' Damon said, mopping sweat off his face with the shirt sleeve, 'but first let's get out of this madhouse.'

The tram they boarded, after a cycle-rickshaw ride to Esplanade, rattled, squeaked, and groaned as if it were about to break apart. Yet it was stopping and starting, taking on fresh loads.

'Did you learn anything?' Pierre said, raising his voice over the din.

Damon shrugged his shoulders. 'Nothing. Police raided the house while we were there. We had to run.'

Thirty minutes into the journey, the tram slowed, shuddered, and came to a halt with a crash of metal.

First, the conductors, then the driver, jumped off the tram. And then the passengers began pouring out of the front and rear exits as if someone had warned them the tram was about to self-destruct.

A man put his head in. 'Can't you see, this tram is going nowhere? Go home. You're not safe here.'

They came out to the pavement.

Pierre asked a peanut seller what was going on. The boy stepped back sharply as if he feared catching an infectious disease from a white man. 'There, there,' he said, gesturing wildly, pointing at a crowd of people at the crossroads, his wide eyes shouting danger.

'Oh, merde.'

'What's going on?' Robert said.

'It's a protest march against the British,' Pierre said, 'I've seen it before.'

People were pouring out of their homes at the same speed as shopkeepers were boarding up their stores. A coolie dropped a sack of rice. In no time, the grain was like white stains across the dusty path. A woman tripped and fell on the tram track. Someone helped her up.

Men in white, espousing the Gandhian principle of non-violence, waving banners attached to bamboo poles, were emerging from a side road. There were young men blowing tin whistles, beating ghee drums with sticks, doing anything to make noise. Then there were the usual firecrackers, not loud or dangerous but enough to add to the clamour.

Pierre pulled Robert and Damon into the deserted tram-stop shelter and watched in horror as police took up position, shields and batons on the ready. The march halted in the east wing of the crossroads. Some sat down on the tarmac to rest their limbs. Others were taunting the police, offering them pieces of oranges and bananas.

The people at the rear were getting agitated. Someone threw

a rock. It landed a few feet from the police line. And then a volley of stones and pebbles rained down on the police.

With the missiles came verbal taunts. 'Traitors, salaa bhanchod, sister fuckers, one who sleeps with the devil, soor ke putter, pigs' offspring.'

Police, like the marchers, were Indians; only the sergeant who led them was a fair-skinned Englishman.

The sergeant gave an order.

The police raised their batons and charged. Striking out indiscriminately. The marchers responded with banner poles, rocks, and whatever else they could find.

Six policemen with rifles materialised, as if from nowhere. An order was issued. Six rifles went shoulder high; the barrels pointed at the crowd.

People in the front row stopped and fell silent.

The sergeant raised a megaphone. 'This march is over. Go home. Go home. Go home.' He was speaking in broken Hindi.

'Did you hear that?' Damon said, 'he speaks Hindi.'

A man rushed into the tram shelter. 'I told you to go home. Didn't I?'

Damon recognised the man from the tram.

'See that yellow board?' He pointed at a shuttered shop about three hundred yards away. 'Go into the alley beside it. I'll meet you there. Hurry, Run.'

They left the tram shelter and ran.

Heads began turning to look at the fleeing Englishmen.

A man put his foot out, tripping Damon into the gutter.

The crowd cheered at the sight of a white man on his knees.

Someone swung a stick at Damon. 'Leave India,' he yelled and spat.

Robert moved quickly to wrench the stick away. He didn't see the fist that struck him across the face. The shock of the blow froze the moment in place. Another blow to the stomach pumped breath out of him.

Pierre rushed in, palms pressed together in a namaste, smiling at the jeering faces. He said something in Bengali.

'Salaa, vilyati gandoo,' a boy, no more than seventeen, hurled insults and pushed Pierre hard. Pierre fell on his buttocks. Still grinning, he got up as if it were a mere schoolyard prank.

Pap, pap, pap. Damon was sure they were gunshots, though he had never heard gunfire before. His heart went into a frenzy; fearful dryness attacked his throat and mouth.

Now everyone was running. It turned into a stampede. The good Samaritan was still with them. 'Quick, quick, this way,' he said and led them into the alley beside the café.

'I am sorry you had trouble back there. Keep your heads down. You'll be all right here. I'll come back when it's safe for you to leave,' he said.

Damon wanted to take his hand and thank him. But he was gone in a whiff, yanking the metal door shut behind him.

The yard was merely twenty feet wide with an open gutter in one corner, drainpipes converging into it. A six-foot metal drum stood by the side wall, giving off a ghastly stench, its rim stained with blood. There was dried blood on the ground, too, embedded with birds' feathers.

Pierre approached the drum, peeked inside and withdrew sharply. 'They slaughter chickens here.'

Robert made a face, threatening to retch.

'If you fellows had not taken so long with Mrs Blythe, we wouldn't be here now,' Pierre said.

'Shut up about that.'

'Shut up, both of you. You're giving me a headache,' Damon said, the sweat-soaked shirt clung to his chest like a second skin.

Pierre tried the wall-mounted tap. It gurgled and released just a few drops of water. 'Bastard.' He slapped the tap with the heel of his palm.

The sun on their head, there was nowhere to shelter. In the street beyond, they could hear people running, shouting, calling out names.

No one spoke for fifteen minutes. They stood against the shop wall to catch a few inches of shade it offered. Damon began slapping his arms. 'Damn mosquitoes. How long are we to wait here?'

'Wait for the man to come back,' Pierre said calmly.

'He could have buggered off home.'

Robert went to the metal door and peeked through a gap.

'What do you see?'

'Nothing, for Christ's sake. We are in a passageway.'

Damon lowered himself onto a stack of bricks, batting flies and mosquitoes with his hand.

The wait felt like hours.

'Did you hear that? Someone's on the other side.'

They stared at the wall, listening for a sign of movement.

First, there was a rustle of leaves. Then two hands appeared over the wall, followed by a face—black hair, dark, alert eyes.

All three stood frozen, unsure how to react.

The rest of the body followed the face, scrambling over the wall and down on their side, landing with a thud in the dust. Another man followed close behind.

'What are you people doing here?' the first man said, dusting himself all over. In his early twenties, he wore a loose, flowing white shirt cut from Gandhian khadi fabric.

Pierre stepped forward. 'Moshai, bhalo, are you well? We mean no harm. As you know, there's trouble out there. A kind gentleman has brought us here. He'll get us out when it's safe.'

'Safe?' the man cried in a mock surprise, and then chuckled, 'There's only one way you can be safe.'

'We are listening,' Pierre said.

'Hmm, listening,' he mimicked Pierre in a mocking tone and began pacing the yard with his hands clasped behind his back.

'Will you help us?' Pierre said.

'We are freedom fighters,' the man replied, 'we want to rid our country of foreign invaders, drive them into the sea.' He poked a finger in Pierre's chest.

'Now hold on,' Pierre said, 'I haven't invaded your country. I am here as a guest.'

'You come as a guest and loot our country. Now it's our turn to loot you.'

'Loot me?' Pierre patted his trouser pockets. 'Empty.'

'We want donations.'

'Donations for what?'

'We want donations for Bengal Volunteers,' he said, 'do you understand?'

'You are from Bengal Volunteers? What's your name?'

'You can call me Raju.'

'Alright, Raju, you get us out of here first, then we will give you a donation for your worthy cause.'

'We set the terms, not you. Empty your pockets.' He waved a finger. 'All of you.'

No one moved, but Raju continued pacing the yard, slowly,

his white shirt damp under the armpits.

A tense silence. It went on for ages, or so it seemed. The street noise had subsided, with occasional shouts and people calling out to their friends.

'Okay,' Robert said finally. He dipped his hand into his trouser pocket and brought out some loose change. 'You can have this.'

Raju stopped, looked at Robert's palm, and then resumed pacing, indicating he had rejected the offer.

Damon pulled out a one-rupee silver coin. 'You can have this.'

Raju accepted the coin and then clicked his fingers. 'More.'

'You're trying to rob us,' Robert exploded.

Pierre made eyes at Robert. Don't be aggressive.

'No robbery. We are asking for donations,' Raju said, and looked at his companion.

'Yes,' the companion agreed, 'voluntary donations only.'

'I'll report you to the police.'

'If you can find the police, why then are you hiding here? Tell me.'

Damon looked at Pierre and saw with dismay that, for once, he had no answers. They were trapped. There was no alternative but to agree to this man's demands. With shaky hands, Damon took out his wallet and held it out.

'Thank you. We will use the money wisely.' Raju pocketed the wallet and then turned to Robert.

'You rascal,' Robert said, 'you already have more than enough.'

Raju continued to glare at Robert.

Robert kept a defiant posture.

Raju pushed his hand down the trouser waistband and pulled out a knife. The blade and his eyes glinted as one as he waved it in the air.

'I don't like doing it, but if you force me, I will. Of that I assure you,' he said to Robert in an extraordinarily polite manner.

Don't be a fool, don't be a fool. Please give it to him, Damon cried under his breath. He was standing as close to the knifeman as Robert, and if he were to lash out, both would be in danger.

Robert lowered his hands from his hip. It seemed he was going to fight.

Damon held his breath, terrified that he would have to join in to help Robert.

Tense impasse.

Robert dropped his shoulders and pulled out his brown leather wallet from the back pocket.

Damon exhaled with relief.

'Throw it,' Raju said, pointing the knife to the ground.

Robert threw it and stepped back.

'Thank you. I'll have that too.' Raju pointed the knife at Robert's wrist.

Robert unbuckled the watch and dropped it beside the wallet.

'Thank you for your donations,' Raju said with a nod of his head.

The assistant dropped to his knees and scooped up the loot.

'Please don't move until we are gone.'

'But you promised to escort us out of this place?' Pierre said.

'Yes, I did, and I always keep my promises. Half an hour,' he said and then yelled, 'Jai Hind.'

'Jai Hind,' the assistant repeated.

Both men clambered onto the wall and slipped down on the other side.

Silence returned to the yard, but it felt like the scream of a banshee. The boys looked at each other and then away. Damon looked at his feet. He knew what others were feeling: rage, guilt, shame, and failure, meshed into one.

Robert massaged his naked wrist. 'Bastards, I don't even know what time it is now.'

'What did he mean by half an hour?' Damon mumbled.

'Someone will be here in half an hour,' Pierre replied.

'Do you believe him?'

'I do.'

Damon shrugged his shoulders. 'I don't.'

No one else had a watch. They didn't know how long they had waited. It felt like hours. There was a knock on the metal door. It clanked and shook violently, and finally, it opened, revealing a man dressed similarly to the two who had left earlier. Slightly taller with dark oily skin and a moustache. He walked right in and looked at each of them in turn, and the yard as if taking stock of merchandise. He crooked a finger, asking them to follow, and started walking back out at a brisk pace, as if he had a busy schedule ahead.

Damon hesitated. 'We don't fucking know him. It could be a trap.'

'It'll be all right, my friend. I know these people. They are members of the Indian National Congress,' Pierre said, and went on ahead. Once on the pavement, he waved at Damon and Robert to come on out.

An old, rickety open-top truck, missing its front bumper, was parked outside.

'Thank you, my friend. What's your name?' Pierre said, catching up with the man and putting his hand out for a handshake.

The man ignored Pierre's gesture of friendship and started walking around to the driver's side.

Pierre opened the cab door on the passenger side.

'Not here, you motherfucker. At the back,' the man growled and spat on the road.

The engine whirred, feebly at first, then coughed, sputtered, and fired up on all cylinders.

'Keep your heads down,' the driver said brusquely through the open rear window.

The truck jerked and began moving.

The boys sat right down on the greasy floorboard, reeking of cooking oil.

'Where is he taking us?' Damon said, 'We should ask him.'

Pierre put his head in the connecting window. 'My friend, where are you taking us? We live in Alipore. Shall I give you the address?'

The driver responded with a sudden brake and an engine rev, throwing Pierre back onto the floor.

No one spoke while the truck growled on, slowing at places, speeding abruptly.

'Fuck it,' Robert snapped finally, 'I don't know about you, but I am getting out. Oi you,' he shouted at the driver, 'stop the truck.'

The driver slammed on the brakes once, then pressed the accelerator. The engine roared.

'I told you,' Robert said, 'he is taking us out of the city.'

Pierre pulled at Robert's shirt. 'Wait, I think we are all right.

I recognise the street.'

'What fucking street?'

'This is Alipore.'

Damon's hand shook as he unlocked the front door. Once inside, he let out a wild hoot.

'What the hell,' Robert said, throwing himself on the sofa, 'there was hardly any money in my wallet, the fools must be cursing their luck.'

'What I don't get is how they knew where we live,' Damon said.

'This calls for a celebratory drink,' Robert said, rubbing his hands gleefully, 'where's the wine?'

'I still don't get it,' Damon mumbled.

'What don't you get?'

'The address. He knew the address.'

'Did you have Uncle Fred's card in your wallet?'

'Yes.'

'Well, there you are.'

Robert pulled the shoes off his feet and threw the legs up. The smell of rotting flesh surged in the air.

'Christ, don't you ever wash your feet?' Damon said, making a face.

'What a day. First, Blythe and her slaughterhouse, and then the riots and the robbers.'

'Damn honourable robbers, I should add,' Damon said.

'I am starving,' Pierre said, 'is there anything in the kitchen to eat?'

'I believe not. Mrs P is not here.'

Their laughter was drowning out the clinking of a bicycle

bell at the gate until someone shouted at the top of their voice, 'Arre bhai, is anyone home?'

'There's someone at the gate.' Pierre said.

'The fools have come to complain, why was there so little money in the wallet?'

More laughter.

The gate rattled again, louder, persistent.

'Better go and see who it is,' Pierre suggested.

'I will go,' Damon said.

A boy at the gate was waving an envelope in the air.

'What do you want?' Damon said, stopping a little short of the gate.

'For Damoon Fini …' The boy couldn't pronounce the name. He shoved the envelope through the bars.

Damon hesitated before accepting it and waited for the boy to cycle away. He turned the envelope over. His name and Burnham Cottage address were handwritten in a writing he didn't recognise. Only his family knew he was in Calcutta, and they were not the type to write letters. He ripped it open, pulled out the sheet of paper and unfolded it cautiously. The paper was blank except for a ticker tape glued lengthwise. It read: UNCLE FREDRICK HAS PASSED AWAY.

A telegram from London. The message landed with a thud on his brain. He had known Uncle Fred was in ill health. But death?

He walked back in with a stunned expression.

'What is it?' Pierre stood up, peered at the piece of paper, convinced it was a message from the Bengal Volunteers.

Damon opened his mouth, but the words caught in his throat. He had been thrown free of the body to become a single black thought. The thought intensified darkly until it had swallowed him. When he found himself again in the body, a whisper left his mouth, 'Uncle Fred is dead.'

So many alleys, each dark and foreboding. He would have to take charge, shut down the house, discharge the servants, and inform his friends and business associates. An enormous responsibility. How am I going to deal with it, miles away from home?

'Before you do anything, you should speak to your dad,' Robert said, as Damon folded the telegram again, until it was an inch-square block.

'How will I tell Nath his master is no more?' Damon muttered.

'That's not important just now. First, you need your father's instructions. Write to him straight away,' Robert suggested.

'The letter will take days to reach. But I can arrange a telephone call for you at the Writers Building. Does your father have access to a phone?' Pierre asked

Damon shook his head.

'What about your uncle's family?'

'No children. His wife died a year ago ….'

'Do you know anyone else in London who can be reached by telephone?' Pierre said.

'My sister. She's a civil servant.'

'Excellent. It's late now, but we'll go tomorrow and place a call,' Pierre said and tried to console him with a hand on the shoulder. 'Take it easy. Everything will be all right.'

'Should I go and see Mrs Blythe?' Damon said as if speaking to himself. He stopped pacing and sat down on a chair.

'No!' Pierre said, 'you mustn't do that. We don't know what

those people want from your uncle. And we don't yet know whether they have found it. My advice is don't let anyone know of your uncle's demise.'

Damon called him over as soon as he saw him at the door of his hut.

'Nath, there's something you need to know. This arrived a while ago from London.' Damon showed him the telegram. 'Your master Fred has sadly passed away.'

Blood drained from Nath's face. His lips quivered as he slipped to the floor and sat down on his haunches. 'When did this happen?'

'I don't have the details just yet. I'll let you know when I hear from London again. However, I want to assure you, whatever happens, we will take care of you and Mrs P. Meanwhile, can you keep it to yourself? No one must know about this until we have sorted everything out.'

Chapter 14

'Which branch of the civil service does your sister work in?' Pierre asked.

'She's a senior Executive Officer with the Home Office,' Damon replied. He understood Pierre was trying to keep him engaged in conversation so he wouldn't fall further into depression.

'At the Whitehall office, is she?'

'I believe so.'

'Whitehall is similar to the Writers Building here.'

'I thought it was a club or meeting place for you journalists,' Damon said.

'Oh, no, no, no, my friend. This place is the headquarters of the Bengal Government. The Governor-General is based here, along with the treasury. It used to accommodate junior servants of the East India Company who did all administrative work with pen and paper, hence the name Writers' Building. The place has a colourful past. Did you know Inspector-General of police, Colonel Simpson, died here, shot by Indian freedom fighters, an underground movement called Bengal Volunteers Corps.'

'Not the ...' Damon trailed off.

'Yes, the very same,' Pierre said, 'an offshoot of the Indian National Congress.'

'For God's sake, Pierre, if you're trying to upset me, you're doing an excellent job. Don't you think I've enough to deal with already?'

'I am sorry, my friend, deeply sorry.'

They alighted the tram at Dalhousie Square and walked over to The Writer's Building with its crowded entrance. At the reception, a small man in a crisp white shirt, lips stained red with betel juice, gave Pierre's pass a cursory glance. 'Good afternoon, sir. How are you today?'

Pierre slapped the desk bashfully. 'You won't be smiling this time next week, you rascal. Our top striker is back in action. You wait and see.'

The man laughed and leaned back in the chair, fingers interlocked behind his neck. 'Mohan Bagan is the best team. No one has beaten us this season.' Orange dots of spittle fell on Pierre's passbook.

'We'll see, my friend. We'll see.' Pierre slapped the table once more. 'You will owe me a pack of cigarettes,' he said and moved on.

He led Damon into the interior of the building, into a long, drab corridor that smelled like the inside of a paper mill. He stopped with a click of his heels at the final door on his right and pushed it open.

A small room with just a desk. On it was a black telephone with wires snaking into a hole in the wall.

He handed Damon his passbook. 'You have a five-minute slot, remember. Give the operator this number and then your sister's telephone number in London. I'll wait for you outside.'

Damon looked at the telephone, a contraption he had used only a few times before, not always successfully, for these things were known to be temperamental with a tendency to hiss and whistle like a boiling kettle.

His heart gladdened on hearing Sally's voice. 'I have five

minutes only, so we'll have to be quick,' he told her. 'How are things at home?'

'Full of relatives, vultures with beady eyes, for they know Uncle Fred was rich,' Sally replied.

'How did he die?'

'He died in his sleep. At least he didn't suffer.'

'How is the old man taking it?'

'Oh, he is happy because he is convinced something is coming to him. But he is trying not to show it.' She chuckled. 'He is waiting for the solicitor who is executing the will, a friend of Uncle Fred. I hear he has an office in India.'

'That's a relief,' Damon said, 'I was worried about how to handle his affairs here.'

'Don't worry. Aunt Frances's nephew has taken it upon himself to deal with it. He will be flying over once the solicitor has read out the will.'

And then she disclosed something he had not expected at all.

'Mother confided in me only last week that she is thinking of leaving him. But don't tell anyone.'

'Does he know?'

She changed the subject promptly and talked about the notorious cousins from Birmingham.

It seemed they had only just begun the conversation when the operator cut the connection with a firm click. He sat back, replaying the conversation in his head, thinking of the extended family assembled at their home: cousins, uncles, and aunts he had never met. You have missed nothing, Sally had said. The news about the old man and his mother separating was a shock. But he felt happy and yet disturbed, for he knew that monster would fight hard to keep things as they were. He recalled the days when a smell would enter the house before father did, a sharp, warm, sour sting that would make him hold his breath. It was the smell of his father's curses which collided with his mother's silence; the fights often ended in a crash, a slap, a muffled sob. With one look at his father – the loose tie, the crumpled shirt – Damon would open his schoolbook and immerse his head in it. Father had two settings at home: silence and shouting. But with his friends and business partners, he was entirely different. With his easy laughter and back-slapping banter, he could make people see things his way. His mother was quite different. A nurse in wartime Europe, in France and Serbia, she often talked of the wounded soldiers in hospitals. How what she saw had changed her. He was seeing her now with the long cane racket in her hand, whacking the woollen carpet slung over the clothesline, and the dust exploding like a bomb, with each strike. That racket was his favourite play tool, used for badminton or tennis. The whack, whack, whack of the racket was still in his ears as he got up and left the room.

As he exited the building, lonely and singular in his mind's eye, he didn't notice the doorman at the gate had given him a salute.

He stepped out into the street and found, not surprisingly, the Frenchman had assembled himself a company. With his back to Damon, he was chatting with three Englishmen under a giant billboard advertising LUX soap: fragrant, smooth, gentle on the skin.

He noticed an oddity in Pierre's body posture. His arms were straight by his side, and he appeared to be protesting about something. The men were looking on unimpressed. Suddenly,

Pierre swung around as if to leave. The men rushed to block his path. And then they were scuffling; Pierre was trying to free himself. A passing bus blocked his view. When he caught sight again, the men had already subdued Pierre. They were frogmarching him to a car.

'Wait, wait,' Damon called as he ran to catch up with them.

Pierre looked back over his shoulder. Their eyes met. And then just as quickly, Pierre turned away. There wasn't a hint of recognition from Pierre, as if Damon were a stranger.

Damon watched helplessly as the car's doors slammed shut and it sped off.

He walked back to the Writers Building but hesitated as though a chasm had opened before him on the broken paving slabs, sensing a danger ahead of him.

He asked the security guard at the gate, 'What was all that about?'

The guard pulled his rifle close to his chest and made a face to say he had seen or heard nothing, though Damon was sure he had.

The air was thick with gloomy silence and Robert's cigarette smoke. Absent was Pierre's incessant chatter and flow of useless information. But his spirit was present, looming large in every room.

'Didn't I tell you, Finnegan, not to invite that man to stay with us? Didn't I say he would be trouble? I was right, wasn't I?' Robert said, quick to score a point: I told you so.

'On the contrary, he was protecting me from those people. He knew I was there right behind him, yet not once did he look at me, or ask for help, not once.'

Nath came in through the kitchen door with an orange scarf slung over his shoulder. Damon guessed from Nath's demeanour that he was about to ask for a favour.

'Sahib, may I have the afternoon off? Today is Nag Panchami. I want to go to the temple.'

'Yes, yes, go,' Damon said impatiently and went back to writing his diary.

'It will be late, sahib.'

Mrs P had already asked for a day's leave, saying she wanted to visit her relatives in the village. Is it a coincidence that both were asking for time off on the same day? Do they know something I don't? Could it be the burglary? He was loath to express his misgivings openly in case Robert would pounce on him with: Didn't I say so?

Robert picked up a book to read. The house was silent again but for Damon's rough breathing and the rustling pages of his diary. The street, too, was quiet for most people had moved indoors for the afternoon siesta.

Damon tapped his pencil on the table and turned over to a new page. He was assembling his thoughts to start the new day when the front door flew open.

'Hi, I am back.' A female voice, chirpy and bright, cut into the silent air—a pause. 'Jesus, you guys look so jolly cheerful. Am I missing something?' she said.

Damon looked up from his diary. The pencil slipped from his fingers as he saw Flora with a little boy by her side. Chubby-faced, fair-haired, sporting short pants and plimsolls, the boy was trying to make himself invisible behind Flora.

'This is John,' Flora said, coaxing the boy to come forward. 'Meet Uncle Damon, and that one is Robert. Leave my skirt and say hello to everyone, Johny baby ... he's so shy with strangers.' She rolled her eyes.

Robert dropped to his knees. 'Hello, Johnny boy, how are you?'

John shook his head, withdrawing deeper into Flora's skirt.

'I've been so busy,' she said as if someone had asked her how she was. She lifted her long hair with a hand at the neck and let it fall back again. She might as well have said, I've been so happy.

But it was the little boy Damon was staring at, suddenly feeling utterly exhausted, reeling from the events of the last forty-eight hours.

The boy looked too young to be her brother, and she seemed too young to be a mother.

'Would Johnny like lemonade – yes? Yes, you do. You wait here with uncles while I make shweety-weety lemonade.'

The motherly gesture. It seemed so strange coming from Flora.

He followed Flora to the kitchen.

'Who is that boy?' he said.

'My son,' she replied without hesitation. 'He's six years old.'

She put her head in the cupboard, which had wire netting around a wooden frame and its four feet standing in bowls of water, a contraption Mrs P had devised to stop ants and vermin from climbing up the legs.

He didn't believe her, and he didn't want to. How could she have a six-year-old when she looked no more than twenty? A feeling washed over him, a feeling of hurt, as if he had been betrayed by someone dear to him.

'Your son? You didn't tell me you were married,' he said and found his voice was beginning to crack.

'Oh, there they are,' she said triumphantly, pulling out a cane basket with a handful of potatoes and five green limes sitting on top. 'Shall I make lemonade for everyone?'

'Flora, I asked you a question.'

'I am not married, Damon.'

'Then how do you explain … who is John's father?'

'It doesn't matter who the father is. Does it? John is my son … and that's all I care.'

'Are you sure? You don't look old enough to have a six-year-old,' he said.

'He's my son, Damon.'

'Why didn't you tell us before?' he said.

As if she had not heard, she picked a lime from the basket and placed it on the board.

He wanted to snatch the limes away. Get out, take your belongings and the boy with you.

'There's something you need to know; my uncle Fred has passed away,' he said.

'Passed away?' The lime slipped from her fingers. 'Your uncle … when? … oh, my God.'

'I am waiting to hear from father. He'll want me to shut down the house.'

'Damon, I'm so sorry,' she said, but did not ask any more questions. Silently and vigorously, she squeezed limes in a jug. When finished, she topped up the jug with water, added five teaspoons of sugar and then stirred vigorously with a ladle.

They walked back to the front room. John was still standing with his face tucked in.

'I can't get him to talk,' Robert said.

'John, say hello to Uncle Robert and come for your

lemonade.' She placed the jug on the table and went back for the glasses.

'Flora,' Damon screamed at her back, 'I need answers.'

He turned to look at Robert to see his reaction and caught a movement outside the window. An Englishman was approaching the front door. Smartly dressed, with a felt topee on his head, his skin was tanned, a Caucasian who has lived in a tropical climate for many years.

Damon's heart gladdened, assuming he was one of Uncle Fred's friends or a business associate coming to offer condolences. How quickly the news travels. At last, someone to tap for advice. And then he realised, suddenly and painfully, how little he knew about Uncle Fred.

'I am looking for Miss MacDonald,' the man said.

'MacDonald?' Damon said.

'Flora MacDonald.'

'Flora?' Damon stared at the man, stalled and confused.

'Who shall I say wants her?' he mumbled.

'She knows who I am.'

'Err … excuse me, where do you think you're going?'

The man had already barged in. He went past the sideboard, the coat-stand and stopped at the sitting room entrance.

Damon followed close behind and saw him fix a choleric glare on Flora, who was handing John the glass of lemonade.

She did not react at first, as if blinded by a dazzling searchlight. And then she screamed, 'No!' She took John by the arm and pulled him between her legs. The glass fell to the floor, spilling its contents.

'You'll let him go now,' he said calmly, civilly, but his eyes were cold as steel.

She did not move.

'I said let him go,' he repeated, politely, and then capped it with a bark, 'NOW.'

Her voice trembled. 'Frank, you said I could have him whenever I wanted to. Didn't you?'

'No, I didn't. I said you can visit him, but only with my permission. Now you'll let him go. Or I'll have you arrested for kidnapping.'

'John wants to be with me. You can ask him yourself.'

The boy looked terrified, his hands cupping his crotch as if he needed to wee.

'I am warning you, Flora.'

She started backing away and hit a jardinière housing a mother-in-law-tongue potted plant.

Alarmed by what was happening, Damon looked at Robert. What should we do?

'Now come on, guys, whatever the problem is, it can be settled in a civilised manner,' Robert said.

Frank gave Robert an angry look. 'You keep out of it.'

Flora dashed around the sofa and then into the hallway. She contemplated running out of the front door, changed her mind, and scrambled up the staircase, pulling John along with her. Frank ran after her, his leather boots clomping on the stairs.

She ran to the open balcony and realised with terror that she had inadvertently cornered herself. She turned around, keeping the boy secure between her legs and faced Frank defiantly.

Damon came running in time to see Frank slap Flora across the face. 'You have gone too far this time. I am going to see that you go to jail, you bitch.'

Flora froze with a hand on the side of her face.

'Don't ever try this stunt again. I am warning you,' he said, and took John's arm and pulled him away from her. 'I'll kill you.' He looked around as if to assess his bearings and then went to the railing. Leaning over, he raised his arm and waved at someone below.

Damon rushed to the railing to see who had received the signal. An Englishman in a khaki safari was standing just beyond the flower beds, looking up.

No one saw her go in until they heard the clanging, as if someone had taken a swipe at a set of knives and forks, sending them crashing to the floor. Damon turned to look. The glass cabinet was wide open, the collection of antique silver was in disarray, and a few pieces had rolled out onto the floor.

A Maharaja silver dagger in her hand, she came running with a rage-filled shriek: a vision, a dream. No, don't do it, Damon cried. But it was only in his head.

Frank had only just turned around; the dagger pierced the lower part of his stomach, without sound or resistance, like a knife in butter. He did not wince or cry as if he had felt nothing.

He grabbed her hair.

This time, she fought back, scratching his face with her nails, peeling the skin in parallel straight lines. He was choking her with hefty jerks, like an alligator thrashing life out of its prey. She was going red in the face. Eyes bulging like two ping pong balls. Saliva spluttered from the lips.

As if guided by a primal instinct, Damon rushed to her aid. He grabbed Frank's right arm and began prying it from her neck. The struggle continued for a minute, neither side getting the upper hand.

'Stop, stop. Let her go, or I'll shoot,' Robert yelled at the top of his voice.

All three turned to look at Robert and froze.

Robert was pointing a shotgun at Frank. 'I'll shoot,' he warned. Kachunk. He released the catch.

'No, no need for it,' Frank said.

Flora pulled herself free from him. 'Get out and let John go,' she screamed.

Frank rubbed his cheeks. Saw the blood on his fingers and appeared confused. His eyeballs appeared to wobble as he looked at Robert again.

Robert shook the gun threateningly.

Frank turned around slowly to show he was leaving. But he refused to let go of John's arm.

'No, you will let him go,' Flora screamed.

He ignored her.

She threw herself at him.

Damon joined in. They pinned Frank against the railing.

Frank flailed and kicked; the bloodied shirt ripped open. Still, he refused to let John go. The struggle continued. Frank appeared to weaken as his upper body went right over the railing. Like a fish out of water, he was thrashing his arms and legs, as if trying to reverse the fall.

The little boy's body slid over the railing, too, as if the two were chained to each other.

'Noooo,' she wailed, throwing herself forward in a futile attempt to catch him.

A scream. A thud.

Damon peered over the railing. Frank was in the flower bed. John was on the concrete path behind a tall bush, only his foot visible from where Damon stood.

Damon turned away slowly and slid to the floor. The world began spinning, as if he, too, had taken the thirty-foot fall. Time appeared to stand still.

From the depths of the house, as if a long way off, he heard Flora, a strange, long-drawn-out cry. Not a scream or a howl but a cry of sorrow, a protracted ooooo.

Damon forced himself up and staggered down the stairs. Death and bloodshed seemed to cling to him like a feeding leech ever since his arrival in India. Why me? Why me?

He didn't want to look. What you don't see doesn't exist. But Flora did exist. She was sitting on the sofa, cradling John and rocking back and forth.

'How is he?' Damon whispered.

Robert shook his head. 'Not breathing.'

'What are we going to do?'

'Can't you see? The doctors must certify him, and the family must be informed.'

'We don't know where they live,' Damon said.

'What about that man, Frank? Know anything about him?'

'No. I've never seen him before.'

'Flora, listen to me, we need to take John to the hospital or send for a doctor … do you want to contact your family, friends, anyone?'

But Flora wasn't listening. She continued wailing and rocking. Fresh tears were meandering over blotches of dried tears.

'Flora, the police will be here any minute. They will want to know why you haven't taken John to a doctor.'

She stopped rocking. 'Police … no police … I don't want police.'

'It's not up to me. Your husband is bound to call the police.'

'He is not my husband.' She looked around her with terror-stricken eyes. 'Where is he?'

'Gone. His friend carried him away,' Damon said, 'Listen, darling, you have had a traumatic experience. You need to contact your family. We can take you there if you tell us where they live.'

As if struck by a flashback, a long-suppressed memory surfacing, she gazed at the fingers of her right hand, at the blood-stained fingernails and the frayed sleeves of her blouse.

'Flora, you're in trouble. You need to act fast.'

'Get me out of here,' she pleaded, 'take me to Madan Lal.'

'Who is Madan Lal?'

She wailed louder in reply.

They hadn't noticed the dark clouds outside until the rain came, a sudden torrential downpour. Bursts of thunder followed, and strong winds.

In the kitchen, Mrs P's calendar of Taj Mahal pictures began to kick the wall as if it were alive. The windows of Burnham Cottage came to life, a surreal waltz of opening and shutting. Bang Bang! Damon ran to bolt each door and window, taken aback by the sudden change of weather, even though Uncle Fred had warned of this phenomenon in India. The tin roof of a garden shed went hurtling down the path,

'I want Madan Lal,' she began chanting as if she were in a trance.

'Who is Madan Lal?' Damon said.

'Just get me out of here. Now.'

'We'll take you to Madan Lal. You have the address?'

'Why not wait for the police so you can tell them what that man has done?' Robert suggested.

'No police. They mustn't find me here with John. You don't know how crooked that man is. You are in danger too.'

'I am in danger?' That hit Damon as if he had crashed into a brick wall. He imagined himself locked in an Indian jail. Father would be furious. I told you not to go to that Godforsaken place, didn't I? And what about the university, the career?

He watched Flora's face, thinking he did not know this woman; it was as though the very thing that had given him aspect had been slowly extracted, her grief feeding on the marrow in his bones. He felt intensely tired and bent over with hands on his knees, and when he looked up, Robert, grim as a jailer, was ordering him to come to the other room.

He followed Robert.

'Why did you let her come here with that boy? I knew she would be fucking trouble. Now you sort this out. I am outta here.'

'How was I to know this would happen? And Fletcher, it was you who was fucking her, not me. And where did you get the gun from?'

'Your uncle's gun. I found it in his bedroom.'

'You could have killed us.'

'Killed you? Killed you? The gun didn't have bullets in it.'

'Whatever. You can't just walk away and leave me with this mess.'

'Hah, I can do what I like. I am outta here, back to London.'

'Fuck you.'

'Right,' Robert said firmly and stormed out of the room, slamming the door behind him.

Damon paced the floor. Leave her and run? He couldn't do that. This was his uncle's house. Go to the police and tell them everything. Or go to Mrs Blythe and ask for help. Nath may return early. The police could storm in any minute. His stomach juices began to swirl and churn as if caught in a storm.

'All right, this is what we are going to do.' He heard Robert's voice behind him.

'What?'

'Sanitise the place quickly before police arrive and then get out.'

'What are you saying?' Damon said, relieved to see Robert had changed his mind.

'I am saying before we leave, we wipe away all evidence so no one will know what happened here .... you understand?'

They ran up the stairs, taking two steps to a stride, to the balcony. As if with solemn genuflection, Robert lowered himself on his knees and then began examining the floor where the stabbing had taken place. There was blood on the concrete, though the rain had diluted it.

The dagger, with veins of blood in its intricate carvings and inlays, lay under the awning away from the rainwater.

'Poor bastard must have lost a lot of blood.'

Damon rushed to the bathroom and came back with towels and a bucket of water. Robert picked up the dagger with a towel and wrapped it carefully. Between them, they began washing the floor and mopping with the towels. They scrubbed the railings next.

'What about the ground where the poor bastard fell?' Damon said.

They ran down to the side of the house. A cluster of plants in the flower bed was lying flattened. Robert set them erect as best he could. 'We're ok; the blood has already washed away.'

The black clouds joined forces with nightfall.

They went back up and collected all the bloodied towels and the dagger, meticulously accounting for each item. 'We will bury these in the garden. How long do we have before Nath returns.'

'About two hours … that is, if the police don't arrive before.'

'Shut up about the police.'

'The gun?'

'We will bury that too.'

Frank's topee with the chin strap was lying under the stairs. Damon grabbed it, went to the kitchen for a torch, and dashed out the back door to the garden.

'We will need a spade.'

Damon went to the shed with the missing roof and came out with a rusty spade, coated in dried mud.

'Over here,' Robert said, 'shine the torch.' He dug his heel at a spot between two trees, a spot sufficiently distant from the house and veiled from the prying eyes of neighbours.

Damon began digging, pushing the spade in with all his might while Robert held the torch. The topsoil surrendered without protest. The going was tough when he reached the lower strata, where the soil was as compact as a rock.

Between the digs, the rain stopped, and an ethereal mist clung to their frame, a shroud of sweat and steam. Damon kept on digging. Snot and sweat were dripping from his nose.

'Animals can smell blood. If we don't bury deep, they will root everything out,' Robert said, 'here let me have a go.'

A car stopped outside the gate. Fuck. Damon switched off the torch. But it was nothing. The car drove off after a minute of idling.

'That's deep enough,' Robert said. He threw the spade to the ground and jumped in with both feet. 'Knee deep. That will do.'

They dropped everything in the hole, and finally, the gun. But it was too long even with the break.

Damon picked up the spade and started again. Darkness had engulfed them, the moon hidden behind the clouds. They could barely see each other's faces, only hear the heavy, laboured breathing.

'I can't do it anymore.'

'It's enough,' Robert said and drove the shotgun barrel hard into the muddy hole.

Damon ran back inside. The toy lay forlorn near the French window, along with John's discarded canvas plimsolls. So small and dainty. A shiver coursed down his spine as he knelt to pick them up, his fingers brushing against the traces of a life now extinguished.

'What's that?' Robert said.

'John's shoes. He must have taken them off earlier.'

They shovelled and pushed the soil back in like dogs, back-kicking dirt over their excreta. Each motion felt laden with unspoken remorse. Finally, they raked the surface, carefully blending it with the surroundings.

Damon went to replace the spade in the shed.

'No, don't,' Robert called, 'they will know someone has used it; it has fresh dirt on it. Throw it in the pond.'

Damon stood at the edge of the pond and hurled it like a javelin.

Robert ran out of the gate and stood in the centre of the lane. The neighbour's servant was standing under a tree, the glowing tip of his lit bidi revealing the contours of his face. Pressing a handful of coins into the boy's hand, Robert asked him to cycle to the Taxi office for a car.

Flora had stopped sobbing, only rocking back and forth, stroking John's hair, as if he were merely asleep. For fifteen minutes, no one spoke or moved. Damon was at the dining table, Robert on the edge of the sofa, smoking a cigarette, taking shallow puffs, producing a stifling cocktail of smoke and fear.

A car stopped outside. Robert sprang to his feet. 'OK, now. Let's go.'

Flora rose from the sofa. 'May I have the bag?' Her voice broke like a Teutonic wind instrument. Her legs wobbled as she walked.

Damon locked the front door and stood back, giving the familiar façade a once-over. Nath will be here soon. His unsullied ignorance will work to their advantage, a perfect shield against police questioning.

Flora sank into her seat and whispered an address to Robert. Robert relayed it to the driver. 'The lady isn't well, can you hurry?'

'Yes, boss. I do my best. This rain is not good, slows everything,' the driver replied and depressed the starter button. The engine whined a few times, then died. He tried again. This time, the engine whined a little louder before going silent.

'For Christ's sake, go,' Robert cried.

'Engine is not starting, sahib,' the driver said, depressing the starter button repeatedly.

Flora stared ahead, terrified. Damon looked back out the rear window as if expecting to see a police car any moment.

The driver got out with a handlebar, walked to the front, inserted the bar in the engine, and cranked it hard. The engine coughed and sputtered, finally caught, and fired off with a sound like a cannon shot.

The driver jumped back in and engaged the gear.

'Who is this Madan Lal?' Damon asked once they were off.

She didn't reply. Her chest heaved as she sobbed.

'Does he know about the man you're running away from?'

'He knows everything.'

'But this is serious, Flora. Can you trust him?

She nodded. 'Yes, he is like a father to me.'

'But that man, Frank, is bound to come for you,' Robert said.

'I'll leave Calcutta. Madan Lal will help me.'

Damon believed her. The pain and the steely determination were clear in her voice. He felt Flora's pain, the stoned-to-death feeling in the soul. He could not, for a long time afterwards, rid himself of the feeling that everything he did was the work of a stranger who temporarily inhabited his skin. He presumed that his mind was deluding him; to protect him from the roar of tragedies, it was offering this illusion that someone else was in control.

Three days later, Damon and Robert returned to London. 'From now on, we must stay away from each other. It's safer that way,' Robert said at the airport, 'and if our paths ever cross, we should pretend to be strangers.'

PART TWO

Chapter 15

London 1939

The girl was standing in The Village Bakery, waiting for her turn to be served.

'What are you doing in a place like this?' Pierre said.

The girl ignored him.

Pierre slid closer. 'I wouldn't buy from here. Didn't you know someone once found a rat as big as this?' He cupped his hands to show the size. 'Baked in a loaf.'

Still, the girl remained steadfast in her refusal to engage.

'I was joking, actually,' he said then, in a tone laced with humour, 'not a mouse … it was a cockroach.'

This time, she eyed him with scorn.

'Where were you born?' he asked.

'India.'

'I can see that. I meant, where in India?'

'Midnapore.'

'Oh, Midnapore,' he said as if he were familiar with the town, 'I've travelled all over India – from Bombay to Delhi, to the heart of Calcutta.'

'Been to Midnapore?'

'No.'

'Then you haven't seen all of India.'

Pierre's eyes locked on her lips, which had parted demurely. He asked her if she would like some marmalade to go with the freshly baked bread and a mug of hot tea.

She smiled.

He took that as yes.

'Come with me.' He walked her across the road.

'Wait here while I check if the landlady is in.' He unlocked the front door and went in, leaving the door ajar.

A minute later, he raised the sash of the first-floor window, thrust his head out and grinned. 'She's out. Come on up. It's the first door on the left.'

She refused to enter a strange house unescorted.

'All right, wait there.' He came bounding down and guided her in.

Under the dim glow of the room's solitary lamp, they sat facing each other, an ocean of stories swirling between them.

'My mother was a simple village girl,' she said, her legs tucked in under her and her hands around a warm mug. 'She was working as a housekeeper at Midnapore military barracks, where she met an English soldier. They had an affair, but it was grossly one-sided, for she was too innocent to say no to anything he wanted. After eighteen months, when she told him she was pregnant, he ran back to England.'

Pierre bit into a crunchy toast slathered with orange marmalade.

'So, when you were older, you came to England to look for your dad?'

She giggled. 'No, you fool. My mother didn't know very much about him, only that he loved his fish cooked the Indian way, and said his name was Adam Smith. Even if I were to look for him, where would I start?'

'You could start by asking around who eats his fish cooked hot and spicy.' He laughed aloud. 'No, no. You're right, Adam Smith may have been an assumed name.'

'I was fourteen when my mother sent me to work as a nanny

for an English family, in Calcutta, to look after a boy of eight and two girls of ten and thirteen. One day, I was taking the boy to school when he mysteriously disappeared. There were people around, but no one owned up to seeing anything. I was terrified they would blame me; I considered running away or killing myself by drowning in the Hooghly.'

'Oh, Priti, good thing you didn't kill yourself, or we wouldn't be sitting here today drinking tea which has come all the way from your country.'

'My mistress didn't blame me.'

'Did they find the boy?'

'No. We heard rumours that it was the work of local, so-called freedom fighters, who wanted to terrorise the white population into leaving India. Police began arresting people indiscriminately. So, what happens?' She placed a finger on Pierre's chest. 'More resentment and anger against your people.'

Pierre threw his hands up in horror. 'Not my people … not my people, I am French.'

'So, when they heard the inspector of police was gone, fired for bribery and favouritism, they gave up hope of ever finding him alive and decided to return to London. My mistress went to meet my mother. She wanted to ask for permission to take me to London with her. Mother didn't want me to go, but she agreed when I promised to write regularly.'

'And you write?'

'I do. However, the amusing thing is that she is uneducated. She asks the postman to read it out to her.'

'So, you've never received a letter from her.'

'No, I am happy with that. It's the day I hear back, I know my heart will break.'

Pierre removed the mug from her hand and placed it aside. He took her still-warm hand in his and kissed it.

Pierre never thought of events in his distant past as evil but rather as mistaken and immensely regrettable. He thought the folly of the world was due to fear and greed, and to call it evil, as if it were the result of purposeful calculation and deliberate wrongdoing, was to show ignorance of human psychology. It was in this way he was thinking, making his way with Priti, his wife, by his side, to the east exit of Paddington station, when he looked up and saw a face in the crowd, a face he had not seen in more than five years and did not expect to see ever again.

He had no doubt it was Damon Finnegan. He recognised the slight build, pale complexion, and flat dark hair.

'Just what are you looking at?' Priti asked. She was leaning on Pierre's elbow. She winced as the loudspeaker crackled, announcing the imminent departure of the ten-thirty to Reading.

'You shouldn't have insisted on early discharge,' he said.

'A hundred times I've told you the maternity ward is for women with newborn babies. Am I one of them?'

He gave her arm a gentle squeeze.

'I asked who that man was you were staring at?' she said.

'Quelque personne du passe,' Pierre replied.

'Oh, please, say it in English.'

'Alright, darling, Priti,' Pierre said, the rhythms of his native French coalescing with English's cadence. 'He's a bloke I used to know from years ago.'

'Why didn't you say hello to him?'

'He doesn't want to know me. I am just a Frenchman, you see, a foreigner.'

Priti paused on the steps of their house overlooking Putney station. Tears were cascading down her cheeks. 'I've spent my whole life looking after other people's children. Yet when I dare to dream of my own, God cruelly takes it away from me.' A mournful lamentation flowed from her lips. She took his hand and pressed it against the womb that held both potential and pain.

'We will have another child one day.' Pierre said, 'There's no reason, the doctors have said, why such an unfortunate thing as a placenta previa should occur again.'

But Pierre held reservations about having a baby, painfully aware of the paper-thin separation between stability and volatility of the ink-stained life of a newspaper chronicler.

Pierre closed the door behind him, dropped the keys on the sideboard, and coaxed Priti to the bedroom. 'Lie down, darling, while I make tea.'

He returned with a tray set with two cups, bread with cheese, and ham.

'What are you doing? I asked you to rest,' he said.

She did not reply but continued stuffing her soiled clothes from the hospital into an oversized laundry bag.

He understood her actions. As with so many, she had succumbed to the myth that busyness is a cure for a fractured heart.

'Leave it to me. I'll take them to the launderette later.'

She snapped. 'Do you think I am invalid?'

'Of course not. But right now, you need to rest.'

'God doesn't want me to rest. If he did, he would have given me the child.'

Chapter 16

Damon stood looking out into the garden. Old memories on wet leaves, a homemade slide that wasn't there anymore, the ash tree father planted when he was five was there all right, towering over the narrow plot. Wood polish, log fire, damp coal cellar, hospital smell on mother's uniform. This was the aroma of his childhood. Now married and with a child, he no longer felt at home in the house on Oaktree Lane, made worse by the fact that his mother had not left his father after all and kept up a pretence of a happy marriage. 'She is a woman of old traditions, Damon. She believes family unity is more important than her happiness,' his sister had said.

Anne was sitting on the cretonne-covered settee, and Mary lay on the floor, kicking with her legs and making gurgling noises. The neighbour was incinerating dry leaves and twigs. Mother shut the kitchen window to stop the acidic smoke from drifting in. She began poking Mary with toys, which the child did not want to play with. On the radio, party officials were screaming at each other. 'We need to be tough with Hitler – don't have the numbers – he will walk all over if not checked – alliances, alliances – ask the Yanks.'

Damon's father, who was sitting at the table, picked up the Daily Mail and gave it a slap with the back of his hand. 'Did you read about that murder? The police in Calcutta have released the man they had detained. All this happened after a mob had stormed the police station. What absolute nonsense, the scoundrels want to wash their hands of the matter – pass it on to the London police.'

'Oh, really.' Damon had missed this later report buried within the inner pages.

'Who is the man they have released?' he asked.

'Your Uncle Fred's housekeeper.'

Damon had known all along they would pick up the poor man and torture him into owning the deed. He couldn't wash away the guilt, even though he had tried hard to rationalise it as: there was nothing I could have done. I was a mere visitor.

'I can't say if he did the crime or not. What I do know is you can't be too trusting of these wogs. Who's to say he wasn't one of those insurgents trying to drive us out of India,' Father said.

Nath, a revolutionary? No. Damon knew the futility of trying to convince Father that the man was not evil; he was a highly religious man with no interest in politics or in the sentiment of the freedom movement. He lived a clean life, preparing modest meals for himself in pots and pans, old and battered like relics from a different age, yet gleaming with meticulous cleanliness. His name was Vishwanath. Translated, it meant a servant of God Vishnu.

Dad continued, 'And that fellow, Gandhi or whatever his name is, is going on about peaceful disobedience. What's peaceful about refusing to follow orders?'

'His name is Gandhi, Mohan Chand Gandhi. A highly regarded man with a massive following. I don't see why they should not run their own country if that's what they want.'

The senior Finnegan shook his head left and right as if exercising his neck. 'They can't run a country, my boy. The only thing they are good at is fighting each other. Do you recall the upheaval they brought to that city? Was it Lucknow? And the savagery they inflicted on that Lord … whatshisname?'

Damon would have liked to be alone at this moment. But he knew there was no possibility of that, now or when he returned home. Anne was sure to bombard him with questions.

Police had started making enquiries here in London. He was beginning to fear a knock on the door by the local constabulary. Where is Robert Fletcher? He imagined Robert was now married and, like him, had moved out of the family home. Had he repaid the loan? It was a certainty that, like his father, he would have found his way into the world of banking and methodically amassed a fortune. Had he seen the report in the newspaper? Probably not. These bankers are too busy counting money and mingling with business magnates to have the time or inclination to peruse a newspaper beyond the financial pages.

'What was all that? You never told me anything about it,' Anne said, finding him alone in the room. She was rocking the baby violently from side to side.

A scene was unfolding around him, and at times, he felt he was not in control, as if he were going down a slippery shaft. If he clawed his way up, what would he find anyway, except Anne telling him he couldn't go on like this?

'It's nothing really. Robert and I had gone on holiday to Calcutta, as you know. We had intended to stay for a month, but when we heard Uncle Fred had died, we came back early. That was a long time ago. Now we hear there had been a murder nearby, and for some reason, they have linked it to Uncle Fred's Burnham Cottage.' He added, for this is what an unaffected third person would say, 'Gruesome. I hope they catch the killers. Five years is a long time.'

'Five years. But that's not what your father has read in the paper. There was no mention of the timing.'

Damon's heart skipped a beat. Damn, damn, damn. Inadvertently, he had said something that wasn't in the public domain. The newspapers carried the report, which was lacking in detail but presented sensationally.

'I don't know for certain, darling. I thought that's what the papers said. Anyway, let's not talk about it; it's too depressing. Is there more tea?'

Chapter 17

Two months had passed. Damon was turning the key to the front door with a tired hand when he heard someone behind him call out his name. Simultaneously, he heard Mary crying. His first instinct was to rush indoors to his daughter and tend to her needs. The man was introducing himself as Detective Inspector Someone-or-other, and could he have a word, 'to clear up some matters.' The words had an air of formality with a hint of a concealed agenda.

Damon felt his stomach muscles twitch. It's happening. He had half convinced himself that the police in London, stretched to the limit, would leave the case pending for months and years and, in time, let it rest for good.

He turned around with a laughing face, this universal reflex when the police come to your door. 'What matters do you want to clear up?'

The detective handed Damon a card. 'May I come inside? Best to talk in private.'

Damon glanced up and down the street and saw a lone walker under an umbrella, the willows nodding to the wind. 'I've arrived home this minute after a long day. Could you come back in an hour,' Damon said, thinking fast, to buy time to prepare answers.

The inspector looked at Damon with remote yet scrutinising eyes as though he was trying to seize hold of something within him. 'As you wish, Mr Damon Finnegan. An hour it is then.'

He put his hat back on, turned and walked back down the steps.

'Damon, you're not in trouble, are you?' Anne said, coming into the room.

Damon stared at the card, frowning. He placed it on the coffee table and fell back into the armchair.

'It's probably nothing,' he said, seeing her feeding Mary at her breast.

The child's presence held a quiet serenity. So innocent, as if she had never cried in her life, wouldn't have known how to. My child. Will they take me away from you? Will I see you again?

Her eyes sharpened towards him. 'A detective Inspector at our door. How can it be nothing?'

'I expect it is about that dead child … you know … the thing in the newspaper, father was talking about.'

'Whose child …?'

'What do you mean, whose child?' he erupted.

'I was just wondering who the child's parent was, that's all.'

'Sorry, it's just that I am tired,' he said, watching his own voice fall to a whisper, 'I expect they want to clear up some matters.'

'Shall I make you some tea?'

'I'll have whiskey.'

'Whiskey?' she raised her eyebrows, 'but you don't drink whiskey anymore.'

'I want it now.' Drink, he reasoned, would make him appear relaxed and so guilt-free.

Anne went to the other room and returned with a glass. 'I've topped it with water.'

'But I wanted it without water.'

'Go and get your own. I'll have this one,' she said and snatched the glass from his fingers.

Her drinking habits had changed lately. From a near teetotaller when he had first met her, she was now drinking most days. There were times he felt distanced from her. And then he would feel he didn't know her at all. She was a stranger; even her face was unfamiliar, not an attractive or loved one, not one he could ever have kissed.

A knock on the door. It startled him, even though he had expected Detective Inspector, whatever his name was, to return within the hour.

Anne rose to open the door.

'I'll do it,' he said, standing up and taking Mary in his arms. The Inspector's hard heart might soften at the sight of a father with his child.

'Come in and sit down,' Damon said, 'a drink?'

'Thank you. Have you ever seen a drunk copper, Mr Finnegan?'

Damon studied the inspector. What kind of reply is that?

Without a word, Anne took Mary from Damon and left the two in the front room.

'My name is Graham Burrows, detective inspector.' He looked around the room. 'A cosy place you have here.'

'You'd better explain why you're here, Mr Burrows. I am a busy man.'

'Quite right, Mr Finnegan. An explanation is your entitlement.' His speech had a nasal undertone. It reminded Damon of a colleague afflicted with chronic tonsillitis.

'The Indian Imperial Police have been investigating the death of a boy in Calcutta. After extensive enquiries, they now believe the culprits may have lived at Burnham Cottage at some point and later returned to London. So, they now seek our aid to bring the case to a conclusion. After a thorough investigation on our end, we believe a link exists between you and Burnham Cottage in Calcutta.'

'The house belonged to my uncle Fred Finnegan, not me,' Damon said, 'how am I linked?'

'I use the word you in a broad sense, meaning your family, Mr Finnegan. Now, could you tell me what you know about this unfortunate incident?'

'What I know is only what's in the newspapers.'

'Could you tell me who occupied the house at the time in question?'

'The house belonged to my uncle. So, it's logical that he was the occupier. Surely you can work that out.'

'Yes, indeed. Did you ever live there?'

'I wouldn't say I lived there. I had stayed there for a few days when I was on holiday.'

'Was your uncle there too, when you visited?'

'No, Uncle Fred was in London at the time. He wasn't in good health. In fact, he died while I was still out there.'

'Who else lived in the house with you?'

'I didn't live there. I have already stated.'

'Yes, yes, you didn't live there. You were on holiday. Who else was in the house with you?'

Damon felt his eyes twitching. That was a loaded question. Should he name names? Robert will be furious. But if I get into trouble, why should he go free? As for Flora and Pierre, he didn't know where they were. Both could still be in India.

'There were four of us, on and off, all friends.'

'Could you give their names?'

Damon gave the names of the other three.

'Are you in touch with them? Can you give us addresses?'

'No. After leaving Calcutta, I got busy with my studies and then with my professional pursuits. I also got married to Anne, whom you have already met.'

'Are you certain about that, Mr Finnegan? People who go on holiday together are usually close friends. It will be strange not to stay in touch,' Burrows said and fixed a staring gaze at Damon. Slowly, the wrinkles around his mouth collapsed. The gaze became opaque.

An inscrutable silence filled the room.

'I've lost touch with them. That's the truth,' Damon said, and strangely felt he was hearing his own voice.

'Very well, Mr Finnegan. I'll accept your words for now. Anyone else you haven't mentioned?'

'There was Nath. He was my uncle's housekeeper and security guard. He lived in one of the outhouses.'

'Anyone else?'

'Look, where are we going with this? I've told you everything I know. There's nothing more to add.'

'Just one or two more questions, Mr Finnegan. In our business, one cannot be thorough enough. It's the same in your occupation, I expect. Your clients would be unhappy if they spotted an error in the accounting. Would they not?'

That surprised Damon. What else does he know about me and my past?

'Were you very close to your uncle?'

'We got on all right. He was fond of me as he didn't have any children of his own. But I didn't see much of him, for he lived so far away from London.'

'Talking of children, did any children live or visit the house while you were there?'

Damon gripped the chair's armrest as if it were a lifesaving device in a tempestuous sea. 'No, I don't recall seeing any children coming into the house. Nor did I meet or see any of the neighbours.'

Burrows paused. 'A wee boy of English parentage, six years old, was in the house. Did you see the boy?'

'I certainly did not.'

'Let me phrase it another way, Mr Finnegan. Did you see a boy of the said age in the close vicinity of Burnham Cottage?'

'No, I didn't see anyone … oh, I just remembered,' he said, 'the cook's little boy. She would occasionally bring him along. The boy appeared happy to play in the garden. But he wasn't English.'

'You had a personal cook?' Burrows cocked his eyebrow.

Damon saw the scar above Burrow's bushy moustache and wondered how he had received it. Was it a schoolyard prank or a drunken fistfight?

'Not mine, she was Uncle Fred's cook. A long-term employee.'

'Was she local, Indian?'

'Yes, she was Bengali,' Damon said and then beat his palms to the armrests. 'Will that be all, Inspector? I've had a long day.' He rose from the chair, carefully casual.

The Inspector stood up too, mimicking Damon's actions and then said as if it was an afterthought, 'there's a small matter, a mere formality to take care of. We will require a written statement from you at the station. Will tomorrow be convenient?'

'I've already told you everything I know, Mr Burrows. Haven't I?'

'You have. I appreciate it. But isn't it best to put it in writing promptly to avoid misunderstandings later? You'll be surprised how quickly people forget crucial dates and times.'

'Come back next week. I'll see what I can do. Now, if you don't mind,' Damon said, heading for the door.

'We are very reasonable people, Mr Finnegan. If tomorrow is inconvenient, please drop by the day after. Like you, we are also busy. You won't believe what time-consuming rigmarole it is to raise arrest warrants.'

Arrest warrants. Damon felt his stomach muscles entangle.

'But if it must be done, then it must be done. What can we do?' Burrows was saying. 'Good night, sir.' And then the front door closed with a resounding boom.

'You look shattered,' Anne said, standing over him.

He hadn't heard her come down. He took a deep breath and collapsed deeper into the chair.

'Your friend Robert was there too. Are they not going to speak to him?' she said.

He was silent for a while, yearning for a glass of whiskey that wasn't there.

'You have told them what you know, why did the man want a written statement from you?' she said, and went to the window and began drawing the curtains in.

Damon closed his eyes and ears. If she asks me any more questions, I'll kill her.

'Are you going to tell your father?' She placed a hand on his forearm. It felt like a policeman's handcuffs. Shut up, shut up. Can't you see I am in no mood to talk?

He got up and went upstairs to Mary's room. A soft strip of light from the landing was cutting through the obsidian canvas, revealing the contours of his daughter's face. So calm and peaceful, cocooned in a quilt and a fluffy pillow.

He stood in the semidarkness for ages, his mind battling an invisible demon, terrified of what Burrows might do, terrified he might lose his child. His vision narrowed as a white light flashed past his eyes. He was looking at the child's face. Why is she so still? Why isn't she breathing?

He felt a vice tighten around his chest. With a cry of terror, he snatched Mary from the cot into his trembling arms. The child woke up and screamed.

Anne came running. 'What the hell are you doing to her?'

'I thought she was dead.'

'You're insane, Damon, out of your mind. Give her to me.'

He left the house and went for a walk to clear his head. Confused and angry. The anger was towards Anne, verging on hatred. Why am I feeling like this? When he had first met Anne, he had fallen in love with her very easily. A month later, they had sex in her bedroom when her parents were out. He had held her tight against him and loved how hot and flushed her skin felt, how perfectly her nipples fitted into his mouth. When he lay on his back, spent, she moved on top, craving it once more. His own desire had not surprised him, but her need came as a shock. It reinvigorated him.

Chapter 18

One could easily miss the police station on Bow Street if one were not paying attention. Damon looked to his left and right and slipped inside like a startled rat dashing for cover. There were three policemen behind the enquiries desk, all of Damon's age, thugs with short hair and trimmed moustaches fogging the room with wreaths of cigarette smoke. Damon gave his name and asked to see Inspector Burrows. One of the thugs flicked his head towards a door behind him. 'Go in. The boss is out today, but his assistant is expecting you.'

Damon went in and dictated the statement to an ill-tempered man in his sixties who was suffering from impaired hearing but appeared in denial.

After it was done, the assistant turned the last sheet around towards Damon and tapped his finger on the lower half. 'Sign here, please.'

Damon took the pen and, as he was poised to sign, said, 'I suppose you will not bother me anymore; this is the end of the matter.'

'The end?' the man glared at Damon as though Damon had insulted him, 'Mr Finnegan, this is only the start. There is a lot more work to be done. No doubt the boss will be in touch. If you wish to speak to him, please wait outside. He will be back in an hour.'

Damon lowered the pen. 'He assured me a statement was all he needed, and that would be the end.'

The assistant pointed at the pen impatiently. 'Please sign.'

Frustrated, Damon picked up the pen. Sign and be done with it. Just then, he heard the door open behind him, and he felt as if a wild animal had entered and was pacing the room. Hearing the silent steps of the animal, sensing his rank breath on his neck, Damon signed the form with a pen with black ink.

Back on the street, feeling humiliated and furious, he hailed a taxi.

At his desk, he scribbled a note addressed to Mr and Mrs Fletcher. He didn't know if Fletchers still lived in the house on Oaktree Lane, but it was worth a try.

He handed a sealed envelope to the office boy.

'Take this to Islington. Don't leave until you get a letter back from whoever is in the house. Did you get that?'

The note that Thomas brought back that afternoon was brief but written with care. It said: I am delighted to hear from you, and glad to know you're well … the easiest way to contact Robert is by phone at the bank … I've no doubt he'll be thrilled to hear from you.

He could almost hear Mrs Fletcher's patrician voice as he read. He was relieved that the Fletchers were still in the house he had first visited when he was thirteen.

Damon dialled the number with his right hand and held the letter open in the other, carefully matching every digit with the one in Mrs Fletcher's writing, his pulse keeping time with the cadence of each ring.

At last, a voice – familiar yet distant – echoed on the line, refrain of a long-forgotten melody. 'Robert, it's me,' he blurted out.

'Sorry, who is that?'

'It's me, Damon.'

'Oh, Damon. How are you?' Robert replied.

Damon held the phone closer to his ear, surprised at Robert's casual response, as if he were expecting the call. Does he know? Has Burrows already spoken to him?

'Hello, Damon, have you lost your voice? No surprises then.'

'Can we meet?'

Robert's slow response added to Damon's fear that the police had indeed spoken to him, and as usual, he had found a way to wriggle out of trouble. Blame others and never show remorse.

'I'll meet you. Where?'

'The Crown at Piccadilly Circus at six-thirty.'

'All right, six-thirty. Wait for me if I am late.'

'Have you heard?'

'Heard what, my friend?'

'Never mind. I'll see you later.'

Damon recognised Robert instantly. His hair was now short with a side parting. He was wearing a stiff collar and a black-and-grey tie, exuding the air of an ambitious office junior. In the long woollen coat, he resembled his father even more.

Damon sat very still. Why should I make it easy for him? Let him find me. He watched as Robert took off his gloves, unbuttoned his coat and scanned the room. He spotted Damon and flashed him a look of recognition. He strode the shortest possible route to Damon's table, situated between two pillars and under a giant cast-iron cooking crock hooked to the ceiling.

'Well, well, after all this time.'

Damon made eyes to say it was a pleasant surprise and waited for Robert to take off his coat.

'I'll dispense with how-are-you and what-have-you-been-doing stuff. If you don't mind,' Damon said once Robert had sat down. He wanted to start on his own terms.

Robert gestured with his shoulders to say that was fine by him. 'But let me get myself a drink first.'

Damon watched Robert as he strode to the bar and demanded attention, which he received instantly. Time hasn't changed him; still, that arrogance of the entitled.

'Guinness?' Damon said, seeing a jar of stout in Robert's hand, 'you hated it, remember, you used to call it old men's drink.'

'I've grown up,' Robert replied, settling back on the chair as if he were in no hurry. He took a sip and ran his tongue over his upper lip. 'How are you?'

'Police have been to my house,' Damon said without inflexion in his tone.

'I asked how you are, but you tell me police have been to your house,' Robert said and smiled, 'same old Damon.'

'They asked me a lot of questions.'

'I know.'

'How?'

'I guessed so when I heard your voice on the telephone. I do read newspapers. What did they want to know?'

'They wanted names.'

'Names of who?'

'People who were there.'

'Did you tell them?'

Damon looked down into his glass of beer.

'Did you give names?' Robert repeated.

'Yes.'

Robert brought his hand down hard on the table. 'For Christ's sake, Damon. I can't afford a fuck-up, especially at this time in my career.'

'What about my career?' Damon retorted.

Robert's lips fused into a thin line. Damon recognised that expression. It meant he was on the verge of exploding.

'This is what I get for helping you,' Robert said, his knee struck the table leg as he shifted position.

'Just what do you mean? You were in it too, threatening to blow that man's head off with a gun,' Damon said and waited for Robert to burst into expletives. But to his surprise, Robert appeared calm as he looked down at the table at a beer mug stain. So, he has grown up, Damon thought.

'I did it for Flora. She was bloody hysterical,' Robert said, looking sideways and rubbing the back of his neck.

Suddenly, an unasked question lingered, suspended in the air between them. Damon was aware, just for a moment, of something strange happening. As if a third person had joined them at the table, bringing with her a scent of herself, dry, salty, and young.

'Would you like another drink?' Damon asked.

'Of course, I want another drink. I may be older and wiser, but I don't let that get in the way of my drinks.'

Damon went up to the bar and ordered a Guinness. White foam slid over the glass as he carried it to the table.

'Still, look at it this way,' Robert said, 'the police can't do anything to us here. They must have solid evidence to make a case. And the police in Calcutta. Laughable bunch. Don't you think?'

'I don't know what to think. It's very well for you, but I've given a statement and perjured myself.'

'Come on, mate,' Robert said, 'you told them you don't know anything. Didn't you?'

Damon nodded.

'Well then, it's for them to prove otherwise.'

'What about Flora?' Damon said, 'What if they have picked her up and forced her to talk?'

'Huh, there's no chance of that. That girl was too clever, even if she was a camera thief. And remember, she knew people.'

They were quiet for a few moments. Robert tapped the tabletop with his finger, and it reminded Damon of his boss back in the office when things were not going well.

'Are you married?' Robert asked.

'Yes, I have a daughter.'

'I can't imagine you married.'

'What's that supposed to mean?'

'Nothing ... did you finish your accountancy course?' Robert asked.

'Yes, I do company accounts now.'

'I am a banker. I landed the job even before I got the degree. They wanted me so badly. And do you know what? I am already in for promotion to senior lending officer, a step closer to a manager.'

'How exciting.' Wants me to believe that nonsense. Got the job because of his father. 'Anyway, I called you over to warn you that if I am implicated, you'll be too.'

'You bastard.'

Damon kept a passive gaze.

Robert stood up and snatched his coat from the chair. 'See you then.'

Chapter 19

Robert was rereading the newspaper, the column where it said the murder enquiry of the dead boy in Calcutta has moved to London. If he had known Flora had a child, he would never have got involved with her. Even so, he had felt no emotional attachment to her while it lasted. He had sex with her a couple of times, and that was it.

The office boy knocked on the door and pushed it open without waiting for a response. 'Your appointment, sir.'

'Send her in,' Robert said.

The woman was handsome and smartly dressed. He guessed her age to be around forty. Not one of his typical customers, most were middle-aged men who carried themselves like weary field horses ploughing rocky earth, day in and out.

He gestured at the chair on the other side of his desk.

'Nice day, Mrs Robertson,' he said, 'what can I do for you?' The words flew from his lips with an air of practised formality. After three years, the role of a lending officer had worn thin on him. Tired of ceaseless repetitions, the familiar cadence of supplication: May I have a loan to start a business, or may I have an extension to the loan?

'I've started a dressmaking business, Mr Fletcher. It is doing well. But now I need capital to expand,' she said.

'Dressmaking? How interesting,' Robert said, conjuring up an image of rolls of fabric stacked into a hill. An atelier alive with the hum of sewing machines, seamstresses bent over benches. 'How long have you been going?'

'Two years. I've been working from home. But I now need staff and premises. I've done the sums. Here it is.' She placed a manila folder on the desk and slid it towards him.

Robert glanced at the folder and let it lie there. 'What's the bottom line, Mrs Robertson?

'Ten thousand pounds. I expect to be in profit in year three.'

'Ten thousand pounds,' Robert repeated, puckering his lips in a whistling gesture. 'What kind of dresses do you manufacture?'

'Good, you ask.' She stood up and began unpacking her wares with meticulous precision as if each piece were an embodiment of her vision.

Robert opened the drawer for his pen. The newspaper slipped out, open to the dog-eared page he had read many times.

The lady unfurled a pink dress and modelled it by draping it over her body's contours. The fabric yielded to the curvature of her bosom.

Robert regarded it from the neck to the hemline and nodded approval. Such acknowledgement was, he believed, the expected response. Was the dress trendy? Was the cut and stitching of the proper standard? He didn't know. But the delicate weave of the fabric reminded him of Flora. He had seen her in a similar dress, though of a lighter fabric that flirted daringly with the summer breeze.

'Right, you will hear from us in due course,' Robert said, leaning back into his chair to indicate the meeting was over. He watched her pack her bag. Once she had gone, he took a long breath, feeling an ache in his chest, sensing a sprouting black bean spreading its tentacles around the heart. He lit a cigarette and picked up the newspaper. When will the police come for me? He began constructing scenarios in which police would raid his house or come to the office and demand an interview with his manager. The word would spread in the office and seep out until it reached home.

A hand slapped his desk with a thunderous force.

He shot up off the chair as if a bomb had exploded in his face. The newspaper fell to the floor.

'Are you deaf as well as stupid?' the man barked, spraying his spittle on the desk.

'Err … no, sir.'

'I've been here five minutes; you haven't even noticed. Dreaming of a holiday, are we? Well, you can forget about it. I've cancelled all leaves. I want you in my office in ten.' He turned and left the office; papers on the sideboard flew in his wake.

At Baker Street station, past newspaper hawkers who were spilling their guts. 'Read all about it … the war is here … read all about it.' Robert ascended the familiar stairway, sidestepping the green slime where water had been dripping from a leaking pipe for many months. Struggling to fall in line with the noise and rhythm of the platform, his boss's words, like a stone rattling in a tin can, were ricocheting in his head. 'Fletcher, you and your team haven't been following the guidelines. You're not conducting due diligence. Here, look at this.' He had waved a sheet of paper in Robert's face. 'Already this quarter, we have three defaults.'

'Sorry, sir, I'll review the cases.'

'I am warning you, Fletcher, if the head office squeezes my balls, I'll squeeze yours. See these hands. I used to be a gravedigger. These hands can squeeze juice out of an apple. You can go now.'

Robert shot up from the chair.

'Sit.'

Robert sat down.

'One more thing, Fletcher. That lady you saw this morning.'

'Mrs Robertson, sir?'

'Her husband is a policeman. Deputy Chief Inspector, City of London.'

Policeman! A powerful force, like a surge of reverse energy, sent his head spinning. Like a piston in a pump, he was sliding in and out of a tunnel. It was dark and eerie, IN, IN, IN … NO, NO, NO.

When he came to, he found himself sitting on a bench, surrounded by people; someone had unbuttoned his shirt and was fanning him with a newspaper. 'You passed out … are you okay?'

'I am all right. I am all right. I've had a turn.'

'Take it easy for a few minutes,' someone advised and then the crowd began dispersing.

His wife flung open the front door even before Robert had inserted the key in the lock. She had become a curtain twitcher. Robert knew the reason. For too many days, he had been coming home late, moving with quiet savagery, irritable and tense. He had told her he was under tremendous stress without going into details. He had not told her about the police investigation.

'Oh, there you are, darling.' He gave her his golden ferocious grin so she wouldn't suspect there was anything wrong. 'I've decided tonight a trip to the cinema is in order. Get ready at once.'

'Oh, how exciting.' She smacked a kiss on his cheek and ran to the bedroom to get dressed.

He settled down on the sofa with a glass of whiskey. As soon as the glass emptied, he refilled it with an extra-large measure. It wasn't long before the spirit travelled through the veins, from the stomach to the extremities of the body, ushering in a warm, satiated feeling. In this haze of liquid courage, he found himself questioning the mental torture he was subjecting himself to. Surely, the police cannot implicate me. Isn't it common knowledge that Calcutta police are woefully inefficient, under-trained and understaffed, manned by Indians? Only the inspectors are English, made of fat and whiskey, the racecourse and whorehouses their favourite hangouts.

He walked over to the bookcase and retrieved a heavy tome. It was a banking journal which he knew his wife would never wish to open. Within its pages was one of his enigmatic treasures - a sepia-etched photograph. He fanned the pages and pulled the photo out.

The photo was of a grand house—a robust Burmese teak front door nestling under a portico. The gravel path was only just visible. The plaque above the door, though hazy in the picture, read "Burnham Cottage." And the banyan tree, its girth so immense, they had fun embracing it, forcing the fingertips to meet. All captured through the lens of a shoplifted Kodak Brownie.

Though Pierre was not in the picture, he recalled the Frenchman's mellifluous voice, a man well-versed in interesting facts, a silver-tongued Gaelic charmer.

He turned the photograph face down, slipped it back into the tome and then replaced it on the shelf among its peers. He replenished the glass again and hid the bottle behind the drape.

The film they were going to see was Alfred Hitchcock's Blackmail. He was familiar with the tale, for he had taken her to see it once before, soon after they were married, in the tender moments of new love. In those days, they would sit in the back rows, cling to each other like bats.

The usher flashed a torch and parted the black curtain. They entered the cinema hall and paused to allow their eyes to adjust to the velvety darkness. A Pathe newsreel was reaching its conclusion, showing a clip of German soldiers marching in a street in Austria, their bodies moving like marionettes. Locals were watching from the doors and windows.

'Bloody fascists!' someone in the audience yelled.

In a rush of blood, he wanted to echo that sentiment.

Ninety days was the length of time Robert held out. Ninety days of battling with customers desperate for loans, or extensions to loans they were struggling to service. Many had gone into receivership. A café owner had fled. No one knew where he had gone. Left the wife and the country, someone had said, clever bugger.

He hated the meetings with senior managers, which were called at ridiculously short notice, giving him no chance to call in sick. Explain why customers are defaulting. He tried to blame it on the economy and the war in Europe. Excuses, excuses, excuses. The bosses wanted action. Call in the loans. Repossess properties. So, what if they are homeless? The shareholders are demanding action.

There were days when his mood matched the dark, polluted air that cloaked the city. You couldn't see a hundred feet ahead.

It seemed like a curse to him. Underlying all this, like the stench of sewer gruel, was the fear of a call from the police.

One day, he took a taxi to Kings Cross, paid the fare and walked down a narrow alley, past tobacco sellers, premises with blacked-out windows, pubs where men drank and played cards for money. Some of the doors had notes pinned to them like nameplates. Luscious Linda, first floor. He knocked on the door and waited. The door opened and sucked him in.

'I think the police are looking for me,' Robert said.

'Why, what have you done?'

'Hmm, something ….' He got up off the bed and began slipping his legs into the trousers. He put a hand inside the tight underpants and rearranged his privates. A pleasant afterglow in the groin. '…. It's not important.'

'Why say it then?' she said. She patted her blonde hair. Her bosoms wobbled as she reached for a cigarette on the side table.

'I killed a boy.' He stood in front of the dressing table, which had a hairbrush, a glass, and a water jug on its dusty surface.

'Phew, you a murderer. I've met all kinds, but not one of them … well, not one who's come clean.' She cackled.

'I didn't mean to … it just happened,' he said, tucking the shirt in.

'Where was this?' she said, taking a drag on the cigarette.

'In India … a long time ago.'

She made a face. 'You serious? They've come all this way to arrest you?'

'You don't understand.' He tied the shoelaces, stood up, and pulled out his wallet. He took out a ten-shilling note and dropped it on the dressing table. 'You won't be seeing me again.'

'Why, you off to India to hand yourself in?' She chuckled, releasing cigarette smoke in short bursts. 'Send me a card.'

'I am leaving London,' he said and slipped out the door.

'Fuck you.' He heard her call out from inside.

Chapter 20

The night had fallen, and as he stood at the back window, gazing out onto the garden, he hadn't heard the knocking at the door. How the dark gathers the last of the leaves, and the leaves do not resist the dark but accept it without protest. Damon wished to be at one with the darkness, to step outside and lie down with it, to let the night pass over him.

The knocking was louder and more persistent, so this time he heard it. Could it be DI Burrows? He did imagine, from time to time, that the police might come back, this time to arrest him. That idea was with him always, like a boil on the skin that wouldn't heal, even though he had replied to all their inquiries. That was over three months ago.

He forced himself to believe it was one of Anne's friends at the door, come for an idle chat or the habitual borrowing of something or the other.

'Good evening, Mr Finnegan.' It was Burrows, alas. 'I am sorry for the intrusion at this hour. There have been developments in the case. I believe you may be able to clarify one or two issues.'

'Yes, yes, how can I help you?' Damon said, showing him a blank face, for that's what an innocent person would do.

The inspector hesitated for a moment. 'Shall we go inside, somewhere private? It's a delicate matter. You never know who might be listening.'

'I fear there's little more I can offer you other than what I've already said. But if you insist, then do come in.'

Once Burrows was seated, he spoke freely, using hand gestures to make his points. 'Mr Finnegan, I know we have been through this, but could you tell us if you ever saw a six-year-old Caucasian boy in the house or on the grounds of Burnham Cottage?' He raised his hand like a traffic bobby stopping a car. 'Before you answer, let me inform you that the boy was seen by a dependable witness around the time you were living there.'

'Not living, Inspector, I was on a short vacation.'

'I accept that may be the case, but please tell us if you have ever had interaction with a boy of the said age during the short vacation.'

'No, inspector, I never saw anyone of that age at the house.'

'Can you think of any reason why someone would say so if it weren't true?'

'I don't know. It could be a mistake.'

'The boy they saw entering Burnham Cottage matches the description of the boy found dead two miles away.'

'If the sightings were two miles apart, how could they possibly pertain to the same person?' Damon said, and at once regretted saying it, for he had intended to take a stance of aloofness, desist from offering opinions.

'I didn't say the sighting of the boy in Burnham Cottage and the discovery of the body were at the same time. There was a three-day gap. What we haven't learned is where the boy was for those three days.'

'Inspector, you really believe I'll know all that?'

'All right. We will leave that aside for now. Now, let me tell you about another person entering the house on the same day. He was male and Caucasian. He was the boy's father. Do you recall ever meeting him?'

Damon's heart kicked the ribcage. 'I've already given you the names of people who stayed at the house on and off. Look, we didn't sit in the house for twenty-four hours a day. We were on holiday; we used to go sightseeing. If anybody came in my absence, I wouldn't know, would I?'

'Could you answer my question? Did you meet the boy's father at Burnham Cottage?'

'I can't say I've seen or met anyone of that description at Burnham Cottage. But tell me, does this man claim to have met me?'

'To confess the truth, no. The poor fellow was six feet under Indian clod before my colleagues learned of his identity, so to speak. The circumstances of his death were untoward … now you look surprised, Mr Finnegan.'

'Do I? I was just wondering why the father didn't report his son's death to the police?'

'I don't recall saying he didn't, Mr Finnegan,' Burrows said, and raised his eyebrows to the hairline. 'Did I? Do you happen to know something that I don't?'

'That's ridiculous … I don't know anything, obviously … I was just conjecturing,' Damon protested. His palpating heart was telling him the trap is of your own making; you should have kept your mouth shut. Just then, Anne came to his rescue inadvertently. She called from the top of the stairs, 'Damon, who are you talking to … not to yourself again, I hope.'

She came bouncing down the stairs and halted midway. 'Oh, I didn't know you had company.'

'Inspector Burrows, darling. He dropped by for a chat. We are just finishing.' He looked at Burrows with raised eyebrows and stood up. 'I hope I was of help, inspector.'

Burrows crossed and uncrossed his heavy legs, appearing dissatisfied. 'Right, Mr Finnegan, let us end our conversation for now.'

Damon led him to the door casually, so as not to appear overtly keen to see him off. Burrows stopped at the door. 'By the way, I understand from my friends at Imperial Police, your uncle's residence, Burnham Cottage, was quite an impressive place,' he said.

'Yes, it was a grand house,' Damon conceded.

'Do you happen to know who owns it now?'

'The inheritor was Charlie, my aunt Frances's nephew. I dare say it was a surprise to everyone because Charlie was very much an outsider.'

'It was a prime property, so many people had eyes on it. Did you know that?'

'No, but I did think Charlie was fortunate. Mind you, all that was a long time ago. I don't really think about it anymore.'

'In case you're interested, there's more to it.'

'Tell me.'

'Rumours were flying about at the time, of back-stabbings, money changing hands, forged documents, the works.'

'Interesting. How do you know all this, Inspector?'

'This I learned recently from a DC from the India Imperial Police who is in London now, retired. According to him, it was the talk of the town for months.' He added after a brief pause, 'I say all this by-the-by, Mr Finnegan, seeing that you might be interested.' He rummaged in his pocket, brought out a cigarette packet, and then shoved it back in.

'Good night, Mr Finnegan.'

As if he had been in a fistfight, Damon felt bruised and pummelled. The inspector was playing games, teasing, and prodding. He had mentioned the boy's father, but not the mother. Why not?

The very next day, he telephoned the bank.

'Sorry, Mr Fletcher isn't in.'

'When will he be back?'

'He won't be back. He's in Plymouth.'

Bastard, bastard, bastard. He must have known what was coming, conveniently slipped away and joined the Navy. It was true that the Navy was looking for volunteer recruits, but he didn't think Robert would be so eager to sign up.

Chapter 21

Every day was a hectic one in the office, with listening, talking, and writing. Meetings with sub-editors, rooms full of smoke, wheezy chests, endless cursing, and the clickety-click of a hundred typewriters.

The world was ablaze with the fever of war. Poland was under the iron fist of Hitler. Paris, a city synonymous with romance and elegance, now found itself in the grim embrace of occupation, its essence fading under the jackboots. Churchill had summoned the nation to stand against the tide of darkness. The evil will perish, and the righteous will triumph.

That's debatable, Pierre mused as he alighted from the bus. The German army is now a mighty fighting force. Priti had just returned from the weekly French lessons and was eager to practice what she had learned.

'I want to be prepared when we go to France to meet your family,' she announced even before she had taken off the coat.

'Forget about learning French,' he said, 'we are not going to France.'

'Why not?'

'Don't you know what's going on? If you want to live in France, you may have to learn German. The country isn't safe anymore. Even England isn't safe. Already, the Luftwaffe has started bombing ships in the channel.'

'Let's go back to India. It's the only safe country now. I have a family there, and you could get your job back with the BBC.'

'There's danger in that country too.'

'How do you mean danger? India isn't at war.'

'I can explain, but it is complicated.'

'Make it uncomplicated for me.'

'When I was in Calcutta many years ago, I got implicated in something and had to come back to London in a hurry.'

'Be serious, Pierre,' she said.

'I had to run away, or they would have put me in prison.'

'Prison? Did you commit a murder or something?' she said in a mocking tone.

He turned to the table crowded with typed papers and writing pads and began stacking them into individual heaps as if it were a task in urgent need of attention.

'Mon Dieu, Pierre, you haven't told me about this. What did you do?'

'It just happened,' Pierre said, still not looking at her directly, 'you remember I told you about the two English boys I met in Calcutta? A well-known businessman was murdered, who was known to them. It was a strange case of double bluff and murder, and when I started asking questions, I discovered something big. If it became public, it would have hurt people at the very top.'

'So, you ran away?'

'Something like that, I was forced to leave the country.'

'Did you warn the English boys?' She dropped her notepad and the book, Advanced French, on the coffee table.

'No, I didn't tell them.'

'Why?'

'Because I didn't think any harm would come to them. They were just college boys out for a bit of adventure. Why spoil their fun?'

'All that is very well, mon cheri, but I still feel you haven't told me everything.'

'But I've,' he protested, though he understood his explanation was lacking in detail. She wasn't the type to forget, though she might forgive. He tried to amuse her. 'Silly Priti, do that Indian dance thing.'

'I am not in the mood.'

'OK, OK. Did I tell you about the Frenchwoman I met in Pondicherry, a Jesuit missionary?'

'Yes, about a hundred times.' She got up and headed for the kitchen.

'Did I tell you?' he called after her, 'she was in India so long she had lost count of the number of years. Didn't know the French had already left Pondicherry, sailed off in boats loaded with vanilla pods and black pepper.'

'Yes, that'll be a hundred and one times.'

PART THREE

Chapter 22

London 1940

Four hundred people died in the first minutes of the Blitz on the seventh of September, and fourteen hundred were maimed or injured that first night. No warnings: no way to know what was coming, or why or for how long. War dropped down and settled.

The new moon had risen over the smoking rooftops. The sky, for the moment, was clear of the bombers. Pierre was pounding the roads, navigating the shifting shadows of buildings, lampposts, and barren trees. His brief was to line up the details and report back what he saw. An enormous task. Even with four pairs of eyes and ears, they would still be insufficient.

He was trying as best he could, etching in words what he was seeing; the snow pile of glass and building rubble, the jumpy impatience of people in subterranean haunts, waiting and waiting for the night to be over. Some couldn't stand it anymore; they'd get up and walk into the street, mad for the end to come and find them.

Weeks into the war, a pattern had emerged in the night attacks. Luftwaffe planes were arriving in droves, passing overhead. The probing searchlight stabbing the heavens. The incendiaries came first, firebombing the darkened city, forcing it alight and ablaze, cutting open a pathway along the river. The bombs came next, banshee wail or eerie whistle, the heaviest ones roaring like an express train through a tunnel. Sirens and dogs bayed at the noise.

Sometimes they released deadly parachute bombs, which floated gently, sinister serenity concealing their deadly intent.

Pierre persuaded his boss to give him a recording machine so that he could bring the sounds of the bombarded city to people's living rooms, transcending borders and continents. He was thinking of France, naturally, a country no stranger to the sinister hums of German planes, or the ominous thud, thud, thud, of jackboots on cobblestones.

He was at the mouth of the bomb shelter at Mile End. The families trudging in the dark, their footfalls measured and deliberate, sounding like ghosts with steel shoes. His tense voice hopped through the night air as he asked them questions.

Another night. He ran to capture the lament of the Luftwaffe's drone. Holding the microphone up to the night sky. 'Do you hear them? They are turning around now. Did you hear the thud? The warehouse behind the station has received a hit. Oh, the flames, the flames, the sky is bright orange.'

Later, when the sirens sounded all clear, Pierre grinned, the weird exhilaration of danger seen and passed by.

The war pressed forward relentlessly. Look any which way, and there were flat waste and doused fires. Home guards in brown uniforms, like eager Boy Scouts, handed out gas masks. Dusty, empty streets, closed shops, and locked factory gates were a common sight. Londoners had found a way to live with it. The exhausted faces of women carrying battered suitcases, surrendering their children to an uncertain fate, bussing them out of London. Pierre arrived at the coach station. 'Speak here.' He held out the mic. 'Are you sad leaving home?'

'I don't know, mister.' Ten-year-old Tom was bewildered and wide-eyed. No one wanted to talk. His older sister pulled his hand. 'Come on, Tommy, they are waiting for us.' The responsibility was on her young shoulders; she was trying to be an adult.

'Go to an anti-aircraft gunnery and report on men in action.' This was his latest brief from the office. 'Don't get yourself killed. We just haven't got the staff to write obituaries.'

Around the four AA guns in Kensington Gardens, men lay huddled under their blankets, waiting. They were taking turns to function as spotters with the night glasses trained at the sky, waiting for the grey dots to morph into bats with fixed wings.

The spotter lowered his telescope. 'Hey mate, this is a security zone, do you have permission?'

'Press,' Pierre said and waved a card at him, 'BBC.'

'BBC or not, I want you fucking out of here,' he said with just a cursory glance at the Press card.

'Harry, pay attention,' someone shouted from under the blankets and then added, 'BBC, you can stay, but don't get too close.'

Pierre flinched as he replaced the Press card in his breast pocket. The voice that had just rippled through the air had a familiar timbre, a low-pitched intonation he had not heard in years. It took him back to Calcutta, to the irritating smells, dry dusty air, and the house in Alipore. Was that really Damon? He peered at the faces under the blankets to locate the owner of that voice. It was impossible. The night was as dark as a blackboard. He pulled out a matchbox from his pocket. A shouted order rent the fabric of the air, 'Put it away at once.' To light a match within two hundred yards of gun emplacements was a hanging offence.

He settled down, pulling his woollen coat over his ears.

All hush, but for the occasional creak of the spotter swivelling his telescope, men breathing, a couple of coughs. Like nighttime in a menagerie. Pierre thought of the dairy farm he had worked on as a schoolboy.

'What are the chances of action tonight?' he asked the nearest gunner.

'As fucking unpredictable as action with my girlfriend.'

Someone chuckled over at the other end.

'Shut up, you two.'

That was Damon's voice for sure. A little heavier, it bore the weight of responsibility. Pierre's heartbeat hastened. He wondered if Damon had recognised him. He yearned to talk, to catch up on the news, past and present.

'Action. Take positions,' the spotter cried. The men leapt, dropping their blankets, hands ready for the gun elevator and triggers. The ammunition carrier flipped the tarpaulin. A hand at the fuse, the rammer poised like a sprinter waiting for the pistol shot. The breech man, vigilant like a meerkat, completed this orchestra of war.

A voice sliced through the charged air. 'Ready?'

'Ready, sir.' A unified response.

Pierre stood up, ready to see and swallow the action, and regurgitate later in the safe confines of the office.

And then the familiar chorus of planes approaching from the west heralded the arrival of the foe. The spotter's voice took flight, calling coordinates guided only by the approaching sound.

Boom. The first shell left the gun. Followed by another. Now the shells were slamming away, stitching a fiery tapestry across the heavens.

'Fuck you, Hitler,' the soldier beside Pierre swore, his cheek against the searing hot metal, 'fuck you, fuck you,' like a prayer. It was a fact that every shot was traceable back to them; every shot could draw the attention of a German pilot, who could turn around in anger and, with the flick of a thumb, rain down death. It didn't matter to them. The men were sweating despite the cold of the October night. Stripped to shirtsleeves and braces, going at their guns with the rhythm of drummers - boom, boom, clack, boom, boom. The burned cordite clawing at the back of their throats. Still slamming shells into the guns, fire, more shells, fire, more shells, until the spotter cried, 'Stop'

The men crumbled to the ground beneath their weapons. The sudden quiet, the release from the explosions, was deafening.

Pierre found his legs trembling. He sank to the ground, exhausted as if he too were one of the gunners.

Before leaving, he took out a press card from his pocket and scribbled his telephone number and a message. 'Could you pass it on to Mr Finnegan?' The gunner, sipping tea from an enamel mug, nodded and accepted the card. A mere boy with the first flush of moustache, sixteen or seventeen. What are the chances he would live to celebrate his next birthday?

So that's it. A newspaper story, only the words remaining to be typeset in leaded letters, to be printed onto paper, folded and rushed to newspaper boys, who would stand on street corners bellowing. On the radio, the story would fly into the air, from lips to ears, like a secret finding its immediate release, pollens exploding from a blooming flower.

Chapter 23

Priti was unable to sleep, so she sat up and looked out the window, hearing the birdsong calling the dawn. This fear that lived in her abdomen moved to her legs when a warplane skidded overhead. She could see buses parked along the bridge, an upended umbrella on the road, the asphalt strewn with shattered glass and a dozen or so women standing beside the lead bus, all huddled in their coats, blowing warm air on closed fists. She knew they were the munition factory workers waiting for the bus to start the morning run.

Pierre turned the key in the door. 'Priti,' he called, closing the door behind him.

'I'm here.' Her voice was weak. She was six months pregnant. The boxroom had already undergone Pierre's deft touch, adorned with vibrant wallpaper obtained from a Woolworth store. A crib crafted with reclaimed timber. 'Sturdy as houses.' He had stepped back to admire his workmanship. 'No way your Charlie is going to topple over.'

They had already named him Charles, after Pierre's grandfather, who had been a sailor on a trading vessel transporting merchandise and slaves to the West Indies. The legend had it that they had caught him secreting food supplies to the slaves, and after the third and final warning, they dropped him overboard in the Caribbean Sea. 'Home is that way, now start swimming.' The captain had bowled with laughter. 'Race you home.'

He ran to the bedroom and drew Priti into his arms and lips. How is Charlie?

'He has been kicking too much. He hears the bombs.' She pressed her palms against the base of her stomach, as if it were likely to roll to the ground. 'There's a letter from mother. She's so worried. Wants me to come home,' Priti said. She unfolded the letter with care, smoothed out the creases and held it up.

Pierre ran a casual glance at the squiggly, uneven slant of the handwriting. 'What has she written?'

'Oh, this and that. She's a meticulous accountant of events in the village; births, deaths, and marriages, of young men running away to cities, others joining the freedom movement.'

Pierre understood why her mother's letter meant so much to Priti. He imagined her perusing every inch of the paper, the dots, dashes, even words cut by whimsical squiggles, the blank spaces too, as if they had a meaning.

He had an image of a simple, unassuming village woman, yet one who was strong-willed. As a single woman, you must be resilient and tough to survive the taunts and gossip of a rural society. You must be able to deflect the lecherous advances of the drunks and the lonely. He constructed a mental image of the future. A distant shore where they would stand together, their child between them, and her mother's open arms.

But right now, Pierre could barely stand on two feet.

'I'll send her some more money from the paycheque next month, I promise.' He rested his head on her shoulder.

'Did you get me the chocolate?' she asked.

This sudden onslaught, this craving for all things chocolate, had alarmed Pierre. He had never seen her eat chocolate or any other kind of candy before. Now she was consuming a bar each passing day.

'It happens sometimes when you're pregnant,' she had explained, 'a sudden craving for something of intense taste or flavour. It doesn't have to be sweet; some women crave savoury, spicy, or crunchy food. It usually happens in early pregnancy. But I am different.'

He produced two bars of Cadbury from his pocket. 'You'll have to ration these. There's a shortage. Smithey tells me all the supplies are going to the army. He may have to shut up shop if it carries on like this.'

'Sorry, I am putting you through all this,' she said and tried to smile to ward off the tears.

A fire engine nearby blasted its siren. A dog barked at the sound. He moved quickly and placed a hand on both her ears. Since the confirmation of pregnancy, loud noises sent her into a panic.

Pierre stood on a chair and finished nailing the blind over the front room window. 'This should do it,' he said, giving a final solid bang upon the tack with a hammer.

'Will that do any good?' Priti asked.

'Not much, but Civil Defence want us to blank out all windows.'

So, this was it. A war had come and settled. Now they will have to live in its shadow. Priti wrapped her arm around herself, as if willing the old strength to rise within her again.

Chapter 24

One hundred bombs a minute rained down on London for five hours. The most devastating single night of the Blitz. Fires were exploding and settling. Even Big Ben, the Parliament Building, and Westminster Abbey were not spared.

Now more than ever, Damon yearned for a night in his own bed away from the boom of the guns. He had worked nine straight nights. In the bedsit in Belsize Park, he sat at the desk with his diary, an honest, bare-all blog of his activities and the seesaw of his feelings. Though he was writing for his own fulfilment, in a far corner of his head was a seed of hope that when Mary was older, she would somehow come upon these notebooks and would then understand why he had left the marital home, that he wasn't an ogre Anne was crafting about him. He was a man driven by nuanced struggles. Meanwhile, the mother and daughter had moved to Lancashire, in the village of Ormskirk, far from the reach of the Luftwaffe.

Anne's sober words reverberated in his head. 'What you're doing won't add up. It's not right. It's not good for the girl.' She was savage in her calm. 'We can work this out.'

He had argued with himself. What is the most noble thing to do? Weighing his guilt against his desire to leave. He pictured her alone in the house, with Mary as her only companion. But finally, and with determination, he said it will never work, that they must part company for good.

He shifted uneasily in the worn chair. The old words sounded in his ears like capes for kings. What he had stumbled on here among the bombs was an alternative reality – a divergent realm fashioned from the most straightforward arithmetic of existence. As simple as one and one make two. An idea of redemption. He had come to understand that each one of us was alive right until the moment of death. And then each one of us was gone. There could be no substitution. What he wanted to say on the pages of the notebook (for Mary) was that if a bomb exploded over his head or a building collapsed on him, he would not hold it against anyone. He was happy to die.

He had barely begun writing when the air-raid siren wailed, followed by a bang. A bomb had found its mark somewhere on his left, too close to ignore. He ran out. There was light now where there had been none. The building had folded into rubble. He heard another whistle and began running toward Belsize Park station. Others like him were dashing into the station too, dragging children, and coercing the old to hurry. He slowed instinctively, intending to take charge and bring order to the mad rush. But he was too tired. Tonight, he just wanted to retreat into the sanctuary and find a quiet corner to rest his limbs.

Down two flights to the platform, he found a space by a passage linking two platforms.

Bodies were stretched out like corpses in a morgue, whose faces he could not see. A man and his wife arrived with a baby wrapped in a shawl, smelling of fear, sour milk, and vomit.

He felt lonely as hell. Only the camaraderie of the men at the AA battery was keeping him going. He didn't expect that to last long. Eventually, the luck would run out, a Kraut bomb would find the target, and they could be stretchered away to hospitals, dead or near dead. He felt the panic that he might never be able to complete his diary. Mary would censure him. Before the war started, he had reread the Odyssey, which he had first read at school and remembered it as the story of homecoming. But it could not have been that. How could the Greeks, who knew that one never entered the same river twice, believe in homecoming? Odysseus did not return home to stay but to set off again.

Someone tripped over his outstretched leg. 'So sorry.'

He pulled his legs back wearily and looked up. His mouth opened, but no sound came out, as if he had been thrown free of his body to become a single black thought, the thought intensifying, expanding darkly. When he found himself again in his body, a startled cry left his mouth and hurtled into the air. 'Flora.'

The woman paused.

'Flora … that you, Flora? … My God. Flora,' he rumbled.

The woman peered down at him, appearing confused and terrified.

'It's me … Damon … remember me?'

'Oh, Damon from Calcutta.' Her voice was a sharp hiss, and her eyes widened to their limit.

'What are you doing? Why are you here? I mean, why are you in London? Oh, I don't know what I mean. Come and sit down.' He gave her his hand.

She took it and lowered herself beside him. An old woman seated by Damon gathered her blanket, creating space for the newcomer. 'Here you go, love.'

'God, what a coincidence,' she said, pulling her coat snugly around her as if to guard against the resurgence of long-buried emotions.

'You can say that again.' He offered her a cigarette and, from the other pocket, pulled out a lighter. She cupped his hand and drew on the flame. Her face glowed briefly. 'You don't look a day older,' he said.

She laughed. 'Your eyes deceive you because it is dark here.'

'I meant you look as beautiful as you did back then.'

'Aw, thank you, Damon. You have turned into such a terrible liar.'

'You mean I lied better in those days?'

'No, you never lied. You used to tell it as it is. Remember?'

He smiled inwardly. In his discerning gaze, the transformation in her was obvious. She had grown up. No longer the brooding ingenue who spurned compliments with a cynical shake of the shoulders, convinced there were ulterior motives to everything anyone said. He remembered her occasional disappearances. She was a mystery and made no apologies for leading people on, offering a tantalising view of her heart but shutting down when someone drew too close. Why is she here? Have the police spoken to her?

A shell hit close by. The walls trembled as the very air seemed sucked up and blown back down again.

Flora cowered, pushing her head into the shoulders, her hands pressed against the ears in a futile attempt to stifle the infernal clamour.

'It's okay. We are safe here,' Damon said with a reassuring smile, a happy smile, 'I am so astonished to find you here.'

Damon pulled the cork from the port bottle. Its resonant plop was an odd sound to punctuate the air this time of the day. But the war had turned the world, traded its diurnal rhythms for a disarrayed dance, and blurred the boundary between night and day.

He offered her a glass. 'Vintage port. You'll like it. I smuggled it out of the officers' mess.'

'I've never had port before,' she said and accepted the glass.

'I remember you as a teetotaller,' he said.

She smiled. 'That was a long time ago.' She gave the wine a swirl and took a sip. 'It's very nice.'

'How long have you been in this dreary place?' he said.

'You mean London?'

'Where else?'

'I've been here a year and a half. Things were getting bad in India. The English were leaving in droves. Only those working for the government are still there.'

'But you're not …'

'I know I am not English. The nationalists consider us Anglo-Indians as traitors.'

Damon got up and stoked the fire. A log crackled, releasing smoke and ash. It was easy to keep the room warm, for it was merely a bedsit with a bed at one end. The dining table and sofa were on the other side of the low partition wall. A full-length hinged mirror inside the front door, in which they had found themselves staring when they had entered.

'Are you warm enough?'

'Yes, yes.'

He came back to sit beside her.

'Do you remember the Frenchman, Pierre?' he said.

'I do, but I know little about him.'

'He's here too, working as a reporter. He loved India.'

'There are Europeans who have fallen in love with India. Yet they don't accept India as it is. They strive to create a mini-Europe to live in.'

‘What about your father?’

‘He loved India for the comforts it provided. Never once went back home in thirty years.’

‘I understand,’ he said. But what he really wanted to know was the events leading up to that day, when she arrived without warning with her son, John. It was a bombshell, for neither he nor Robert could even have imagined her with a child. Did she know the police in London were investigating? He chose not to say anything until he knew more about her and the reason for coming to London.

He leaned over and replenished her glass.

‘Are you trying to make me drunk, Damon Finnegan?’

Her smile and those eyes took him back to the day all three had sat on the balcony and chatted late into the night. Nostalgia veiled over him, distant memories unfurling in sepia tones. She was Robert’s girl, but secretly, he was in love with her.

‘Of course not, I am only trying to make you happy.’

‘Happy? I’ve never been happy. Have you?’

He thought for a moment. ‘Yes and no. There have been times when I’ve experienced happiness.’

He took out a handkerchief from his pocket and dabbed at the drops of spilt wine on the table. Two ruby red smears appeared on the white cloth. A long silence followed, punctuated by a murmur of voices on the street outside and hurrying footsteps.

‘You said your father was a priest in Calcutta.’

‘Yes, but he resigned from the church after a few years.’

‘Why did he resign?’

‘Because of me.’

‘Because of you? I don’t understand.’

Chapter 25

Calcutta 1930

'Tell me about you?' Flora said to Madan Lal.

'What's there to know about me? I am a simple man, Flora baby. I was born in a sleepy village twenty-four miles from Calcutta, in Serampore. When the British arrived and established cotton mills and jute factories, the village expanded. They built homes, shops, and a courthouse. People came to visit and settled, including Hindus, Christians, and Muslims. Clerks and babus looking important with Parker fountain pens clipped to breast pockets.'

She slapped a ball of dough on the wooden board and began kneading it with her knuckles. 'Why did Papa go to live in Serampore?' she said.

'That I don't know, Flora baby. But he did. They had built a new church in the village, near an ancient peepul tree. I had gone inside to look because I was curious. There, I met Master Larry for the first time. He saw me and called me over. He said he was looking for a cleaner for the church. Would I be interested? I said yes, I'll do it; I needed a job.'

'How old were you then?'

'Oh, Flora baby, you shouldn't ask questions like that.' He shook a finger in admonishment. 'Age isn't important.'

'All right, all right. Don't tell me then.' She punched the dough with a fist.

'Don't do that. If you overdo it, the chapatis don't come out right. Here, shell the peas if you want to do something useful.'

He took the ball of dough away from her. 'Then six months later, he made me his personal servant, washing and ironing his clothes, cooking, and doing little things here and there. Your father was a very punctual man, and everything had to be set exactly to his instructions. He dressed for dinner, even if dining alone. That was twenty years ago.' He counted twenty on the fingers of both hands, tapping each digit twice. 'So many years before baby Flora came into the household.'

She felt her lungs explode. It was the way he had said it, the tone, and the manner that suggested she was an outsider who had arrived at the house and stayed.

'What did you mean by that?' she said.

Madan Lal did not reply. He focused on roasting brinjals as if it demanded his full attention. 'Oh, Ho, Ho,' he cried and pulled his hand away from the open fire. The half-roasted brinjal fell to the floor. 'See, I nearly burned my hand. You're distracting me with your questions, questions, questions.'

'Madan Lal, did you not hear? Speak to me.'

He picked up the brinjal from the floor.

'Tell me, tell me, Madan Lal, what is it?'

'You have blossomed into a young woman. I've known you when you were so little.' He brought his hands together as if cradling a newborn. 'You'll be of marriageable age soon, and we will be looking for a husband for you, and as you know, it's not an easy business these days. The husband's sides are very, very fussy. It is right that you know these things, so you're prepared.'

The logs in the fire hissed and spluttered, stimulated by dripping ghee.

She coughed. 'Go on, go on,' she gestured.

'I am only a servant in this house. It's improper for me to say these things, and I don't want to hurt you, Flora baby.'

'You don't worry about hurting me. And haven't I promised I'll never tell anyone?'

'Then I'll tell the truth. The woman you know as your mother isn't the one who gave you birth.' He paused and gestured at her to sit down.

She did not see his hand move. Her eyes were fixed on his lips. Have I misheard? But he appeared sincere in what he was saying.

'In those days, when Larry sahib managed the church, everything was going well. Then, one day, Larry sahib met a girl. She was the daughter of a court clerk from Bandu Busti. He started meeting her in secret in another town. Doing things like that isn't good. It sometimes catches you off guard, and then it's too late. Yes, what can I tell you, Flora baby? I didn't know until the sahib came home one day and told me the truth. He said the girl was carrying his child, and if his superiors in Calcutta discovered the truth, his career would end. He appeared more worried about his job than about the girl … Are you all right, Flora baby?'

'Yes, go on.'

'I was forthright with him. I told him that for an unmarried girl to be carrying a child is very, very shameful. Her family will throw her out of the house, and the villagers will throw the family out of the village. I told him there was only one thing to do: marry the girl and save her honour. Larry sahib said he couldn't do it because he was a catholic priest.' He paused again and looked at the Christian poster pinned to the wall. 'I told him then it's best he leaves the church and saves the girl. But he refused. He was hoping the girl would leave the village and move somewhere far, and that everything would be all right. But these kinds of things don't go as you wish. The girl gave birth to a beautiful daughter.' He turned his head as if he couldn't look Flora in the eyes. 'And then two months later, the mother was dead.'

The kitchen walls appeared to swell like sails caught in a tempest. She held the worktop as if for dear life.

'It is rumoured she killed herself because she felt so ashamed. Whatever the truth, the family had a child on their hands, and they were too old to look after her. Still, sahib was like a heartless monster. He had shut his brain and was refusing to listen to anyone. For many days, we didn't hear anything from the family. And then, one day, a noise at the door woke me up. I thought it was another homeless man desperate for shelter. But there was no man at the door, only a homeless little child wrapped in a shawl.' His voice wavered, as if he was about to break down.

He cleared his throat and continued, 'She had a vigorous cry in the lungs and no visible deformities. Baas, after that, I was very firm with Larry Sahib. Boss, I'll not let you harm this child, I told him. She is your daughter, your very flesh and blood, and you must look after her. That was the only time I saw him cry. He said, Madan Lal, do you think I am a monster, that I don't have a heart? But what can we do? We can't raise her by ourselves, two men. I told him there was a way out. First, he must leave the church. Secondly, find a mother for the child. He looked surprised when I said that. Find a mother - what do you mean by find a mother? Do they sell them in the market?' Madan Lal rolled his eyes. 'You see, these angrej, Englishmen don't understand matrimonial matters. I explained that he must look for a woman to marry, a good woman who would be willing to accept this girl as her own. But sahib was still moaning. Where will I find such a person, Madan Lal? Where?'

A guava seller stopped at the window with a basket balanced on his head. Move on, move on, she gestured impatiently.

'You see, I knew a family; good, decent people, who had a grown-up daughter of marriageable age, a quiet, homely type of girl. They had been struggling to find a husband for her. You know what it is like in our society: men make big demands of dowry, asking for this and that. And if you're unable to give them what they want, you fall short by one rupee, they walk away.'

Flora stopped him mid-speech. 'Madan Lal, you're not to tell this to anyone.'

'Bap re bap.' He touched his earlobes solemnly. 'My mouth has stayed shut all this time, and it will remain so in the future. I am telling you all this, so you're better prepared for the life that awaits you.'

He paused and shook his head.

'Flora, baby, you must keep a sober head. I am here for you. You come to me whenever you have a problem. You're like my own child.'

She put her arms around him and dug her face into his shirt. When she pulled back, she saw a wet patch on the front of his shirt.

For many days, she was like a soulless sleepwalker, not talking or listening. Whenever she looked out the window across the courtyard, she would see Deenu, Madan Lal's son, who was the same age as her.

Yet she must stand and stare out the window. It had become a compulsion. She noticed the dormant trees were beginning to swell. Soon, they will open their buds to see the spring light again. The strength of a tree lies in its ability to live through the dark season and emerge alive and stronger, year after year. It was then she saw her fear was no more; in its place lay strength and daring. She made up her mind to leave.

Father and Mother were getting ready to go to the Club to attend a housey-housey party. He was scraping chairs, banging wardrobe doors, and complaining about the maid. She hasn't ironed the trousers properly. Even a one-armed monkey could have done better.

In the front room, she sat down on a chair by the window, opened a book and held it to her face. Anyone looking would think she was reading, and if they paid close attention, they would also see that she was sweating, even though the weather was temperate. A breeze was flowing through the room, cool to the face, as if it were reading her mind and trying to calm her, calm her, calm her.

In an hour, they would leave the house. And then she would leave ten minutes later. She looked at the clock on the wall and then the leather attaché case with her belongings, just the essentials. She had been walking to school for the last few weeks, saving the money her mother gave her for the bus fare and tiffin. She kept the money in a Bata shoe box, along with her make-up.

Madan Lal came into the room to fetch something from the dresser. Their eyes met briefly before he left.

Chapter 26

The day had turned out surprisingly bright for late October. The time was ten-thirty in the morning. Damon closed the curtains, throwing the room into semi-darkness. Daylight still managed to seep through the curtains' edges, making a vase on the wall. Flora understood that he did this to catch up on sleep.

'I'll make you something to eat,' Flora said, 'breakfast before you go to sleep.' She smiled. 'Doesn't it sound odd … breakfast before bedtime?'

'I'll do it. You stay put,' he said.

'But you have had a rough night.'

'I can manage. Remember what I do?'

'Have you shot down many planes?'

'We try our best. But it's not easy, especially on a moonless night, which is every day.'

'You're so brave.'

'Ah, it's nothing really,' he said on the way to the kitchenette. 'I've just six eggs and dry ham, I am afraid. I always seem to miss my slot at the ration shop.'

'Eggs? Splendid. They will do,' she said and slipped out of her sandals.

'I don't think we need two people to break an egg. Do we?'

'You are right. Move out of my way,' she said and snatched the pan from his fingers. The onions were in the cupboard. As she bent down to retrieve them, she sensed his eyes on her.

'Pass me the knife,' she said.

'But you were only going to crack the eggs,' he protested.

'Where's the oil?' she demanded.

He passed her a jar of goose fat. 'I don't have any oil.'

She scooped a spoonful and dropped it into the pan. The fat began to spit and sizzle. It quietened as she poured two beaten eggs over it. The room filled with the inviting aroma of frying eggs. She repeated the process with two more eggs.

Finally, she placed two plates of ham omelette and bread on the table.

'Isn't it strange,' he said as he dived into the omelette, 'I qualified as an accountant and turned into a gunner.'

She watched him closely as though it was possible to absorb an exactness of him, the resting expression of the body, the mind's inner light voiced in the busy hands of an accountant turned gunner.

'And when I first met you, I could never have imagined you would be a soldier one day,' she said. 'I thought you were a pacifist.'

'I am a pacifist. I hate killing. But I don't have a choice,' he replied. 'Mother said the same thing when I told her I was signing up. I thought you were a pacifist, she said, and clung to the word, pacifist. Someone who doesn't rush off to join a war. Someone who stays behind and doesn't break his mother's heart.'

'What did you say?'

'I don't have a choice, I told her. Of course, you always have a choice, she replied. What if something happens to you? And then she placed a hand on my head. I saw she was crying. She said, Son, I am offering my blessings. You go ahead and do what's right for the country.'

'Your mother is brave.'

He nodded, yes. 'My sister is the same. Someone once said that when she spoke, she made people feel naked against the world.'

'I like you the way you are,' she said and settled into the arms of his conversation, the short sentences, the fuzzy baritone, the warmth of what he was saying.

'Tell me what it was like growing up in Calcutta,' he said.

'As I told you, my mother was Bengali and my father a Scotsman, both faithful to their own cultures. My childhood was unhappy as far back as I can remember, for I could not please either of my parents. Everything I learned was full of contradictions. I went to school dominated by Indian culture, while at home, my father held fast to Scottish tradition.'

Chapter 27

Calcutta 1927

Thirteen-year-old Flora was sitting on the floor in her new blue frock, copying illustrations from an old comic into her notebook. Father and mother were on the lawn with their afternoon tea, discussing where to spend the summer months. Her ears were alert to the conversation while her eyes concentrated on the drawing.

'She refuses to go to Nainital.'

'That girl is becoming far too rebellious,' father said, 'she needs discipline.'

'What are you going to do then?'

'Send her to the convent in Darjeeling. Fresh mountain air, just like bonny highland and nuns' iron fist will do her good.'

Three years sped past in Darjeeling. She didn't care about the religion nuns forced down her throat, blended with hot Ovaltine at bedtime, as if the sweet cocoa taste would make Catholicism more palatable. But she enjoyed the freedom, freedom from the tyrannical strictures imposed on her by both her father and mother.

One day, she was summoned to the head nun's office. 'You're going back to Calcutta,' Mother Superior said.

'Why? I don't want to.'

'Not my decision. The letter is from your father.' The fat on her arm rolled as she waved the letter at Flora.

The matter came to a head when Madan Lal said on the first day of her return from Darjeeling, 'I've prepared your favourite jhingra fish and cauliflower in coconut sauce. It's to welcome you back home, baby Flora.'

Flora eyed him fiercely. 'I am not a baby anymore.'

'You'll always be a baby to me, no matter how old you are,' he replied with the confidence that his master would back him.

The dishes on the table were steaming. The family dog was on another chair, her tail thumping against the armrest.

Father looked up and fixed his gaze on Flora. 'I am sending you to Glasgow to live with your grandparents.'

That surprised her. He rarely ever talked about Glasgow, his birthplace, let alone sending someone to live there.

'I don't want to go.'

'Yes, how can you send her to live with folks she has never met?' Mother said.

'Why must you contradict everything I say, woman?' he barked, 'There are some good schools in Glasgow.'

'Like the one you went to,' Mother said with a laugh tainted with mockery.

The ex-priest hit the table with the knife handle and let out a censured grunt.

'Stop it, both of you. I am not going anywhere,' Flora said, 'and that's final.'

The ex-priest grabbed a spoon and noticed soup was missing. 'Madan Lal, where is the soup?'

'Sorry, I forgot. It's coming, coming.' The harassed cook ran to the kitchen

The ex-priest brought down his fist. 'Soup after the main course?'

Through the doorway shuffled the cook, balancing bowls of mulligatawny soup and muttering. 'See what I've to deal with, and I am not even young anymore. Terrible to be poor in this country. No one cares or respects us ...'

'Stop babbling on, Madan Lal.' The ex-priest tapped the soup bowl with the spoon. The dog's tail started wagging again, mistaking the tapping as a signal for feed.

'Well, lass,' he addressed Flora, 'if you'll not take my advice about your education, what I believe is good for you, then I've nothing more to say. I'll let your mother deal with it.'

'I believe we should let the girl be in Darjeeling,' Mother said.

'We cannot afford the fee. The nuns are getting greedier by the day,' Father growled.

'Then how can you afford to send her to Scotland?'

Flora got up and ran to her room, feeling alone and unwanted. She lay down on the bed and wandered down blind alleys of thought as she fell asleep. She woke up later in a dark room, feeling as though she was being watched by whispering faces and her parents. Her suitcase lay undisturbed where Madan Lal had dropped it that morning. No one had come in to check on her all afternoon.

She looked out the window and saw Deenu, Madan Lal's son, crossing the yard whistling, his long legs carrying him tall and carefree. She wanted to be with him, to be like him. And then she saw with closed eyes her mother's flared nostrils and hand raised like a sword to slice Flora's head off. How dare you mix with the servant's son?

It was late afternoon. Mother was out. Father was sprawled out on his bed, dead like a basking lizard.

She crossed over to the servants' quarters, two small rooms at the rear of the house. It was a forbidden territory. We don't go there; they come to us, Mother had said, don't you ever forget.

The door was slightly ajar. She pushed it open and slipped inside. Seeing Deenu asleep on his string bed, naked from the waist up, she sat down beside him and watched his chest rise and fall. 'Wake up,' she said softly and dropped her hand on his chest. His skin was moist and slippery. She ran a finger down the centre of his chest, through the puddle of sweat that had gathered in the hollow of the stomach, to the spiral pit of his navel. A line of fine hair snaked downwards, disappearing into the waistband of his cotton shorts. She touched the filaments with the tip of her finger, brushing them backwards against the grain. He stirred and opened his eyes. She felt his fingers on her face, tracing the shape of her nose and her lips, following the curve of her chin down to her throat. When he reached her neckline, she stopped him.

'But you touched me first,' he said.

She had no answer. She sat still as he fumbled with her blouse and released her petite breasts. She felt his palm on her nipples as she stroked his sides with her hands and ran them down the cage of his ribs. A lock of hair came loose at her temple as she leaned forward.

'You're the most beautiful girl in the world,' he whispered.

Neither knew what to do. Their bodies slipped, fumbled, until he manoeuvred himself on top. And then she felt the kindling of a great flame of pain between her legs and cried out loud.

She returned the next day and the day after, whispering and giggling. She was so happy that she no longer missed her friends in Darjeeling.

One day, Parvati, the cleaner, saw Flora slipping out of Deenu's room. 'Flora baby,' she exclaimed. Her eyes narrowed as they followed Flora running. 'What were you doing there?'

'Oh, nothing, nothing … I was just talking to him. He wanted to borrow my textbook for his homework.'

'But he doesn't go to school.'

Flora ran up to her room and locked it from inside. Her heart racing, she flung open her school satchel, pulled out her notebooks, and spread them on the desk before sitting down. The notebook open, pencil in hand, she lowered her head, appearing deeply engrossed.

Late afternoon. The house was strangely quiet, and then she heard her father's booming voice downstairs. 'Get out. I don't want to see your face here again.'

She heard Deenu sobbing, hiccups convulsing from the stomach. Her heart burned, and guilt ravaged her insides, for she was powerless to help him.

'Get him out of here. If he comes back, I'll throw you out too and see to it that you never work again.'

And then she heard Madan Lal's grovelling voice. 'No, sahib. He won't come back. I'll send him away.'

Flora started crying again. Tears rolled down her cheeks, landing on her maths homework. Though her father had never hit her, only threatened to do so, this time she expected a beating.

For three hours, nothing happened. Why are they ignoring me?

It was getting dark. She got up and looked out the window. The streetlights had come on. She spotted the man from number fifty-five walking his dog.

Finally, there was a knock on the door. She recognised the tap's pattern. 'Flora, baby, come for your dinner,' Madan Lal said, his voice subdued but with a hint of urgent concern.

'I am not hungry.'

'But you have to eat something, na,' he said.

She crept to the dining room, expecting father and mother to pounce on her. But they weren't in the dining room. Just then, Father came in. He saw her and teetered towards her. She smelled alcohol on his breath as he tried to balance himself by holding her shoulder. She could see he was smiling. It meant nothing. She knew Father often laughed when drunk, laughed for no reason. Suddenly, his expression changed. He wasn't smiling anymore. He was making a face as if in great pain. And then he threw up, yellow liquid with pieces of solid all over her blue skirt and blouse.

'Dad,' she screamed, stepping back. She was disgusted but glad, too, that he wasn't angry, that he was incapable of anger.

When Mother came home that evening and heard what had happened, she called Flora to her room.

'You cheap slut, don't you have any shame?' Mother screamed and rained down slaps, pulled the hair, and sent her crashing into the furniture.

And then she heard Madan Lal's voice, though she couldn't see him. 'Memsahib, have mercy on the child. Beat my son if you must.'

'You Madan Lal,' she screamed, 'I want you to call the police at once. I want that boy arrested.'

Chapter 28

Damon got up, switched on the radio and tuned it to the morning news. They were reading the war tally, like a cricket scoreboard. Only this was grim. It tallied not runs and wickets, but the dead and the wounded.

After finishing breakfast, Flora carried the plates and cutlery to the sink and turned on the tap. The pipe groaned like a buffalo before water began flowing.

'No, no, leave the dishes for me,' Damon said and came up behind her.

She felt his body against her back, and then a finger scraping the nape. It sent a current shooting down her spine.

'There are only a few dishes. I'll be done in no time,' she said.

A hand came from behind her and took the dripping plate out of her fingers. She didn't protest. She could hear his breathing on her neck, and as he took her shoulders and turned her around, she felt the power of his arms.

'I should be going, you have to catch up on your sleep,' she said.

'I am not sleepy,' he said and took her head in both his hands. Their eyes met, and she felt her head spinning.

'Careful, my hands are wet,' she said and raised her arms above her head. She felt his lips on her and pulled away. 'I've to go,' she gasped.

'What's the hurry?' he whispered.

'It's not right,' she said.

'But who is here to judge what is right or wrong?'

Suddenly, her will to resist crumbled. She wrapped her arms around his neck. Their mouths met, eager and urgent.

'I must go,' she mumbled half-heartedly. They were holding each other tight and then split to pull each other out of the kitchenette. A saucer fell on the floor and smashed. They moved across the room to the bed and began fumbling with their clothes, undressing each other.

They fell on the bed in each other's arms, panting.

She froze suddenly.

'What's the matter?' he whispered.

She lost her tongue.

'Tell me. What's the matter?

A sob, hard as salt, welled up in her throat. She caught it, and the tears fell freely, but before they could drop from her chin, he brought his face down and licked the tears. 'They are salty,' he said.

That made her smile.

He got up, naked and unashamed, ran to the mantle and picked up a slab of chocolate. He dashed back and lay down beside her. 'Do you want to taste it?' he said, tearing the wrapper.

'Hm.'

He bit a piece of the chocolate, held it on his tongue, and brought his mouth to hers. Their tongues met.

'Nice,' she said.

He did it again, this time with a bigger chunk.

He turned over and straddled her hips. 'Don't move,' he said and rubbed the melting chocolate over her left nipple, going around in tiny circles. And then he brought his face down and licked the erect nipple. He did the same with the other nipple and then in the valley between her breasts.

'Did you like that?' he said.

'Hm, yes,'

He slid further down her body.

She looked at the ceiling and then at the hair on the crown of his head.

Finally, they lay back exhausted and fell asleep.

Damon woke up sharp at four in the afternoon. His body clock was set to jolt him awake at that hour.

He got out of bed, put the kettle on the stove and ran to the bathroom to wash and dress. He had to be with his unit by six before nightfall.

An hour later, they were out on the street.

Breathing freezing air into the warm, dark living cavities of her lungs, she nestled in Damon's arm. His one hand rested on the belt of her coat, and he reached for her with the other; they held hands and strolled as if they were skating. He didn't look at her, but she felt his hips against hers.

He released her when they reached the top of the lane. 'Shall I walk you home?' he asked.

'No, I am all right. You'd better hurry, or the German pilots will wonder why you're not at your station.'

'Don't worry, I'll get them this time.' He aimed an imaginary gun at the sky. BAM

She smiled. 'Write your name on the bullet, so they'll know who it's from.'

He cleared his throat. 'You're to go straight home before it gets dark.'

She watched him go, taking purposeful strides. His frame appeared bulky in the woollen trench coat. A saddlebag slung across the shoulder. It held a flask of tea and some sandwiches.

What if he doesn't come back? The thought suddenly dropped on her head like an unwieldy lump and stayed there. She heard a shout in her head. Don't go, the shout said. Please, don't go. A group of schoolboys passed by her. She wondered if their thoughts were full of war. If they were turning the idea of volunteering for the army into something sweet, like candy. If they were waiting for the right moment to tell their mothers.

Instead of going home, she went for a walk and, without a purpose, entered a graveyard. It was in disarray, with many half-finished graves paired with mounds of earth, a dull open sky above it. The quietness rumbled in her ears, accentuating the rustle of dried leaves and the clanking pedal of a passing bicycle courier. She saw the amber flame of a matchstick as the caretaker lit a cigarette. Lost to time and space, thinking of the strange turn of events, she had come to London to escape the turmoil in India, unaware of the far more deadly chaos that awaited her in England. She had considered writing to her mother and father. But what to write? I am all right. Are you well? Even if she scribbled a few words on paper, she would end up throwing it away anyway. Now, meeting Damon in an air-raid shelter, of all places, was a coincidence most strange. A boy, reticent and timorous, who preferred a book as a gift rather than a cricket bat. Now a changed man, a quietly confident soldier.

As the light faded, butterflies awakened in her stomach, for she associated darkness with the Luftwaffe's awakening. She heard quarrelling magpies in ash trees as if foretelling disaster. They say: Don't tempt fate; it catches up with you.

She turned onto the pavement at a hurried pace. First, she heard the wail and then the thunder of a freight train. She knew what was coming. She cursed at herself for the stupidity of not going home earlier. The explosion was close enough to lift her in the air. Rubble rained down on her, followed by dust clouds. She couldn't see beyond ten yards, but she could hear with clarity shrieks and cries. A child's plaintive wail added to the discord. Christ! She tried to rise, but her body would not cooperate. While she lay there, time crept back and handed her the last three hours. Damon was pointing a gun at the sky. BAM, BAM, BAM.

Finally, she pushed herself into a sitting position, then stood up slowly. Christ, that was close. It felt as if she were the intended target. She took two steps, her face in a grimace as though tensing for the arrival of more bombs, for the shattering of bones and haemorrhaging of blood, for the release into darkness. But they didn't. Emboldened, she broke into a trot. She had reached the end of the street when a boom rocked the pit of her stomach. For a moment, it seemed the world had been silenced, a silence belonging only to the hollowed-out buildings. She had lost all sense of direction. She heard a voice calling, 'This way, love … come down.' She ran towards the voice and hurled herself all the way down the steps. A door opened. Mysterious hands pulled her inside. 'There you go. Safe now.'

She slumped against a wall. As her eyes adjusted to the dark, she was astonished to see there were others like her. Breathing, coughing, and talking in hushed voices as if not to betray their location, or the bombs would seek them out. A game of hide-and-seek played with deadly intent.

'Take it easy, miss,' someone said, 'best to stay put until morning.'

'But I want to go home.'

'Don't we all miss?'

The air smelled moist and stale, an olfactory testament to the lives suspended within this makeshift haven. There were paper bags containing scraps of leftover food and toiletry bags. She realised people had come prepared to go straight to work from here, wash and change in the factory toilets.

Resigned, she lowered herself onto the floor and stretched her legs out, watching the past go by in mocking parade, whispering to Damon about the bombs, watching his brow come down under the weight of rage. She must have dozed off, for when she opened her eyes, she didn't know where she was. A woman sat up, looked around her, and cursed as she adjusted the blanket over her daughter.

At daylight, people began rising. The family beside her stirred, pushed themselves up off the floor and began folding the blankets with practised efficiency. Others had draped the blankets over their shoulders to preserve the warmth as they ventured out.

She patted down her coat, smoothed her hair, and followed them to the exit. A boy of eleven or twelve was standing at the entrance, staring out the yawning doorway where the winter morning had crept down the stairs into the basement. She recognised him. The boy lived with his mother three doors from her apartment building.

'Hello, where is your mother?' she asked the boy.

His round eyes took her in, but he didn't answer.

'Is she inside?'

'She has gone to fetch grandmother,' he mumbled, his eyes on the verge of tearing up.

Flora knelt to his level. 'How long has she been gone, darling?'

He shook his head. 'Don't know, miss. She said she'll be back soon.'

It was apparent that the mother had been gone a while.

'Do you know where your grandmother lives?'

The boy nodded. 'Yes, not very far.'

'Come, let's go there. Maybe your mother is late due to an emergency.'

The boy's hesitance succumbed to the pull of her compassion.

As they rounded the bend to his grandmother's street, the boy held back, seeing the devastation that lay before him. The centre of the explosion appeared to be a house on the left. Its roof had sheared off along with the roofs of five or six surrounding houses. Parked across the pavement were a fire engine and an ambulance, but there was no sign of activity. She followed the boy who was now staring at the brutalised entrance of a house. The remnants of shattered windows bore witness to the force that had torn through its soul. She could see into the front room, its walls wearing the ashen scars of a merciless blaze.

The boy ran up the steps. 'Mum!' he called at the house, the way a child calls for his mother, expecting to hear something like, 'yes, I am here,' or 'come in, the dinner is ready.'

'Mummy,' he called again, louder.

As if in response, a fireman came out of the door. Dust all over his green uniform, the helmet askew. Behind him, another fireman. Between them, they were carrying a stretcher. Weary faces, concentrating on the job of saving a life.

Following close behind was a neighbour. She saw the boy, and her steps faltered. 'Oh Archie,' she said.

And then the boy crumbled where he stood.

Chapter 29

November winds had stripped the trees bare. Chimneys were throwing out smoke, which fell away and drifted in hairy, drawn-out strings before dispersing.

People were enduring the weather. Children with their hoods up, facing up to school, while their mothers rushed to the clothesline, looking up at the sky, hardly daring to hang anything at all.

The coal merchant said to Pierre, who had stopped by for a brief chat, 'If things continue as they are, I'll soon not need the lorry.'

Pierre sympathised with him. 'Stick in there. No war goes on forever.'

Back home, Pierre lay beside Priti. 'Shhh, don't say that – go to sleep,' he said softly to her restless spirit.

The fear of losing Charlie was plaguing them both. 'I can't help it. I am tired of feeling like this.'

She fell asleep at last. Pierre was wide awake, thinking of the future. Once the war is over, he would take Priti and Charlie to France, to meet his relatives, and then to India, the very cradle of Priti's heritage. He hoped to reveal the plans at the last minute, on February 19, as a surprise birthday present.

The echo of running footsteps alerted him. Two pairs of feet were pounding on the pavement, but there was no vocal accompaniment. That's odd, he thought, for drunks of the night never moderated their voices or restrained their words in consideration of others. The cadence of steps eased, it seemed outside his own house, and then the letterbox flap clanked twice, and he knew whoever the nocturnal wanderers were, they had deposited something in the letterbox.

Priti and Pierre were no strangers to receiving vitriolic missives, such as wogs go home or similar messages, scribbled on pieces of paper, or venomous words hurled from a safe distance, the perpetrators laughing and running away. Once a package had arrived similarly, and it held no written words, but the message of hate was clear, for it held a clump of dog faeces.

'Ignore them, these people are fools, jealous that we have a home while they live in hovels.' But his words could not staunch the sorrow that gripped Priti's heart and put her off from going out or meeting friends.

The feet that stamped kicked at a tin can in the street. The can clanged from one gutter to the other. The sound grew fainter.

He put the light out and felt the tenseness slowly recede. Silence had returned to the street. He would sleep for four hours before rushing out again to report on the tally of death and destruction, the ugly truth and pretend bravado that concealed the tremors of every heart. How could it be otherwise when faced with the flash of bombs rending the fabric of existence?

A smell tiptoed into his consciousness, gently mingling with his dreams. Half asleep, he thought for a moment it was dog faeces he was smelling from the package posted into the letterbox. And then a crackling sound awakened him fully. He jumped out of bed, and the acidic odour of scorched furniture, furnishing and paintwork hit his lungs. He ran across the room and threw the door open. A whoosh of flame rose into an inferno as if it were lying in wait for him. The hall was engulfed, sucking the oxygen out of the air.

He realised escape through the front or rear doors was impossible. The flames were climbing the stairs, devouring the bannisters like a molten serpent with an insatiable appetite. He retreated into the bedroom, slamming the door behind him and felt the finality of his isolation.

He threw up the window sash. A great tongue of flame shot at him from the bay window directly below. He recoiled as the fire entered the bedroom, curling and pirouetting in a macabre dance of death.

He saw the neighbours on the street; blankets stretched out like hammocks. 'Jump, jump, jump.'

He ran back to the bed and picked up sobbing Priti in his arms. His legs collapsed mere three feet from the window.

Chapter 30

Damon clanked the lion head door knocker and waited. The girl who opened the door saw Damon standing and took a sharp breath.

'Is Flora awake?'

'Awake? She has hardly slept. Come in, I'll fetch her.'

The apartment was suffused with femininity, with the odour of newly washed hair, and casually discarded gold-strung slippers. Raincoats in shades of pink and lime, slung on hooks. A sideboard was adorned with crocheted mats. A pair of her flatmates were in the kitchen. 'Well,' one of them restarted the conversation Damon had interrupted, 'why doesn't she go for an Essex boy then, you can't be too picky these days?'

'She doesn't want a nice Essex boy who has grown up chatting with his nan in the kitchen.'

'What does she want then?'

'She wants a Clark Gable with a master's degree.'

The first girl snorted. 'Good luck to her.'

'Damon, I wasn't expecting you till later,' Flora called from the hallway, the housecoat flapping around her legs.

'I thought I'd drop by to ask if you would like to come back for a cup of tea.' His voice was hoarse from the cordite fumes.

'Yes, I'll. Give me two minutes to change.'

The girls in the kitchen had gone silent again. Damon sensed their eyes were upon him. Do they think I am an Essex lad too, still living at home?

Flora appeared in a grey raincoat and stood facing him, looking into his eyes, as if waiting for him to claim her.

He took her arm and pulled her closer.

Life was back on the streets. People were inspecting the damage. Someone cursed Hitler and kicked a fallen tree trunk. Two Home Guard volunteers were painting a white line on the pavement, running lengthwise.

Flora halted; her gaze fixed upon a weathered door. 'I thought I was going to die right here. See that door there. That's the entrance to the shelter. I didn't see it in the dark until someone pulled me in.' Her voice trembled as she recounted the near-death experience.

'I am sorry. I should not have let you walk home alone,' Damon said.

'And that poor boy. He reminded me of John. Oh, Damon,' she whispered, and two lines of tears trickled down her cheeks, landing on the layers of dust on the pavement.

He gathered her close to his chest and held her, so the tears were shaping a wet patch on the shoulder, an unspoken communion of shared pain.

Past the night shelter, they turned into the park instead of his bedsit. The park, a fragment of its former self, now lay deserted, half turned into vegetable plots. Grow vegetables wherever you can. We must become self-sufficient in food. That was the wartime decree from the government, and people were taking heed, enthusiastically digging the frozen sod with spades, rakes, even knives and forks, whatever tools came handy.

Damon and Flora sat down on a bench which was sprouting lichen on the damp surface. Faint outlines of children's hopscotch grids were visible beyond the railings.

'You want to talk about it?' Damon said, placing a hand on her arm, 'They say time heals the injury.'

'No, it doesn't,' she protested, 'one simply learns to exist with it.'

He didn't contradict her. How could he? He thought of Mary. She was still alive, though he hadn't seen her for months.

Voices drifted their way. A woman was explaining how to bake a cake on a coal fire.

'She reminds me of my mother,' Flora said, 'she used to bake biscuits and offer them to everyone she met. Her friend said it's because she didn't want to be fat alone.'

She drifted into silence, and he could see that her thoughts were far into the past, to John.

'May I ask you this, Flora, where did you go after that day?' he said

'Where else could I've gone, but to Madan Lal. He took charge and found me a safe place to live.'

A sparrow flew down and landed by her feet. Another came to join the first. 'Shhh, don't move,' she whispered, 'or you'll scare them away.'

He pretended he hadn't understood and stamped his foot. The birds flew.

'Ah, you cruel thing.'

He gave her a boyish grin.

'How did you get involved with that man, Frank?'

She sighed and opened her mouth as if figuring out how to give the thoughts in her head a verbal form.

He kept quiet to encourage her to talk, to make sense of her past through speech.

'It's a long story, Damon. I was sixteen when I learned the

truth. The truth is that I was an unwanted child. My father wished I didn't exist, for I reminded him of someone whom he wanted to forget. Mother couldn't bring herself to love a child not of her own womb. That's when I decided to leave home. I went to my uncle Sean and told him I wanted to live with him. He was against it at first. He said his was a bachelor's house. How could he have a teenage girl living there? But I was adamant.'

Chapter 31

Calcutta 1931

She was trembling all over.

He leaned over and opened the car door from the inside.

'Go,' he said and then pulled out a watch from his pocket, looked at the dial and shoved it back in.

'Go on,' he said again, 'Jitun will carry your suitcase.' He tapped the driver's shoulder from behind.

The driver opened his door and stepped out smartly.

'Uncle Sean, please …' Her voice was trembling.

'No, there's no other way, you can't stay with me anymore. You must go home.'

She sensed the pain in his voice and realised he was compelled to be harsh. Without another word, she slipped out of the car, started walking towards the front door, unsteady, against her will. The door opened as she reached the steps. She saw her father standing inside as if he were expecting her. She flinched as he took her wrist and began guiding her towards his room. She went along without protesting.

The first slap sent her reeling to the floor. It was from Mother. She had been waiting inside. She raised her hand again.

Father put his arm out to stop his wife. 'Come and sit down,' he said to Flora.

She pulled herself up off the floor and sat down in the chair.

'Tell me all about it.'

She closed her eyes.

‘I said I want to know what you have been doing.’

She stayed silent. The house was silent. The kitchen was quiet. She wondered where Madan Lal was. She didn’t want to face him. Not because she didn’t like him, but out of shame.

‘I am a patient man,’ he said, ‘until you speak, neither of us is leaving this room. Was it that boy Deenu?’

She kept her mouth sealed. Her nose was beginning to run. She wiped it with a handkerchief.

‘It was him, wasn’t it?’ Father barked, this time in a strong Scottish accent. He lapsed into his childhood accent whenever he was angry. ‘Right, I am going to ask Madan Lal to bring the boy here.’

‘No, it wasn’t Deenu,’ she said, ‘no, no, no.’

‘Then who?’

‘No one.’

‘Are you saying you’re not pregnant?’ Mother said, placing a hand on her arm.

She pulled herself away from her mother, but the touch remained on her skin. She rubbed the feeling away.

‘Are you, or aren’t you?’

She didn’t reply.

‘It’s easy to find out. I’ll call Dr Sengupta.’ She made it sound like a threat.

‘Frank,’ she said in a monosyllable, as if the word had slipped out of her mouth accidentally.

Both mother and father crowded over her. She could see his silver ring with the blue stone on the middle finger.

‘Who is Frank?’

‘He used to come to the house.’

‘What for?’

'Friend of Uncle Sean. They used to discuss business. He was nice to me.'

'So, you were carrying on with your uncle's friend. You slut,' mother hissed.

'No, it wasn't like that. He was like an uncle, like Uncle Sean. One day, he asked me if I wanted to see Calcutta from the Grand Hotel's roof terrace. He said the views were stunning.'

'Did you go?'

She nodded. 'He picked me up from school.'

'And then what happened?'

'He took me to a room in the hotel and forced me.' She trailed off and began weeping again as if she were reliving the horror. She remembered him talking to someone in the hotel lobby, and then he walked her all the way to the top, to the open roof terrace. Look over there. She could see the river, the boats appearing tiny like toys, and the façade of the Victoria Memorial. It looked so different. 'The Chinese restaurant,' he said, pointing at a line of twinkling lights, 'that's the Outram Ghat.' And then he led her downstairs. She thought he was going to show her more. She remembered going into a room. It looked so grand, classy. Even when he locked the door from inside, she didn't think anything of it.

'Didn't you scream for help?'

'He hit me and forced me to take off my clothes.' She began shivering as if she were very cold.

Suddenly, she began missing her steel tumbler. She wanted it in her hands, to hold it tight. Where is Madan Lal? Ask him to fetch it. She remembered the kindly old man who came to the neighbourhood once a week, shouting something she didn't understand. One day, her mother called him over and gave him a small steel tumbler. Flora watched as he sat down, spread his legs, held it between his feet and then began hammering it with a steel pen. Dot after dot, her name began to take shape. Job done, he buffed it with a leather cloth and handed it to her. Get four annas from your mother, he said.

'Why didn't you tell Sean?'

'I didn't tell anyone. He said he would kill me if I did. I believed him.'

Father and mother exchanged glances.

At first, she thought they hadn't believed her, that she was protecting Deenu. She took a deep breath when her father said, 'You're not to leave this house without my permission. Is that clear?' He leaned over and patted her on the shoulder.

And then mother added, 'I'll call Dr Sengupta.'

Through the window of her hospital room, she could see buses and cars glide down the road, their taillights blinking as they turned left at Ballygunge Phari before disappearing into dark clouds of their exhaust. In the patch of green between the maternity ward and the warden's block, she saw a little girl on a green bicycle circle around a flower bed. A man beside her, a hand holding the seat at the back, half running, half walking. The girl's excited shrieks, asking her father to let go of the bicycle.

She had a headache, and her legs hurt. The bleeding hadn't stopped. She was changing pads every two hours.

She walked back to the bed, smoothed out the sheets and sat down. The baby, wrapped tightly in a blanket like an Egyptian mummy, lay in the cot by the bedside. She looked at the face, the tiny hands, the fingers curled up, the chest rising and falling. She wanted to pick him up, but they had told her never to disturb a sleeping baby. He'll wake up when he's hungry. That's when you should hold him close so he can feel your heartbeat, smell your body oil.

She lay down on the bed, pulling one leg up and then the other. She considered switching on the table lamp, then changed her mind. Her thoughts drifted to the recent past, to Dr Sengupta. She had overheard the doctor and mother's conversation after she had been prodded, had a needle inserted to draw blood, had a torch shone in her eyes, and had her blood pressure checked. 'No, nothing can be done now, it's too risky,' Dr Sengupta was saying. 'Whatever you have heard cannot be from a medical professional. If the child stops breathing, we may have to cut her open. There's the risk of infection, and the risk that the girl may not be able to conceive again. She's only sixteen.' 'That's exactly my point. She's too young to be a mother,' her mother had asserted.

For four days, no one visited her. On the fifth morning, father and mother came to the ward.

'How are you feeling?' Father said, pulling up a chair. He was shaved and smelled fresh.

She nodded. 'A little better.'

'They say the baby is coming along fine.'

Again, she nodded. 'I want to come home.'

'Yes, you'll, you'll, soon. They say you'll be home in three or four days. Make the best of it while you're here. I hear the food is excellent.'

She forced a half smile. 'What about school?' she murmured, 'I am missing my friends.'

'Darling, first get fit and healthy, then we will discuss the school,' mother said.

She felt her father's reassuring hand on her shoulder.

'Your mother and I've been thinking about your future. You're still a teenager. There's a whole life ahead of you. We've decided it's not right to lumber you with the responsibility of raising a child.'

A bell tolled in her head. This doesn't sound right. She raised her head to look at his eyes. 'What are you saying?'

'We have decided to give him up for adoption. Frank came to see me. He says he wants to take the boy. His wife is keen too, as she is unable to conceive. Says they have always wanted a child.'

'NO,' she screamed. Her eyes shot to the door as if expecting Frank to come barging in.

Mother came forward to restrain her. 'Calm down, Flora, we're only trying to help you.'

'Think of your future,' father said, 'when you're older, you'll get married, won't you, then you can have as many children as you want.'

'How can you? After what he did to me.'

Father looked at the headrest above her head. 'But we must be realistic, darling. I believe this is the best solution for you and the child.'

She turned to her mother, pleading. 'He is my son. How can I give him up? Won't you help me, Mum, please?'

'Help? Yes, I've helped bring up one illegitimate child. I am not doing it again.' Mother's eyes were like two cubes of ice. 'You sort this one out,' she said to her husband, walked to the other end of the room and stood with folded arms.

Later that day, she was given an injection they said would

help her sleep. For a few days afterwards, she remembered falling in and out of sleep. There were people around, sometimes doctors, other times nurses, but no one talked to her, asked her how she was or handed her the baby to breastfeed.

One day, she woke up to find herself on the settee at home. She recalled her father's face, looking at her gravely. Madan Lal was offering her food on the tray. 'You must eat, Flora baby.' She couldn't understand why he was bringing food to her bedroom. She felt he was staring at her with long, questioning stares. Sometimes she sensed he was speaking to her without moving his lips. What are you saying? Speak. I can't stand it. The next moment, he wasn't there, as if she had been talking to the walls. And then she was gripped by an urge to break down the walls.

When she awoke next, she found herself in a strange place. The smell, the light, the walls, everything was unfamiliar. A hall about four times the size of her bedroom. High windows, light coming in fractured and refracted, like so many rainbow-coloured arrows. She sat up, alarmed at the sight of the girls. There were at least twelve, the same age as her. They were crowding around her, staring.

'Where am I?' she said.

The girls didn't reply. They led her to a smaller room where a carved statue of Jesus Christ sat on a shelf, alongside two oil paintings on the wall, one of which she recognised as the Virgin Mary.

'What's this place?'

One of the girls stroked her hair, helped her sit comfortably in a chair, and then they left without saying anything.

A man came into the room. He was wearing a white robe.

'My name is Father Brown. What's yours?'

'Flora MacDonald.' It was an effort to speak. The throat felt as if someone had scraped it with sandpaper.

'Well, Flora, you're welcome to stay with us as long as you want. You're very safe here.'

She didn't understand why he was offering her accommodation.

'Do you know where you are?' Brilliant white teeth appeared to spring out of his mouth as he smiled.

She shook her head.

'You're in the Church of the Virgin Mary. It's a shelter for girls who don't have a home. We found you last night sitting on the steps. You were saying you had run away from home. Do you recall?'

'No.'

'You were in a terrible state. We had to call the doctor. He said you were hallucinating, overdosed on tranquilisers.'

Chapter 32

London 1940

The park was quieter now, except for the tap, tap, tap of someone knocking a stake into the soil.

She felt Damon's hand on her shoulder.

'I believe you're brave. I do,' he said.

She took a large gulp of air as if swallowing grief.

'How did you get back to your son?'

'After about a year and a half, I found out Frank's wife had left him. I suppose she had had enough of that evil man. And he had employed ayahs to look after my son. I also found out they had named him John.' She smiled and then coughed. 'I would have preferred a different name, but still, John isn't too bad. Is it?'

'Not bad at all. It's an honest Christian name.'

'I longed to meet John, but I didn't know how to go about it. Then one of the Indian girls in the shelter offered to help. She suggested going to the house and speaking to the ayah. Somehow, she managed to persuade the ayah to leave John with me for an hour or two at a time, of course, always in secrecy. Those were the happiest hours of my life. Once I managed to take him to Alipore Zoo to show him the monkeys.' She paused. 'After six months, Frank found out and put a stop to it. He threatened to kill me if I came near his house. What could I do? I would stand at a distance, watching for hours to catch a glimpse of John. I started doing odd jobs, so I would have money to live on.' She dropped her shoulders and glanced sideways. 'I would go over to Bow Barracks. I knew I shouldn't be there, but I didn't care. Anyway, that was about the time I met you two Englishmen.'

'Ahhh, so that makes sense,' Damon said, 'you must have taken us for naïve fools?'

'Not fools, but I could see you were new to India, not yet the hardnosed, money-grabbing, entitled scamps they become after a while. That's why I wanted to be with you.'

A man wearing a raincoat passed them, pushing a rusty handcart put together of scavenged parts, the wheels screeched like alarmed magpies.

'Let us be off then, you and I,' Damon said, 'with the time that does not but fly.'

'What's that?' she said.

'Nothing. Just a poem I composed.'

'I didn't know you were a poet. I want to hear more.'

'Are you sure? It's nothing really.'

'I want to hear it.'

'Alright,' he said and cleared his throat.

'Let's go thru' these wrecked streets
Run, quick, run to the cavernous retreats
You cry, you wake, you leave
No, let's not go thru' these wrecked streets
One-night hotels where lovers meet
Of insidious intent? My heart is freed
Oh, do ask, what is it?
Let's be off then, me and thee
Lest time does but skip and flee.'

'Damon, that's so nice.'

'I am in love with you,' he said.

The tone was still poetic, she noted, and she looked in his eyes, searching. Is he merely reciting a poem, or are the words coming from deep within his heart?

'Damon.'

'I am in love with you

I am not in the business of denying myself the simple pleasure of saying what's true

I am in love with you.'

'Damon,' she repeated with a hand on her heart.

He stood up and pulled her to her feet. 'Let's go.'

As if it were an accident that they were on the street where Archie's grandmother lived. The scene was as she remembered from that morning. On the pavement, someone had collected fallen bricks and timber and arranged them in separate heaps, like two funeral pyres.

She stopped by the dust-covered path where Archie had stood and called out to his mother, now marked with imprints of countless footsteps.

'I want to tell you something.'

'Yes,' he said.

'Tomorrow is John's birthday. He would have been thirteen, about the same age as that boy.'

'I am sorry,' he said.

'I miss him so much,' she said. Her eyes moistened, and her lips quivered. She placed a hand on her mouth.

'I am so sorry.'

She felt his strong arms pulling her into his embrace. When she closed her eyes, the earth turned too fast, and she opened them. She could see the fine threads of his eyebrows sitting on the upper ridge of the sockets in curly waves.

‘Please don’t cry. Everything will be alright.’ She heard him say and in her bewilderment she didn’t know if those words were spoken, or if he had only wound his arms around her, held her so tightly, with such continual changing pressures that it seemed he had more than two arms, that she was surrounded by him, demanding and renouncing all at once, that he was telling her not to give up, be strong, only weak people cry.

Chapter 33

London, September 1940

When he arrived at the apartment the next day and knocked on the door three times, a hollow silence greeted him. He wondered if Flora had gone to Whitechapel, where she worked, even though she had indicated she didn't work on Saturdays. His ponderings were interrupted as the door opened, revealing an elderly woman he had not met before. She ushered him with a wave of her hand. He noticed her eyes were regarding him with keen interest.

'Are you Damon?' she asked.

'Yes, I am. How did you know?'

'It doesn't matter. Flora is dead,' she said. Her words cut through the air with such unvarnished directness that he thought he had misunderstood, that she meant Flora was dead to this world, fast asleep.

'Oh,' he said, forcing a half-smile to accompany the humour.

'She hanged herself last night. Look, I am sorry, but I don't see the point of beating about the bush. You're a grown man.'

Hanged herself? It didn't make sense. Who is this woman telling me she has hanged herself? He could see that she was the type who made difficult decisions and took control of things that mattered.

'I am sorry. You'd better come in,' she said.

At least there was warmth in the way she spoke, punctuating her words with energetic use of her hands.

He looked past her into the hallway, and the door from which she had appeared, wearing a housecoat. He had a sudden urge to rush past this woman and look into the room, to catch a whiff of the air and see how she had arranged her bedroom.

'What time did this happen?' he said.

'Very early hours. We sent for the police. Bless them. They came sharpish considering … the doctor has been here too.'

'I had no idea,' he mumbled, and suddenly felt terribly weak, and his head felt heavy as a boulder.

'How did you know the girl?' she said.

'She's a friend from long ago,' he replied.

'I live next door,' she explained, 'how hysterical the girls were, poor things. They didn't know which way to turn and asked for my help. Do you know where her folks live? But before you answer, come, come, come, sit down. You appear as if you're about to keel over.'

He followed her in silently and sat down on a chair she pulled out for him. She fetched a glass of water from the kitchen and handed it over to him. 'Girls don't appear to know anything about her family. Do you?'

He wasn't surprised Flora had kept her past a closely guarded secret. Perhaps she thought the only way to live was to ignore the past, shut it out of her brain.

'She may have relatives in Scotland. But I don't have any names or addresses. She had no relationship with her father and mother,' Damon said. He felt sadness wrapped around every word that came out of his mouth.

'That's a pity,' she said, 'if we canna find her folks, I am afraid it will be a pauper's funeral. What a shame for a lovely lass like her.'

'I'll pay for the funeral. She deserves only the best,' he said quickly. A cry, a strangled grief, threatened to erupt from his stomach. He wanted to howl.

'Excuse me, I need some fresh air.'

He rushed out of the apartment as if he were about to retch. Out on the street, he began pacing up and down and kicking dust. He didn't know how long he had been there when a white van pulled up. Its rear doors opened, the hospital's huge red cross split into two halves, like pieces in a sad jigsaw puzzle. Two men came out with a folded canvas stretcher. They knocked on the door, even though it was open.

Fifteen minutes later, they appeared at the door; this time, the stretcher was open, a white sheet draped over it. One man in front, the other at the rear. They walked around the van to the rear and, with practised efficiency, slid the stretcher onto the floor.

The sheet had slid off her right foot. Damon could see the polished toenails he remembered seeing many years ago. Painted vermilion red.

Chapter 34

London, October 1940

Dressed in a black suit, Damon arrived early and sat at the back of the visitation room. He expected most of the forty chairs would remain unoccupied. Only her flat-sharers, or her colleagues at the shop where she had worked since arriving in London, would bother to attend.

People started to arrive, walking around the coffin draped in purple cloth, her favourite colour. Faces he had never seen before were kneeling next to Flora, or standing over her to look, touch the coffin, and then move on. The room quickly filled up with about thirty men and women, dressed solemnly.

Mrs Simpson, the neighbour, dressed in a new frock of sombre colours, was standing at the front, nodding at people or exchanging subdued words. She saw Damon and signalled with a nod to come over.

Damon got up and walked down the makeshift aisle between rows of chairs, keeping his gaze fixed on the casket. An excruciatingly long walk, all the while sensing eyes were upon him. He could see her as he approached. Her hair was as he remembered, carefully laid out, the face cocooned in plush satin lining. It appeared plasticised, but still, she was Flora.

As he knelt, he realised they had closed her eyes, and that he would never again see her brown pupils. 'I'll always love you.' He placed a hand lightly on her chest. 'Rest in peace.'

But peace had never been with her, he realised now; she was a restless person. What was it in that face that was a self-serving source of wonder to him? Each time he looked away, he found he had forgotten it; he couldn't memorise its features. Yet he could count them in her absence: the brown-black eyes, the small forehead, a black mole on the left cheek, the complexion which wasn't dark but not white either. Was this evanescence the key to the peculiar power over him? Did the fierceness with which he took in her presence cause him to lose focus? A hunger for a presence that her presence couldn't sate.

He stepped back and looked up. People were still watching him as if they knew who he was. He felt a rage swirling within him. Who are you? What do you want?

Mrs Simpson led a man around the coffin, an odd-looking man with a ship's prow of a nose, orange hair and freckles on pale skin. He was wearing a waistcoat over a stiff-collar shirt and long breeches. Mrs Simpson brought him over to Damon.

'This is David MacDonald, Flora's uncle. Police were able to trace him in Glasgow,' she said, and then to David, 'Damon … he was a friend of Flora.'

Damon sensed the old man watching him as if his mind could be seen, the mind that had drifted into an absent state.

'Da-mon,' he said after a long pause, making the name sound French.

'Hello,' Damon said, 'did you know Flora was in London?'

He nodded. 'Aye, I did. She sent me a letter when she first arrived.'

'Yet you didn't bother keeping in touch with your niece,' Damon said.

'Nay, it wasn't like that,' he said. 'I wanted to meet her.'

'Why didn't you then?'

'She didn't give me an address. She said she'll write after settling down proper. But I nay hear nothing. An old sailor like me didn't have the strength to go look for her.'

The curtain parted at the back of the hall. Father George appeared and smiled. A smile as crooked as his gait, as he took position behind the coffin. He cleared his throat proudly. The room went silent. 'Dear friends, ladies and gentlemen, we are gathered here …' The right words spoken in Latin, the gesture of ritual began to unfold, flowers and incense, and hymns.

He began talking about Flora as if he had known her personally. '… in death as in life she'll be an inspiration to us all … hear us dear Lord … please have mercy on the soul of our sister Flora.'

His sonorous voice carried a note of tragedy. 'I'll tell you, brothers and sisters, this beautiful, bounteous country looks like paradise.'

A few members of the gathering cleared their throats.

'But there are moments, and this is one of them, when it feels as if we are in exile, amongst the seed of Cain, and the Lord's face is hidden from us.'

Sighs of relief from the congregation when he said, 'Let us return to the sacred space of the Garden of Eden, where Flora now dwells. Now let us pray.'

'Hello mate.' A familiar voice whispered in Damon's ear.

'What the hell. How did you get here?' Damon cried, momentarily transported to the carefree past.

'I spoke to your mother.'

'I heard you were in the navy, somewhere in Portsmouth, or is it Plymouth?'

'Yes, I signed up. I had to mate, I had to, like you.'

'But you're here. Have you jumped ship?' Damon whispered, keeping his eyes on the minister.

Robert smiled. 'No, I've a two-day shore leave. Anyway, you'll fill me in on Flora later, won't you? What a shocker.'

'There is nothing here for you,' Damon said. 'She didn't come to London looking for you. It's a misconception if that's what you're thinking.'

'How did you meet up?'

'I'll tell you another time.'

'What about that Frenchie? Ever found out what happened to him?'

'His name was Pierre. I have spoken to him.'

'You didn't think of informing him about Flora?'

'He's dead. Died in a house fire. I read in the papers,' he said and then lowered his head and closed his eyes. He didn't want to talk anymore. In his right ear, Robert whispered, 'We got to pray, right?'

'For Christ's sake, Robert, pray.'

Mrs Simpson came over fifteen minutes later. 'Would you like to be a pallbearer?' she asked softly, a reassuring hand on his arm. 'We must hurry, looks like the rain is coming.'

Damon nodded, though he didn't want to walk to the grave. He didn't want to see Flora lowered into the ground. He didn't want to toss in a handful of dirt. He certainly didn't want Robert to see him grieving.

'Me too,' Robert said.

Damon and Robert were the lead pallbearers. The rest were the undertaker's employees; hefty fellows dressed in black ties.

The priest invited the guests to throw clumps of sod on the coffin. Dirt to dirt. Ashes to ashes.

The rain finally came, like a cheap redemptive symbol in a story. It had no prejudice. It fell from the grey sky onto rich and poor, happy and unhappy, the living and the dead.

The funeral done, he was walking away, in every sense, leaving it behind and crying, of course, stinging salt tears. He felt liberated. He was going to shed the memories of the street where he grew up. He was going to clear his mind so that he wasn't just another self-invented man with no belongings in the world.

They walked to The Windmill, one of the few local pubs still in business. Damon picked up a book from the shelf behind him and began reading. His beer lay untouched.

'You think you can ignore me?' Robert said after a few minutes of silence.

A steamroller started up on the road, tarmacking a portion of the road under the lamp post. Damon turned a page. He was reading a report about corruption in the tax office, but he didn't absorb a word of it. He felt a pulsing in his temple and tension mounting behind his eyes.

'Say something. I won't leave until you do.'

And knowing that Robert would sit there until he spoke, Damon responded without lifting his eyes. 'I am reading. Can't you see?'

'What happened? Why have you changed?' Robert said.

'Didn't we agree when we left Calcutta that we would go our separate ways?' Damon said and turned another page. He could sense Robert searching for words.

'But we are here now?' Robert said, 'In the same room.'

Damon's head snapped up in agitation as the stream roller coughed and clanked. The smell of hot tarmacadam reached his nose. 'Our friendship is over, Robert,' he said.

‘I don’t care about the friendship. I want to know what was going on between you and Flora, and why she was such an idiot to kill herself.’

Damon could feel his own pounding heart. There was something disembodied about his rage, knocking him out of himself. He stood up and punched the table. The glasses rattled as he threw punch after punch. When it was over, he stood back, dizzy and out of breath, shaking out his numb hand.

‘Is your friend alright?’ a man in a navy boilersuit asked Robert, ‘he must have hurt his knuckles.’

Someone at the back chuckled. ‘Never mind the knuckles, check if the table is alright.’

Robert said nothing as he leaned over and straightened the glasses. He glanced over at the bar to see if the publican had noticed.

‘Now get out of my sight,’ Damon said.

But it was Damon who turned and walked away.

Chapter 35

London 1942

When the guns were no longer roaring in anger, celebrations had run their course, Damon travelled to Ormskirk to meet Anne and Mary. He intended to seek consensus so he could spend time with Mary, maybe even bring her back to London for long weekends.

Mrs Wood, the landlady, opened the door.

'Ah, you are Anne's husband. Do come in. I have distressing news for you. Anne was rushed to the hospital three days ago. She has a failing heart,' she said.

Damon lowered his head. He felt as if a sack of cement had been poured inside him and quickly hardened.

'Take off your coat and sit down,' Mrs Wood said and signalled at her husband, who promptly left the room and returned with a four-year-old girl in a light-yellow frock, her hair tied into a ponytail.

'We have been looking after dear Mary as our own daughter.' Her kindly smile convinced Damon that she was genuine.

Damon almost didn't recognise his own daughter through his moist eyes as his arms shot out, expecting Mary to rush into them. But the girl didn't come running. She walked into his embrace as if he were just a family friend.

'Mary dear, he is your dad,' Mrs Wood said. 'Well, we will leave you two alone.' She left the room, taking her husband with her.

Damon lifted Mary off the floor and hugged her as he had

never hugged a child before. The girl flailed her arms and made a face as if impatient to be freed. He made her sit on his knees and pulled out a bar of chocolate. Mary's eyes widened. Damon felt his heart crying with gratitude and happiness. He knew she probably never had a chocolate bar gifted to her at any time other than a birthday.

'Where is mum?' he said.

'In hospital,' Mary replied.

'Shall we go and see her?' he said.

'Yes,' she replied shyly.

The Ormskirk Hospital on Wigan Road was a fifteen-minute bus ride.

They entered the ward through a side door and immediately spotted Anne through the glass partition. He stopped in his tracks. Dishevelled hair, a pale, sunken face; she could be an old woman if he didn't know better. She was asleep with her mouth half open as if she had been shouting at someone and forgotten to close it. A book was lying on the side table. He was surprised to see it was a Jules Verne novel, whom she considered an overrated author with an old-fashioned writing style.

'Mum,' Mary cried.

The head nurse stopped her from going near. 'Your mum has been awake all night. It won't be wise to disturb her now that she has fallen asleep.'

'Nurse is right, darling. We'll come back later. We can go to the park instead,' Damon consoled Mary.

His dream of taking his daughter to a playground, watching her run around, playing on swings, while she ate candyfloss, was about to become reality.

It was late afternoon when they returned home.

'I'm going back to see Anne,' he told Mrs Wood after they had tea and biscuits. 'I'm staying over at The Feathers Inn on Edge Hill Road. And tomorrow I will be going back to London.'

Damon reached for his raincoat and tried to slip it over his jacket. For a moment, he was struck on the threshold of the door, doing battle with the coat.

'I assure you, young man, your daughter has a good home here. Now go with an easy heart.'

This time, he found Anne awake. She saw him coming but didn't appear surprised. The nurse must have told her about me, he thought. He went and stood by the bed. Neither spoke for a few moments.

'So, you have come,' she said in a dry voice, as if merely stating a fact. And then added, 'What do you want?'

'I heard from Mrs Wood that you have blocked arteries,' he said.

She shook her head weakly, as if it was nothing.

'I wasn't informed, or I would have come earlier,' he said, 'how are you feeling?'

She didn't reply. Stared at a fixed spot on the ceiling. He looked around the ward and noticed the woman in the other bed looking at them. He turned his back on the woman.

'I've come to see you and Mary,' he said.

She raised her head a little and looked at his face, as if to study the expression and then dropped back on the pillow with a sigh of disappointment.

He became aware of the creaking trolleys, bronchial coughs, clearing of throat, and loud conversations.

How can anyone get a rest in this place? He wanted to shout

at the nurses. He realised it wasn't the noise but the guilt that was maddening him. He hadn't come to see her, and yet he had. He wanted to turn around and run. But he couldn't. The legs felt as if they were cased in lead.

'Your landlady is very kind. Mary seems happy there,' he said after a long silence.

She didn't reply.

'I am going back to London tomorrow,' he said. He expected her to explode. You have come for one day. You might as well not have bothered. I'll get by on my own. Haven't I been doing it for the last three years?

But she replied in a calm, reasonable voice, 'I understand. You need to be at work.' She was savage in her calmness.

Chapter 36

Damon shifted to a more spacious house in Hammersmith. It's an easy commuting distance, he told his work colleague, who lived in Hammersmith too, promising to meet up in the tavern opposite Hammersmith Palais.

The colleague shook his head, as if he wasn't impressed. 'The real reason is Mary. Come, why don't you admit it?'

Damon smiled guiltily. 'If she ever comes to London, she should have her own bedroom. Don't you agree?'

He had already installed a new bed in her room, a wardrobe, and a dressing table with many drawers for her jewellery, makeup, and whatever else teenage girls collect these days.

'When my son comes home, he happily sleeps on the sofa,' the colleague replied.

'Girls are different, you can't expect them to rough it out.'

On one of the visits to Ormskirk, Damon asked Mary if she would like to come home during the school holidays. He referred to his house as her home even though she had never set foot in it. And she appeared unconcerned whether she did or not. Friends at school were more important to her.

At the age of fifteen and a half, she had grown taller than most of her friends and intellectually more mature.

'By the time she is nineteen or twenty, she will be a stunning young woman, very bright too,' he told his friend and colleague.

'I can't wait to meet her,' the colleague said, 'another pint?'

Damon looked out the window of the pub, at the hull of a

small truck, burnt out and rusting, ash that lay upon the leaves and upon the cars, dust in the air and still falling, it seemed, upon the sycamore that stood near the fire station with half its trunk scorched as though some vandal had tried to set fire to it. Some of the windows on the street were still sealed with refuse sacks.

Would Mary be happy living here?

He went to Ormskirk the very next week.

Sitting in a teashop, the market opposite was bustling with housewives carrying cloth bags, barrow boys yelling, and children screaming on the mini carousel. He turned to Mary, who was sitting in the chair with an air of malevolence, as if she would rather be somewhere else.

She cried out at him, 'You left my mother, you sent her away, didn't you. You're nothing but an evil man.'

He found himself frozen, his hands, his mouth quivering. His eyes dropped to watch his feet when he heard the truth fall from his mouth. 'We had fallen out of love.' He told Mary everything about the trip to Calcutta, why he married her mother, and why he left her. His life since he returned to London had been lived against a backdrop of Flora, even though she was thousands of miles away and didn't expect to meet her ever again. Yet the memory of her in the daily and ordinary world would not retreat. Everything changed when she came to London. That was the happiest time of his life, fulfilling and everlasting, as he had hoped. But it turned out too short. Now she is dead.

His heart pained as he watched the girl's frowning disbelief, the sliding look in her eye, her mouth slumped, and then she buckled silently, wrapping her arms about her chest. 'Sorry, Dad.'

‘I shouldn’t have burdened you with all this.’ He admitted afterwards.

‘Yeah, well, maybe not,’ she said and then added a moment later, ‘I forgive you, Dad.’

He suspected she loved her mother more than she loved him. She would naturally blame him for breaking the family. He looked at his daughter. She was drinking tea with her hands wrapped around the cup, her upper lip curled. He could see Anne in that face.

He called the woman with the pinafore and ordered a pork pie and more tea.

‘Are the police still looking for you?’ she asked.

‘I don’t think so. The war has changed everything. Now India is independent, and we have nothing to do with that country anymore.’

He was slicing the pork pie with a knife; his hand began to shake like a mad hatter’s. He couldn’t loosen his fingers to drop the knife. Mary leaned forward and pried his hand open. She ran her cool hands up and down his arm. Later, she phoned his office to say her father was sick and would not be in for two or three days. She stayed with him in The Feathers Inn until he was well enough to return to London.

A few days later, Damon called his mother, if only to hear her voice – as a comfort against the howling wilderness inside him.

‘Is everything alright, son?’

‘I hope people are not being hard on you because of me and Anne.’

‘Let them say what they want. I know my son.’

As he heard those words, words he had heard before, he wished he had not called her after all. He closed his eyes and tried to imagine himself weightless, without the burden of a judgmental society. It was impossible.

On a later visit, he asked Mary what she would like to do after finishing school.

'I will go to university, or maybe not. Oh, I don't know what I want to do,' she replied. She appeared flustered as if she was being asked to do something against her will.

Chapter 37

London 1955

Another seven months went by.

Mrs Wood had a telephone installed in her house.

He called Anne from the office. 'I am coming over this weekend to see Mary.'

'Mary has gone camping in Scotland with friends,' she replied in a plain, hurried voice, 'I thought she had let you know.'

'No, she didn't.'

'Well, that's between you two.' She put the phone down.

A week later, he received a card in the mail, an ordinary wish-you-were-here type of card. She had scribbled a few words: Dad, I am in Edinburgh. Mary.

He telephoned a month later.

'Didn't you know?' Anne said.

This time, he stayed silent, not deliberately, but for want of suitable words to express his surprise, or disappointment, or dread.

'She came back from Scotland, and then two weeks later took off again. This time, she said she was going to France. She has a friend whose brother lives there.'

'But … but … she doesn't have any money.'

'That's because of the pittance you send us every month. I have had to go back to teaching to make ends meet.'

'When is she coming back?'

'I don't know. Two or three weeks,' Anne replied.

'You let her go just like that. Without a firm commitment?' He was angry. 'You are sure she has enough money?'

She didn't reply, although he could hear her breathing. He realised in that silence that all was not well. He knew Anne was suffering from depression and was flying off in rage over minor issues.

'Is there something you're not telling me?' he said in a threatening voice.

'What does that mean? There is nothing to tell you.' She slammed the phone down.

He closed his rain-soaked umbrella, opened the front door and stepped inside. A letter was lying on the doormat. He held his breath as he bent down to pick it up. It was a card from Mary. *'Hi, Dad, I am still in France. Love you, Mary.'*

There was no address, nor an indication when she would return to England. Why wouldn't she say when she's coming back? How is she surviving with no money? He was furious with Anne for letting her go.

He set the card on the mantle beside the one she had sent from Edinburgh and went to the kitchen. Just as he placed the kettle on the stove, the recently installed phone burst into life, startling him. He had yet to get used to its ringtone, which to him sounded like the bells of a fire engine.

He rushed to the hall and picked up the receiver. He recognised Anne's breathing in the receiver and a light cough even before she spoke. He knew instantly it was an emergency. She had never called him since leaving London for Ormskirk.

'Damon, have you heard from Mary?' she said. Her voice

was thin and reluctant, as if she had swallowed pride in making this call.

'I have not heard but received a card from her this morning.'

'She has been gone for two months. I'm worried,' Anne said.

'You said she is with some friends. Have you spoken to their families?'

She was quiet for a few moments. 'I don't know who the friends are. No one at school knows anything.'

'How can you be so stupid? You let her go without checking who the friends were and where she would be staying?'

He drove to Ormskirk in his Ford Anglia.

Mrs Wood opened the door and solemnly led him into the inner room.

Anne was sitting at the table with a mug of tea. She didn't get up or greet him.

'Would you like some tea?' Mrs Wood asked and gestured at her husband to put the kettle on the stove.

'Thank you,' Damon said and walked over to Anne, who refused to make eye contact but stared straight ahead.

'What do you know about the friends she is with?' he asked.

She shook her head and spoke to the mug of tea. 'Nothing. They used to come for her, but Mary never invited them in. I've only seen them from a distance.'

'Go on,' Mrs Wood said to Anne, 'tell him about the headmistress.'

'I went to meet the headmistress, and we interviewed her classmates. According to them, she had many friends outside the school. They may have been from Burscough.'

He got in the car and rushed to Burscough police station.

The sergeant tapped a pencil on the desk. 'Why have you waited so long to report your daughter missing, Mr Finnegan? In any case, technically, she's not missing since she has been sending you postcards.'

'She may have been abducted,' Damon said.

'Have you received ransom demands?'

'No.'

'What fool will abduct someone for fun? You tell me.'

'I am telling you something is not right. She has been taken to France against her will,' Damon said, placing a closed fist on the table.

'France is outside our jurisdiction. You should contact the police there. Is there anything else I can help you with?'

'Have any other parents reported missing children?' he asked the sergeant, who had stopped tapping the pencil and appeared distracted by screams from an adjoining room.

'Mr Finnegan,' he replied sympathetically, 'these are difficult times. There has been a war going on out there. Families get separated for many reasons, but in the end, they do find each other. I am sure your daughter will return safe and well. Have faith in God.'

Damon thanked him and left. He wasn't so sure about a helping hand from God, but never gave up hope that Mary would return, more mature and worldly-wise.

Over the days and weeks, he began concocting stories of Mary waiting for him at the doorsteps. Dad, where have you been? I've been waiting for hours. Or she is sitting patiently on the steps, reading a book. She now speaks French, making her bilingual, like Pierre. Other times, he sees a young man with her who speaks only French. Sometimes he pictures Mary springing out from the side alley, waving her arms in the air: *Tadaaa*, it's me.

He received eight more cards from Mary over the next five years, from France and Switzerland. In the final one, she had put in a few extra words to say she was alright, that he shouldn't worry about her.

And then they stopped coming.

Chapter 38

Acton, London 1965

I had flown into London from my home city of Calcutta. My family had registered me at Acton Technical College for the essential A levels before I enrolled at a university. At my father's behest, the college liaison officer had arranged accommodation for me in a house on nearby Mill Hill Road. It was a three-storey early Victorian building, with the rooms converted into bedsits and a shared bathroom and kitchen on each floor.

Away from home for the first time, I found myself in an unfamiliar culture, which shocked and confused me. For four months, I kept myself confined to the room, leaving only to walk to college. The other occupants of the house were students like me, or single working men, who tended to leave early and return late, sometimes drunk, banging doors and caterwauling in locked rooms.

In this unregulated pattern, two certainties stood out. One, a woman used to come on Monday sharp at seven in the morning to clean the house, starting from the entrance and working her way up to the top, muttering all the while about the dirty animals who lived there, that a pigsty was a haven of cleanliness in comparison.

The second certainty was the landlord's arrival on Thursday evenings to collect the rent. A man of medium build with a greying beard, he wore loose-fitting corduroy trousers and olive-green sweaters. He used to visit each room methodically.

Of course, the house used to fall silent on hearing his gruff voice, incessant clearing of the throat. The boys would lock their rooms, tread the floor as if walking on a bed of burning coals, throw themselves on the bed and pretend to be asleep. I was an exception. I used to dutifully open my door at the first knock with the money ready in my hands. He only stopped long enough to place a tick in his ledger book and then gave the room a once-over. He rarely said anything of substance, other than a nod or two or 'I'll be back next week, boy.' He would tap the pencil on the ledger book and move on to the next room. I found the man intriguing, often wondered if he had a family and, if so, how large it was.

On one of those visits, he did the customary inspection of the room, walked over to the sash window, and tugged at it. This time, he did something he had not done before. 'Do you feel the draft?' he said.

'Yes, only when it's windy,' I said guardedly, not wishing to appear ungrateful, though the window was like a square block in a round hole. I worried that he would ask me to leave.

'I'll get it fixed, boy, don't worry,' he said. As he was leaving, his gaze fell on two photographs of my cousins and other family members on a picnic to a famous landmark in Calcutta, the Victoria Memorial, and its vast open parks. I had received the photographs in the mail only the other day. In nostalgic memory of home, I had pinned them on the wall above the bed. He stopped and inspected the photographs up close.

'Is this Calcutta?' he asked.

'Yes, that's the maidan opposite Victoria Memorial,' I replied.

'Are you from Calcutta?'

'Yes, that's my city. Have you been there?'

He didn't say yes or no, but I noted the change in his demeanour. He appeared less forbidding.

Hmm, he pulled out a chit from his ledger book and handed it to me. 'Here is my number, call me if you need anything.'

The name handwritten on the paper said Damon Finnegan.

Over the next few weeks, he began spending more time in my room, wanting to know more about me, about Calcutta, hanging on to my every word. I asked him one day if he had ever considered visiting the city.

'I've been there, boy,' he replied, 'I've been there a long time ago, when I was a student like you.' He began to tell me more, mentioning a house in Alipore, the people he had met during his short stay, and the mafia-like businessmen. He didn't go into detail. However, it was apparent there was much more under the surface.

One day, he asked me what I was studying. I told him all science subjects, like maths and physics. He wanted to know if I was happy. I told him I prefer history, arts, and literature, but my father believes the future is in science.

'You should study what interests you most. I defied my father and refused to join the army. You say you're interested in history. How much do you know about the war?'

I admitted I knew little. It wasn't a subject taught to us at school; neither was it discussed at home. I suppose the elders thought I was too young to understand world affairs.

On later visits, he gave me books. They were all about the wars.

One time, I caught a cold with pneumonia-like symptoms. When he heard about it, he came to see me the same day and called in a doctor. 'It's the English climate, you're not used to it, my boy. Be very careful.'

A year later, I left the house to move near the university. I did not see Mr Finnegan for the next ten years, though at his insistence, I kept him informed of my movements by letters. One day, I received a letter from him, asking me to visit him. The very next day, I took the Piccadilly Line tube train to Acton Town and walked to Mill Hill Lane.

My first reaction was one of shock, for Mr Finnegan appeared to have aged more than ten years. His hair had fallen out; his complexion was pale grey as if there was no blood in his body. His head shook involuntarily as he spoke.

'Come and sit down. Are you wondering why I look the way I do? I am suffering from bowel cancer. Doctors have given me six to twelve years.' He laughed, which was more like uncontrolled clucking. 'It's actually six months, and if I am lucky, hurray, a year.'

I felt guilty for not visiting him sooner. He had been so kind to me when I was a struggling student.

'I am sorry,' I said feebly, for I couldn't think of anything else to say. I had never faced a situation like this in my life. What do you say to a man who has mere months to live? Don't worry, it will be all right!

'Do you ever dream of living in the clouds? Look out the window at the sky,' he said, 'tell me what you see.'

I did as he asked. It was a clear spring morning. 'Beautiful blue sky and woolly clouds are floating high above, lots of them,' I said brightly. It reminded me of the Wordsworth poem I had learned at school: I wandered lonely as a cloud, that floats on high o'er vales and hills, when all at once I saw a crowd, a host of golden daffodils.

'In those clouds, the wind blows at one hundred and fifty

miles per hour, the temperature is thirty below zero, and there's no oxygen. You'll die instantly if you happen to be there,' he said as if it were a well-known fact.

I understood the message he was trying to convey in his own way.

'You must be wondering why I asked you over, boy,' he said.

I shook my head. I noticed he was still calling me a boy as if I were a teenager.

'When I first told you about my time in Calcutta and about my life before and after, you appeared interested. I want to tell you everything about me so you can put it down on paper.'

I laughed, taking it as an attempt at humour.

'It's my only wish before I die.'

I still took it as a joke.

'Marge,' he called and tapped the side table with his knuckles.

The woman, in a white nurse's coat, who had let me in earlier, entered.

'What is it now?' she said wearily.

'Bring it,' he said.

I thought he had asked for some medicine to take at this hour.

Marge returned with a battered, dusty cardboard box.

Damon's lips quivered as he opened his mouth to speak. 'I want to give these to you. They are yours. I would have burned them if you had not come along today.' He swallowed saliva as if to moisten his throat and gestured at Marge to open it.

Marge placed the box on a chair and lifted the lid.

I could now see that the box contained a thick pile of notebooks, the type a child would use for schoolwork. They were dog-eared and a little mangled.

'These are my personal diaries,' he said, 'I permit you to go through them. But there's a lot more than what's on those pages, you understand.'

I sat listening to him for three hours, keeping my attention rapt so he wouldn't feel I was merely being polite. It was easy to do, for I indeed was interested in what he was saying.

I went and sat with him for days afterwards as he filled me in with intimate details which were in his head only.

I started writing when I had an hour or two to spare, after office hours or on weekends. A year later, one day, as I was about to leave home for work, the phone rang. I recognised the voice of Damon's faithful carer. My heart slumped on hearing her voice. I knew Damon had finally succumbed to cancer. After that, I didn't have the heart to continue. The project stayed stalled for ten years.

One summer, while on holiday, I picked up a book someone had discarded. It was a kind of biography, a true story of a man of Jewish faith born in Egypt who fled to Israel after the Yom Kippur War. How marvellous, I thought, this book could be a blueprint for my project.

I started again and resumed reading his diaries in chronological order. It struck me how enthusiastic a lover he was and how deeply personal a man he was, with deeply ingrained principles. One of the diary entries from the later years revealed his love for Flora. Here I quote a passage: … I was secretly in love with her … even though she had concealed the truth that she herself was a mother, mother to a child of mere six tender years. The doleful impression she cultivated was of a girl without a family, weaving a narrative of orphaned vulnerability. It was an artful deception that hid the truth of the bond that tied her to motherhood.

In another section, when his marriage with Anne was over, he wrote this beautiful piece: I've a duty to people, and somehow, I'll discharge it. I also have a duty to myself. I've discovered this essential identity through my feelings for Mary. Although she doesn't know it, that emotion has ripped open my self-protective layers. I see now who I am. It's not a question of happiness. I don't value my own more or less than anyone else's. It's something more urgent than that, and more lasting. It's a question of being faithful to oneself.

I could tell the way he scribbled the words with a blunt pencil, slanting back and forth haphazardly, that he must have been in a troubled state of mind.

Soon after he met Flora in London, he wrote this piece: People talk of the agony of moral choice. It's true, I feel agony, and it makes me tremble. But I don't have a sense of choice. To be with her, be part of her, is a natural imperative because, in a sense, she is me, my inner self.

In one of the later notebooks, I was surprised to find a black-and-white photograph glued to a page. It was of Damon, alright, a much younger version of him, looking grumpy as if he didn't want to be there. A girl, who appeared older than he was, was standing beside him, holding his hand. She was Damon's older sister. The writing below the photograph said: I've a picture of myself taken when I was ten in my parents' house on Oaktree Lane, it requires no effort to return to the room. The house's spaces live in my bones, but I must work harder to penetrate the young strangers in the snapshot. Sister's hair is in a ponytail, and mine is short back and sides, which I hated. Neither of us looks comfortable in front of the camera, but we have acquiesced to the command 'cheese.' When I look at the photo now, I clearly see its banality and what it hides. As a vehicle of memory, it resists inner reality. The feeling that ran between us. I hated her guts, but I also admired her, grudgingly, for she was so knowledgeable. I now realise that she loved me, not just as an older sister, but also as a protector from my father. There was sadness in her, a wound that lay beneath the brisk, bright persona. I found out years later that she was a lesbian.

After the doctors had diagnosed his debilitating illness, Marge told me he had gotten a typewriter because he found using a pencil painful due to the onset of arthritis.

I reproduce an early typewritten entry here. It's not dated. I expect he must have overlooked. But it's easy to assess the date. He's addressing a bottle of Thresher whiskey, his favourite tipple at the time.

This is my tenth day of being a teetotaller. Sheets of newspaper block the windows, and electricity drips through the cord into the 40-watt bulb above my head. The typewriter cackles and clanks, as though protesting at the darkness I feed its parts. For ten days, I've abstained from you. The doctor says the two of us are mortal enemies. But it's not strictly true, for I feel no enmity towards you. In truth, I am pretty fond of you. It's you who is my enemy, for you are hellbent on killing me. The Irish tenants gamble and scrape their chairs in the room above. I curse and bang the ceiling with a broom. I don't go out. I hunch at my desk and tap at the keyboard with fingers stiffened by cold and arthritis, as single-minded as a prisoner tunnelling out of solitary confinement with a teaspoon. Do you know what it's like to die? They say that staying in the host body past the end date is an offence. So, I must hurry.

The mouse now rests on the rubber mat, its job done. Its shiny surface, where my hand rubs on it a thousand times a day, catches the light from the table lamp. There's silence in the corner of my house. I've backed up the manuscript on a disc and printed it all on crisp white paper. They now lie on my desk, in an uneasy pile; each page is asleep, covered with the other. A glass paperweight, embedded with pretty flowers, sits on top like a crown.

My next task is to find a publisher. I'm unsure how to proceed at this stage. But I'll find a way. At first, I didn't know why Damon was so eager to have his memoirs published. But I know now. It was for Mary. He reasoned she would come across them somehow, somewhere, sometime. He didn't know where in the world she was, or if she was alive or dead. But he was an optimistic man.

Dear Reader,

I was brought up in Calcutta (now Kolkata). I made many friends at school, some of whom were Anglo-Indians.

In the summer of 2010, I travelled from my current home in Berkshire, UK, to Kolkata to seek out those old friends. But I could find none. They had all dispersed, with some moving to within India and others to countries far and wide. One friend I remember well. His name was Damian. His mother was a Bengali Indian, and his father, a Jesuit priest, was born in Glasgow. When Damian was still an infant, his father abandoned him and his mother and returned to his homeland, settling in London. There, he married an Anglo-Indian girl who had emigrated to London from Kolkata the same year.

The Passage East 1934 is a work of fiction loosely based on a real-life story.

Thank you so much for purchasing this book. If you enjoyed it, please consider leaving a review and recommending it to your friends.

To learn about me, the author, please visit my website and leave a message.

www.anilnijhawan.com

About the author

Born in India, Anil Nijhawan now lives in the UK. His career has embraced working in the computing industry and running his own business. A fitness enthusiast, he has run the London Marathon several times. His hobbies include global travel and painting.

www.ingramcontent.com/pod-product-compliance
Ingram Content Group UK Ltd.
Pitfield, Milton Keynes, MK11 3LW, UK
UKHW040914190126
10169UKWH00040B/400

9 781919 438306